✓ **W9-BUC-337**

# IF I
# COULD

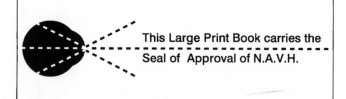

This Large Print Book carries the
Seal of Approval of N.A.V.H.

# IF I COULD

# COULD

Donna Hill

**Thorndike Press • Waterville, Maine**

Published in 2003 by arrangement with Kensington Books, an imprint of Kensington Publishing Corp.

Thorndike Press Large Print African-American Series.

The tree indicium is a trademark of Thorndike Press.

The text of this Large Print edition is unabridged.
Other aspects of the book may vary from the original edition.

Set in 16 pt. Plantin.

Printed in the United States on permanent paper.

**Library of Congress Cataloging-in-Publication Data**

Hill, Donna (Donna O.)
    If I could / Donna Hill.
        p. cm.
    ISBN 0-7862-4994-3 (lg. print : hc : alk. paper)
    1. African American women — Fiction.  2. Divorced
mothers — Fiction.  3. New York (N.Y.) — Fiction.
    4. Unemployed — Fiction.  5. Large type books.  I. Title.
    PS3558.I3864 I38 2003
    813'.54—dc21                                    2002075044

FICTION

5/03

*In loving memory of my dad, Floyd Hill. You always told me I could do anything I set my mind on . . . and you were right.*
*This one is for you.*

# ACKNOWLEDGMENTS

Many thanks are extended to my editor, Karen Thomas, for providing me with the opportunity to write this book. I truly appreciate your faith and the risk you took to make this a reality for me. To my wonderful children, Nichole, Dawne, and Matthew for being the best kids a mother could hope for, and my grandson, Mahlik, who makes everyday special. To my soulmate, Robert, for all your love, encouragement, and guidance that made the journey and completion of this book possible. To all the fans who through the years have continued to inspire me with their kindness and support. And most of all to God, who continues to bestow me with the magnificent gift of words and their ability to touch lives. Yes, I am truly blessed.

# PART ONE
# That Was Then

# CHAPTER ONE

*Pregnant!* She should be happy, damn it. It was a miracle. And she was happy — almost — off and on. What sucked the joy out of it was that she knew what this was going to cost her and she had no one to blame but herself. At least she was married, she reasoned. She wouldn't be a statistic. *But, damn, why now?* She grabbed her knapsack, slung it over her shoulder, and jogged down the stairs and out into the bitter November afternoon.

A light snow had begun to fall as Regina got behind the wheel of her brand-new 1985 Toyota Celica and pulled away from the Columbia University campus on Broadway and 120th Street. Her heart beat just a bit faster. Bad weather meant bad traffic and a long trip home. Russell was always more disagreeable if he arrived home before she did. She glanced heavenward. *Please don't let this weather get worse.*

By the time she'd reached the Triborough Bridge, a bare ten minutes later, a steady stream of pure white enveloped all in its path and traffic slowed to a crawl. It would be beautiful to look at, and maybe even enjoy — some other time. But today she was tired, bone tired, mentally and physically, and her day was nowhere near ending. The nerve beneath her right eye began to tic. She still had to pick up her daughter from her mother's house and get home to prepare dinner for Russell, a task he refused to do even if he was home all day — along with laundry, cleaning, and food shopping. All no-no's in Russell Everette's book. Not to mention taking care of their two-year-old daughter, Michele.

"That's your job, Gina. You wanted to go back to school, to fulfill whatever it is you think you need to fulfill, so you figure out how you're going to get everything done that needs to be taken care of around here," he'd told her in no uncertain terms when she'd asked for some help around the house. "That's the problem with women these days: they want all this independence and equal rights and then when they get them, everything else suffers."

"Russell, I just want to do something for myself besides sit home all day and watch television and think about what to cook for

10

dinner," she said, looking at her hands instead of into his eyes, wishing that for once he would hear her, really hear her.

"Don't I take care of you and Michele, Gina? Aren't I a good husband and father? I bought you a beautiful house, give you enough money so you *don't* have to be out in that rat race, and it's not enough. I don't understand it, Gina. You have the luxury of staying home to raise our child, something that children nowadays desperately need. You and I talked about this," he quickly reminded her. "And you still complain. Do you know how many women would love to be in your shoes?"

The weight of an unnamed guilt settled and lodged in her throat. She twisted her hands in her lap and swallowed over it. "I know . . . it's just that . . ." She glanced up at him and recognized the censorious expression on his face.

"Just what?"

"Nothing. You're right." She shook her head in dismissal. "I can handle it."

"You're going to have to. I *let* you make this decision to go back to school, so you deal with it."

Regina sighed as she reached over the visor and took out her money for the toll. Absently she thanked the clerk for her

11

change and gingerly pulled off, momentarily wishing that there was someplace else for her to go besides home. But that was ridiculous, of course. She was a wife and mother. And wives and mothers didn't have thoughts of leaving their husbands and children. Especially pregnant wives and mothers.

*Pregnant.* For an instant she relished in the momentary wonder of it. But just as quickly, that euphoric sensation of knowing she carried the life of another within her disappeared in a single breath. She'd have to tell Russell sooner rather than later, and she knew he would put an instant stop to her pursuit of finding herself.

She'd been back in school for six months, and it felt like ten years. At twenty-three, she wasn't the oldest student in her journalism classes but she felt like she was. More days than she cared to count, she wanted to just chuck the whole thing and return home to curl up in front of the soaps and the court TV shows and think about some exotic meal to cook instead. Maybe Russell was right. He always was, and her mother, too. This whole school thing *was* a stupid idea. What was she trying to prove anyway? All it was doing was draining her energy and

12

straining her relationship with her husband.

She was lucky to have a man like Russell, a man who made sure that his home and family were taken care of. Even her two best friends, Antoinette and Victoria, said so. Then why was she so unhappy?

When she'd married Russell three years earlier she was completely fascinated by him — his looks, his take-charge personality, and a sexiness that rolled off of him in waves. He was striking in appearance: tall, built like a seasoned athlete, and with the smooth, dark brown complexion that she'd always longed for. Everywhere he went women took second looks, but he had eyes only for her — a phenomenon that fascinated her almost more than he did. She knew she wasn't bad-looking. Not really. But she was certainly no raving beauty. She struggled with her fluctuating weight all her life — and having a baby only added to the problem. She still maintained fifteen pounds she couldn't seem to shake. She had pimple breakouts whenever she became too stressed — which seemed to be too often lately — and she tended to be quiet and reserved — a trait that was just part of who she was, but unnerved the people around her. Yet right from the beginning, Russell didn't seem to care about any of those things. He would take her shopping and pick out clothes he said would suit her figure, and send her to the hair salon whenever he thought her hair wasn't just right. He bought her all kinds of creams and lotions for her skin and even set up an appointment with a skin specialist, who he assured her would help with her problem.

Regina was touched by his kindness, his thoughtfulness, and the attention he paid to her. She was accustomed to having someone manage her life for her, make her decisions — know what was best for her. That was all she'd known, from her overbearing, overprotective mother, to Catholic school, where the nuns ruled with an iron fist and reminded you daily about hell and damnation, and any unique thought or action was considered sacrilegious. Russell's entrance into her life was only more of the same. He took care of her, took the pressure of daily living off her shoulders and onto his. But he came with the added benefit of being a man, a man who awakened the sleeping giant of her sexuality — who made her feel like a woman. It was the only area of her life where she felt she mattered — in which she participated and was appreciated.

She shivered, uncertain if it was from the cold, or from the fleeting erotic thoughts of her husband's touch, their nights together, the heights they reached, and her growing feelings of worthlessness and shame the mornings after.

Often she wished that she could share her traitorous feelings with Vicky and Toni, but she couldn't. They had perfect lives, great careers, came off as being sure of themselves, and knew what they wanted from life. She couldn't stand to be diminished in their eyes. She wanted to belong. She wanted what they had, or at least wanted to pretend that she did. How could she ever admit that things were not as they seemed? Not to them. And the more alone she felt in her marriage, the tighter she clung to their friendship.

Regina turned on the radio in the hopes of tuning out her troubling thoughts, but that served only to muddy them for the moment. If she could just hang on for three more months, she thought, she would have her master's degree, and the editor at the *Daily News*, where she was doing her internship, assured her he'd take her on full-time. He liked her work, thought she had a lot of potential and a keen eye for detail. "I think you'll make one helluva reporter one day, Regina," he'd said. But how long would that last once her pregnancy became obvious? *Damn!*

Finally, after a grueling two-hour, stop-and-go, slip-and-slide trip that should have been no more than forty-five minutes, she eased into her mother's driveway in St. Albans.

Reluctantly she shut off the engine of her Toyota, stepped out of the car, and her bootless feet sank into a layer of icy white snow. She inched her way to her mom's front door, instinctively wary of falling and the harm it could present to the budding life she carried. Maybe a new baby would soften Russell a bit, change his attitude about his role and hers in the house, she mused. He had to give her some assistance with a toddler in the house and another baby on the way. She couldn't imagine that his macho attitude would overrule her and the baby's health. He'd been an absolute Prince Charming when she was pregnant with Michele. There wasn't enough he could do for her.

She silently prayed for those days of bliss-filled happiness to return to the Everette household. In the meantime, she must deal with her mother and the lecture

16

she was sure she'd receive about something the instant she set foot across the threshold. She stuck her key in the door and switched her mind to "off."

As always her mother's neat little house was in immaculate condition. Every item was in its place, every surface was clear and dust free, and the air smelled as fresh as springtime. And as always, even moving toward the dinner hour, Millicent Prescott looked as if she'd just stepped off the cover of a magazine. Her red-brown skin was perfectly made up, not a hair was out of place, and her still-trim body was stylish in a designer pantsuit in a soft mocha that did wonderful things for her light brown eyes — the only trait Regina had acquired from her mother. She felt an overwhelming need to check her own reflection in the mirror. Her mother had a way of doing that to her — making her feel self-conscious and vulnerable without uttering one word. It was in the unflinching set of her eyes and her strident attitude.

"Hi, Mom. Sorry I'm late." She dropped the keys in her purse and walked toward her mother, her arms outstretched for Michele.

Millicent's mouth was drawn into a tight line.

Michele started to tear away from her grandmother's hand and dart toward her mother, when Millicent's no-nonsense voice halted her in her toddler tracks. "What did Grandma say about running?" Her voice cracked like a whip. The little girl turned wide eyes on her grandmother. "Little girls don't run; they walk — like ladies. Remember?" she said a bit more softly, making direct eye contact with Michele, then gave her a tender kiss on her cheek. "That's my girl," she said in her sweetest voice, the voice that always came after the tongue-lashing, that soothed the sting, the one you longed to hear to make your wrong go away.

She stared at Regina while talking to her granddaughter. "I'm sure your mommy doesn't allow you to run." Her smile missed her eyes. "I taught her better than that."

Regina's insides suddenly heaved as waves of unforgotten childhood anxiety swept through her. She breathed deeply, pushing them away as Michele walked ladylike into her arms. "Hi, sweetie," she whispered into her cottony soft hair. She held her tight against her chest for a moment. *Michele, the one thing she'd done right in her life.*

Millicent crossed the room, her posture impeccable. "That poor child just goes from hand to hand," she moaned in that martyred way of hers that curled the hairs on the back of Regina's neck. "You know how much I love that baby — and you — but there's no reason on God's green earth why this baby should be traipsing across town all kinds of hours when she could just as well be home with her mother."

"Mom, please. We've been through this a million times. I'm in school. I need a sitter so that I can go. You said you would do it, that you didn't mind," she went on, going down the list. "I don't want to leave Michele with just anyone and you know that."

"I really don't see why you can't wait until this child is older before you do whatever it is that you're doing. It's ridiculous and so selfish of you, Regina." She pressed her hand to her chest. "I would cry every day when I had to go out to work and leave you. I only wish I'd had the kind of husband who could have taken care of the two of us. If he could, I wouldn't have been forced to work, to leave my only child every day to be raised by strangers." Her entire expression tightened, making her smooth, brown face and sharp Indian features appear as if they'd suddenly been cast in plaster. She turned mournful eyes on her only child. "You have everything I ever dreamed of, Regina. I made sure of that." She stepped closer. "A husband who loves you, provides handsomely for you, takes care of everything so that you don't have a worry in the world, a beautiful daughter. You owe him a lot. Sweetheart, don't ruin that. Family comes first. You have time to pursue these dreams of yours. Think of your daughter, your husband." She lowered her voice, as if afraid that some unseen person would overhear. "Russell talks to me, Regina. He always has. You know he's like a son to me." She paused. "He's not happy, Regina, not happy at all. I can't blame him. And unhappy men . . ." Millicent arched a finely tapered brow.

Regina's stomach tightened. She knew very well what her mother was implying. She lifted Michele into her arms and pushed out a long, exasperated breath. "Well, this may all be a moot point, anyway," Regina said, feeling the cape of defeat settle around her shoulders.

"What are you saying?"

Regina shook her head. At least for now her secret was one thing she could call her own. She could savor this one bit of happiness awhile longer. "I'll talk to Russell," she said on a breath. "We'll work it out."

"I certainly hope so," Millicent said with a note of skepticism in her voice. She loved her daughter — there was no question about that; she'd sacrificed more than she could ever hope to regain to ensure that Regina had everything. During those years when her own marriage began to crumble, all she had was Regina, her daughter, her baby girl. They built their worlds around each other, just the two of them, and she prepared Regina as best she could to be ready for the life of a good wife and mother. Russell was the perfect man for Regina; she knew it the instant she met him through a former coworker. He was strong, driven, knew what he wanted and how to get it. So much like her own husband, Robert, had once been. Russell was just the kind of man her daughter needed, someone who could continue to guide and care for her with a strong hand, the way she had done. She knew her daughter possessed nothing exceptional in looks; men didn't flock around her, so her choices weren't bountiful. There was no way that she would let Russell get away.

But they were both worried about her

now. Neither of them understood this phase she was going through. Millicent was certain it would pass. If there was one thing she knew about her daughter, it was that she wouldn't resist what she knew was right. And being there for her family was the right thing. Women sacrificed, that's what they did, and the sooner Regina accepted that, the happier she would be.

Regina focused her attention on getting Michele into her snowsuit and out of her mother's house. She was suffocating, the air of her own thoughts sucked out of her. It was hard to explain how she felt each time she stepped across the threshold of the home of her youth, other than to say that she felt like a child, incapable and inexperienced, and she behaved accordingly. And as much as she understood that this bizarre transformation did take place, she was no more able to do anything about it than she could fly without a plane. That knowledge ate away at her day by day.

Hauling a bundled Michele up into her arms, she headed for the door. "I'll call you during the weekend, Mom."

"I was hoping you and Russell would come by for Sunday dinner. I'll fix your favorite, macaroni and cheese casserole," she cajoled. "You know how lonely I get over the weekend. There's nothing worse than eating alone." Then she suddenly waved her hand in dismissal. "No, no. You have dinner with your own family. I'll be just fine. Whatever I fix will just have to serve me for the week. Don't you worry. I'll be fine," she repeated. Her eyes seemed to have lost their sparkle, and the forlorn, downward curve of her mouth was not lost on Regina.

Regina sighed. "Sure, we'll come. I'm sure Russell would love it anyway."

Millicent perked right up, just as Regina had known she would. Millicent clapped her hands together. "Wonderful. I'll fix all your favorite foods and that pound cake Russell loves so much. And I'll get to see my baby again." She cooed and gurgled, nuzzling Michele's cheek.

"I gotta go, Mom. I'll call you."

"Drive safely, sweetheart. You know how you are when you get yourself upset."

Regina tugged in a breath. "I'm not upset, Mother."

Millicent, ignoring her comment, pecked Regina's cheek, then held it in the palm of her hand. "You know I love you, Regina. I only want the best for you," she said in that patronizing tone that made Regina want to shake her. "Don't damage this marriage of yours. Talk to Russell; try to see his side in all this." Her gaze ran a quick inventory over her daughter. "I see your face is breaking out again, and you could use a touch-up," she added, rubbing the roots of Regina's hair between her fingers.

By now she could hardly breathe at all; it was like those horrid times when her mother would make her play piano in front of all of her card-playing friends on Saturday nights when she'd just learned the piece the day before. She'd feel all clammy, her head would pound, and her heart would race as if it would burst from her chest. But she played anyway, because she slowly began to realize that the sooner she did what her mother demanded, the sooner she could breathe again.

She stepped outside and gulped in a lungful of air.

Regina carried her overdressed, sleeping two-year-old daughter on her hip, draped Michele's baby bag over one shoulder and her duffel bag of books on the other. She entered the house from the side door that opened onto the kitchen. And of course it was empty. Not even the sound of boiling water could be detected in the spotless kitchen. She shouldn't have expected anything different — but, damn it, maybe just once.

Huffing with her load, she let her bag fall with a dull thud onto the jade green marble floor. Russell would just have to fuss, she thought, her frustration and weariness beginning to take a toll on her. Michele whimpered and shifted her body, nearly causing Regina to lose her grip. She hoisted the sleeping baby a bit higher on her hip and mounted the stairs to the bedrooms above.

She heard water coming from the shower in the master bath as she gingerly tried to undress Michele without waking her.

"Just getting in?" Russell's heavy baritone crept up behind her.

She stiffened, keeping her back to him, and finished undressing her daughter. "Yes," she mumbled. "Traffic is pretty bad with the snow." She put a light blanket over Michele and tiptoed away. When she turned, Russell's imposing frame blocked the doorway. He looked down at her.

"Why are you doing this, Regina?"

She blew out a breath and stood her ground. "Doing what?" Really, she didn't want to have this conversation again — not today. She'd exhausted all the reasons to justify her "rebellious" behavior, as her friend Antoinette called it. Vicky just called it plain stupid. "Why go through all that drama if you don't have to? If the man wants to take care of you, let him."

"You know what I'm talking about, Regina," he said, cutting into her train of thought. "This whole school thing, not being home, so involved with books and papers that you don't have time for me — and for Godsake the newspaper." He turned away in disgust and headed for the bedroom. Regina followed and shut the door behind her.

"I'm doing the best I can, Russ."

He spun to face her. "The best you can," he said incredulously. "You're kidding me, right? You can spread yourself just so thin before something finally snaps, Regina."

"Maybe things wouldn't snap if you didn't place the whole responsibility of this family, this house, this marriage on me. You're a part of this, too. Doesn't it matter to you what I want, what I need?"

"As long as I'm the provider, as long as I take care of you and my child, then yes, the rest is up to you. And as for what you need and want, I don't think you know what that is. You said you wanted to be married, raise a family. But you don't act like it. You're acting like our marriage and this family are the last things on your list. An afterthought."

"That's not true."

"Isn't it? Tell me why it's not. I want to hear this for myself." He folded his arms and waited.

Suddenly she had a flash of the nuns from grammar school, waiting for her to explain why she'd missed Sunday mass. It didn't matter what explanation you gave — short of death — you were wrong and you would be punished accordingly. That's how she felt now, that no matter what she said it wouldn't make a difference. But she had to try, just as she had all those years ago. And she would take her punishment in stoic silence, and think up another reason to give the next time. There was always a next time. She would make sure of it by playing sick on Sunday morning, oversleeping or taking too long to get dressed. It was the one time when she could feel in control, feel significant — just for those few moments.

"I want to be a whole person, with outside interests," she finally said. "I want to be able to talk to people about more than recipes, household tips, and diaper rash. I'm good at what I do, Russell, but you never notice. You don't want to notice.

Not once have you ever asked me how my classes are, what I do at the *News*. Never."

"I know you're good at what you do. I don't need to ask you. Why do you think I miss your touch around here?"

"Russell —"

"Shhh." He stepped up to her. "Hey, careers, this school thing, there's plenty of time for that. We need to concentrate on us. You got time."

"Russell, it's not going to get easier." She moved away from him and sat on the bed.

"Ask any of your friends what they would do if they had a choice." He sat beside her. She eased away. He put his arm around her and she shuddered. Russell smiled in anticipation.

"Russell, this isn't about my friends. It's —"

His mouth covered hers, silencing her. Her body stiffened. He pulled her closer. "Baby, I want us to work," he breathed deep in her ear, his hot breath flooding her in waves. "But I need your help."

"Russell, just listen to me."

"We have all the time in the world to talk." His fingers began playing with the back of her neck, and electric waves ran along her spine. She sucked in air through her nose and held it in her chest. He pushed her baby soft hair aside and kissed her behind her ear, then in it. Her eyes slid close, and she silently screamed.

"I'd do anything for you," he said in a hoarse whisper. "You know that, don't you?"

"Yes." And she felt sick inside as her body began to involuntarily heat against her will.

"Then let me, baby. Let me take care of you." He ran his hand across her breast. She pulled back and he took it as a tease. He laughed deep in his throat.

"Russell . . . please . . . !"

"I know — me, too." He covered her mouth again and eased her down on the queen-size bed. He unbuttoned her plain white blouse and unzipped her jeans.

Her body weakened, softened as it always did, betraying her. She knew she was saying the words, but he couldn't hear her. She was telling him to stop, she knew she was, but it was pointless. He wouldn't hear her even if she screamed. It was always this way between them. He'd cut off her thoughts, stop her words, by filling her body with his. And she was helpless to resist. She hated this part of herself more than anything, this weak, needy part that begged to be heard. This part of her that sang in the pleasure of his touch, for his connection to her, even as her mind tried to resist, even as the unspeakable rush of her climax held her, shook her until tears of anguish streamed from her eyes.

"Yeah," he said with a groan, "that's my baby. You're mine. No one can make you feel like this," he ground out through his teeth.

He was right, she thought through the haze as yet another apex ripped through her. She needed this, needed to feel this — this one thing in her life that made her believe she was capable of anything — if only for a moment. If she closed her eyes, let the sensations flow through her, she became powerful, strong, visible. She was beautiful and desirable. With a thrust of her hips she could weaken him. She could be heard if she cried out his name, moaned in pleasure. He understood all that. If only for a moment.

Russell shuddered once, twice, before his body collapsed atop her. He didn't say a word, didn't share a tender touch, a thought. He simply rolled over and quickly fell into a satiated sleep.

Regina curled into a ball, pressing her fist to her mouth to keep from howling like a wounded animal. She turned her head, looked over her shoulder at her sleeping husband. She should feel something — anything. Her body still tingled, satisfied beyond words, but her heart and soul were so very empty, needy.

Tears of sadness rolled down her cheeks as she thought of the child she carried, the sleeping baby in the next room, the vows spoken before God and man, and she wondered how she would get through the rest of her life if everything in it didn't change.

# CHAPTER TWO

Victoria sat in the black-and-chrome swivel leather chair, with a pink plastic cape draped over her clothing.

"Is it burning?" the technician asked, checking Victoria's scalp for any immediate damage.

"No," Victoria uttered from between clenched teeth, trying to stifle the urge to holler from the torturous sting of the cream relaxer. "It's fine." Just a few more minutes, she told herself. A few more minutes and they could wash this mess out of her hair. But she wanted to be sure that every strand was bone straight, every kink as smooth as silk. And if it took being a little uncomfortable, the hell with it. She'd rather deal with that than with those telltale beads that sprouted up around her hairline and the back of her neck.

She closed her eyes and shut out the pain. She'd been coming to John Atchinson's salon since her college years. It cost an arm and a leg, but it was worth it. His technicians and stylists were some of the best in the business. And she refused to settle for anything less than the best.

Female voices whirled around her to the backdrop of piped-in music. They chatted ceaselessly about their lives, their jobs, their men.

"I wouldn't date a man darker than me," one woman was saying. "And I definitely wouldn't marry one."

"That's right, girl. I ain't trying to have no black, nappy-headed kids."

"And you know those light-skinned brothers are fine. Most of them got good hair, too."

Victoria opened her eyes and looked in the direction of the two women. They immediately reminded her of her two older sisters, Janice and Kim. The same sisters who had made her young life a living hell. They were what you called high-yella, with hair down their backs and eyes that were almost green. They took from the Creole side of the family, their mother was proud of saying — her side.

The three sisters shared a single room in a two-bedroom project apartment in Atlanta. Victoria's days were bad enough, with the children in school leaving her out of activities and conversations. At least in school she could run away and not listen to their mean chants. But at night, closed up in that room, she couldn't get away, and the ugly, callous words seeped through her pores and settled like cement around her heart.

"I don't know where Mama got you from," Janice would taunt. "Can't even see you when the lights go out."

"She's adopted," Kim would chime in, laughing wickedly. "She don't look nothing like us."

"She so black, even if she married a white man her kids would still look like tar babies," Janice added.

"What you cryin' for, darkie?" Kim demanded. "You know it's true."

The two sisters laughed and laughed, then talked about other things, leaving her out as if she weren't there — just a spot in the night.

And she never forgot their cruelty; it lived and breathed inside of her, growing until it consumed her, and all she wanted was to stamp it out — make everything they ever said untrue.

Even her mother added to her torment by reminding her of what colors to stay away from — like reds and yellows. "Your sisters can wear them things," her mother admonished her one day when she came home with a red blouse she'd purchased. "You can't. It just clashes with your complexion. You know you take after your father's side of the family." She shook her head sadly. "Your grandma always told me never to marry no man darker than me." She laughed lightly. "And Lord knows she was right." She patted Victoria on her narrow shoulders. "But you gonna be all right, fix yourself up, dress proper. You just gonna have to try harder, is all."

Try harder, Victoria thought, shutting her eyes again. Right up to now, years later, she was still trying, but she wasn't sure if it would ever make a difference. But she was damn sure not going to give up. She'd prove them all wrong.

One of these days she was going to have a life just like her friend, Regina. She would have a husband who loved her and took care of her. She would have a big house, travel around the world, and she'd be together, so important that no one would dare tease her again.

Regina didn't know how good she had it. She was damned lucky to find a man like Russell Everette. Although for the life of her, Victoria couldn't figure out what Russell saw in Regina. She was sweet and everything, but she was so . . . so ordinary. Regina was the kind of person who, if you didn't get to know her, you'd go right past her without realizing she was there.

It had been that way since the time they all met in college, doing their undergrad work at Columbia. Victoria was a business major, Antoinette was studying social work, and Regina . . . She frowned in concentration, but for the life of her she couldn't seem to remember what Regina was there for. Maybe it was something to do with writing, since that was what she'd gone back to school for. And she vaguely remembered Regina always carrying around some sort of journal.

Actually, that was what made her take a second look at Regina in the first place. . . .

Victoria had arrived at the Miller Theater on the Columbia campus at least ten minutes after the start of the program. The theater was packed. Although she'd been at Columbia for nearly two years, she never realized there were that many black students in the entire university. But she supposed since Benjamin Hooks, the president of the NAACP, was the guest speaker, they'd come out in full force.

She inched her way along the back wall of the theater, trying to locate a vacant seat. She had no intention of standing indefinitely. She didn't care what the attraction was.

Weaving in and out of the pressed-together bodies, she zeroed in on a lone empty seat. Moving quickly, she slid into the seat right next to who she later discovered was Regina Prescott.

At first Victoria didn't pay her much attention. She was sort of nondescript, not the type she generally associated with. But when Regina briefly glanced at her, smiling shyly, Victoria noticed her incredible light brown eyes. Her first impression was that they were those colored contacts that were becoming the rage. But taking in the rest of her, the simple white oxford shirt and khaki pants, unpolished nails, and short, natural hair, Victoria didn't think she seemed to be the type of person who went for fads.

Pushing the thoughts aside, she settled back into her seat and tried to catch up with the speech being presented. But her attention kept drifting back to Regina, who was furiously taking notes.

Victoria tried to peek over Regina's shoulder and was surprised to notice that they weren't notes at all, but some sort of journal entries, or a diary or something.

"Strange place to come and write in a diary," Victoria dryly commented.

Regina's hand slowed, then stopped. She turned to Victoria, embarrassment splashed across the small patches of eruptions on her high cheekbones.

"I try to write whenever I can," she said almost apologetically in an incredibly soft voice.

"Oh," Victoria mumbled. "Sorry to disturb you."

Regina closed her journal. "You haven't missed much," she offered. "Are you here for a class assignment?"

"No. Not really. I'm a business major," she said, as if that were extremely significant.

Regina didn't comment.

"Why are you here?"

"I thought it was important that I show my support."

"Even if you aren't paying any attention," Victoria joked, lifting her chin toward Regina's journal.

Regina smiled. "Yeah, I guess so."

"What year are you? I haven't seen you around before." Not that she would have noticed anyway.

"Second. And you?"

"Second in September." Victoria was

quiet for a moment, then asked, "You ever go to Leo's? Everybody does." Leo's was the favorite diner hangout the "in" students frequented.

"No."

"So what do you do in your spare time?"

"I have a part-time job at the investment office where my mother works." She shrugged slightly. "It keeps me pretty busy," she offered, as if to explain away her lack of knowledge about Leo's.

"You should come sometime. You'd meet some pretty cool people." Victoria made it a point, a goal almost, to be sure to be seen in all the right places with all the right people. She had big plans for her life, and the foundation she set in college, the connections she made, would be the keys to her inevitable success.

"I don't know, maybe," Regina mumbled.

"There you are," a voice whispered behind Victoria's head. "I been looking all over for you, girl."

Victoria turned to see Antoinette standing behind her. Antoinette was one of the few people she actually associated with on a regular basis. They'd met at Leo's and clicked right away. Antoinette, or Toni as she preferred to be called, was smart, funny, and drew men to her like a magnet with that shapely, compact body of hers and her headful of curly hair. Which was all the more reason for Victoria to stay in close contact with Toni. Her good looks and dynamic personality reflected well against Victoria's more reserved, almost smug persona. She softened her somehow. They balanced each other in an odd way.

"Let's get out of here. All this talkin' is boring the hell outta me," she said in a loud whisper.

"Where to?"

"Leo's, where else?"

"Cool." Victoria picked up her bag from between her feet on the floor and stood. "See ya," she said to Regina.

"See ya."

Victoria made a move to leave, then stopped. There was something in Regina's eyes. She'd seen that look before — in her own eyes. That look of need, of wanting to be accepted — hiding behind a facade of "other things are more important anyway," even when they weren't.

"You want to come and hang out for a while?" she asked abruptly, surprising herself with the invitation. "You'll find plenty of stuff to write about at Leo's."

"That's for sure," Antoinette said wryly.

Regina glanced at Antoinette, who shrugged. "The more the merrier. But whatever y'all gonna do, let's get going. I have a date tonight with this fine brother," she announced with a dramatic toss of her head. "He's a senior in the Social Work division. We're going to . . . exchange theories," she said with a mischievous laugh.

Victoria and Toni turned waiting eyes on Regina.

"Okay," Regina finally agreed.

And they'd been together ever since. She never could figure out why they seemed to remain friends. They were about as alike as the seasons. She could sort of understand her and Toni's friendship. Both of them were driven, determined, although Toni was the most flamboyant and talkative of the three. Regina . . . what could she say? She was easy. Always there if you needed her. She wasn't pushy like Toni, didn't always act like she knew everything, and would rather listen than talk. Whatever she and Toni decided to do was always fine with Regina. She was just . . . Regina.

Funny that of the three of them, it was Regina who was the first to land the drop-dead-gorgeous husband. Wound up with the house, the car, and kid. Didn't have to work. She envied her more than she would ever admit. And now Toni was all over this guy Charles. She was sure, if Toni were to tell it, that she and Charles would be the next ones down the aisle. And Victoria was the one, as always, who would be left out.

But her time would come. And when it did they would all stand up and take notice.

"Let's get that stuff out of your hair," the technician said, tapping Victoria on the shoulder, effectively shutting down the rerun movie of her life.

If she could get out of there within the hour, she could get back to the bank and put in some overtime, work on the big loan application that had come in earlier. She was determined to get a promotion to account manager. She was the only black female in her department, and she knew she had to prove herself — work harder. And she knew she would.

# CHAPTER THREE

Antoinette sat quietly at her desk in the small, overcrowded office of the clinic, listening to her sixteen-year-old client tell her about the second baby she was carrying, while her first one, less than a year old, slept in a dirty stroller at her side.

She wanted to reach across the desk, snatch her by the neck, and shake some sense into her cornbraided head. This child had no clue as to what she was doing to her life, to the lives of her children. She had no education to speak of, could barely string two coherent sentences together, and would probably be on welfare for the rest of her life. The saddest part of all that was the girl didn't see the problem — or maybe she did and wouldn't admit it. That was the first step toward change, accepting the fact that there was a problem.

"I kin take care of my kids," the girl challenged, a bright gold tooth in the front of her mouth adding to the mumble of her speech.

"You think that living on welfare, in your mother's apartment, is taking care of your kids?" Antoinette leaned forward. "Wanda, part of being a parent is being responsible, able to take care of yourself independent of anyone else, being able to offer your child a future. What kind of future can you have with no education, no skills, no job, and no experience with life? You're just a child yourself."

Wanda sucked her teeth. "I don't know why I gotta keep comin' here no way," she grumbled.

"What about the father? Is he planning to help with the baby?" Antoinette pressed, undeterred by Wanda's attempt at evasiveness.

Wanda looked uncomfortable for a moment, then shifted her bottom in the hard aluminum chair and peeked over at her baby. "He gone."

"Gone?"

Wanda turned hard eyes on Antoinette, eyes that had seen too much at sixteen. "I don't need him no way. My mom got eight kids. She takes care of us just fine without no man around."

Antoinette felt ill and terribly sad. So many, too many, of the kids who came to her had the same fatalistic mentality. What happened to hope — the desire to have more than your parents did?

It was a story she knew all too well. One too close. Looking at this young girl, hearing the hopelessness in her voice, seeing it in the empty stare of her eyes, she saw her own sisters whom she'd left behind in Algiers, Louisiana. She'd been afraid that if she stayed, she'd get sucked into the quicksand of their malaise, their defeat. So she ran as far away as she could to better herself, to distance herself from the ugliness.

Perhaps that was why she was drawn to social work. A part of her believed that she'd failed her family somehow. That maybe there was something she could have done and hadn't. So she tried desperately to do for others what she'd failed to do for them.

She was different from the rest of the family; where they seemed to shun reading and writing and advancement, Antoinette never did. There was always something mysterious and fascinating about books and learning that triggered Toni's imagination since she was little and her first-grade teacher had given her her first book as a Christmas gift. She'd steal magazines from the store to bring home because she never had money to buy them, and she'd sit up late into the night reading a book a classmate loaned her. Her mother, Beth, and her father, Albert, hadn't gotten beyond second grade and saw no reason to put stock in books and learning. Education and finding ways to climb out of the hole of poverty were topics that weren't discussed in her household.

Her father was a hard man, hardened by the life he'd lived, the pain and suffering he'd seen. Life had taken whatever spirit he might once have had in him out. "Books ain't gon' get Negroes nowhere in dis world," her father often said. "Dis here is our life. You best get use to it."

Her mother, always looking beaten and broken from endless hours of working in the cane fields, then dragging herself home to tend to her family, said little or nothing, offered no guidance or encouragement for her daughters.

So her three younger sisters sought love and affection outside of their home. Lynn had her first baby at fourteen, her second at sixteen. By the time Ann Marie and Gloria were seventeen they had three children each. And they all lived in the tiny, beaverboard shack.

Antoinette, the oldest, tried to talk with

her sisters, monitor their behavior, encourage them to stay in school. All to no avail. There was so little offered to blacks in Algiers in terms of resources. And she couldn't turn to her parents. They believed she wanted more than she was entitled to. She couldn't believe or accept that this life they laid out before her was all there was. Poverty and ignorance were a way of life for them, accepted as the norm. It was almost as if they were afraid of learning, of wanting more, because upon discovery they'd realize all of what had been robbed from them.

Frustrated, and nearly beaten down by the enormity of their defeat, she left and kept on going, pushing Algiers, her parents, her sisters, the dirt, the hunger, the longing behind her. She built a new life, a new history.

She hadn't been back home in more than eight years, and secretly it haunted her, this lie of a life she led. The guilt of her abandonment was like a shadow that followed her no matter how far she traveled. She tried to put it all behind her and failed. Just like this child in front of her who was pretending that everything was fine and as it should be. How was she any better?

"You finished?" Wanda demanded with the impatience of her youth.

Antoinette blinked, bringing her back into focus. She cleared her throat. "Are you still going to the parenting classes I set up for you?"

"Yeah."

"Good. And you're still studying for your GED?"

"Yeah."

Antoinette nodded, moderately pleased. Maybe she couldn't change the past, but hopefully she could have some impact on the future.

"Then I'll see you next week."

Wanda stood, her rounded belly poking out in front of her. She grabbed the handle of the stroller, pushed it ahead of her, and left without a word.

Toni lay next to Charles, unable to sleep, staring up at the uneven ceiling. She sat up. They'd been living together for about six months — maybe not really living together, since she still maintained her apartment in Riverdale. But she spent most nights with Charles, as much as she disliked the tiny space. But sometimes you made concessions to get what you wanted. And she wanted Charles. So what was a few nights of being uncomfortable, stacked against the possibilities of what could be?

But tonight the walls seemed to close in on her. The room grew smaller.

She felt Charles stir, and hoped he wasn't asleep. She needed to talk.

"Charles," she called in a hushed voice, mindful of the thin walls.

"Hmm," he mumbled.

"I'm thinking of going home."

"This time of night?"

"No. Not to my apartment. Home, to Louisiana. To see my family."

He rubbed his eyes and sat up. "What brought that on? You never even talk about your family."

She sighed deeply. "I know. But I need to see them. Okay?" she snapped.

"Hey, whatever you need to do," he said, not wanting to get into a thing with her. He knew her well enough to know that once she made up her mind about something it was a done deal. He turned on his side, his back to her.

"I want to go and come back before the holidays."

Charles turned back around. "That soon? You know I can't get time off from work with such short notice, especially this time of the year. Why don't you wait until I can get off?"

"I need to do this by myself," she said, partly in truth, but also understanding that she could never allow him to see that side of her life.

"Are you all right, Toni? Did something happen?"

"I'm . . . fine. I just need to do this."

He stared at the outline of her body silhouetted against the darkness of the room. Her knees were drawn up to her chest, her arms crossed over them, her chin resting there. "Is there something you need to tell me?"

"No. That was it. I'm going to check on flights tomorrow."

"How long are you planning to stay?"

"Just a few days." She stretched out her legs and lay down, then turned her body toward his, needing his warmth.

"I love you, Toni. You know you can tell me anything," he said, pulling her closer.

"I know," she said into the night. But she knew she could never tell him the truth of who she was, what she had come from. It would ruin everything. And she couldn't risk losing him because of it. But if she did go back, would she lose another part of herself?

★ ★ ★

The Shark Bar on 73rd and Amsterdam, Nick Ashford and Valerie Simpson's place, was crowded as usual on a Friday night. The trio had been coming to the trendy after-work spot since they'd graduated from Leo's. It was Victoria's "new" favorite hangout.

"I told you I was going to get that promotion," Victoria stated smugly, then took a sip of her white wine. "It's just a matter of time before I make VP." She glanced again at the menu.

"That's great, Vicky," Regina commented.

"Yeah, it is. But I just don't see how you can deal with all those numbers and anonymous faces," Antoinette said. "I need to deal with real people, real issues."

"It's where the money is," Victoria tossed back. "And the people with money — and connections."

"That always was your thing," Toni added. "I guess it'll pay off one day — no pun intended," she said laughing.

"Well, I know one thing: I have no intention of being holed up in some one-bedroom apartment for the rest of my life. My man is going to be into something."

Antoinette pursed her lips, breathing

51

deeply. She knew Victoria thought of Charles as low-class because he was a chauffeur. But she also knew that Charles had great things in store for him. She would see to that.

Regina gauged the tension brewing between her two friends — typical for their usual monthly Friday-night get-togethers. She generally tried to stay out of the line of fire unless things really got ugly. As much as these gatherings sometimes bothered her, in a strange way she needed them, needed to be with these women. It was her one outlet, her one way of stacking the cards of her life against theirs, and the one thing that Russell didn't have an objection to. So she savored these few precious hours for as long as possible, even when they flipped her stomach.

Victoria turned her attention to Regina. "So what's up with you, Gina? How's married life?"

"Okay, I guess."

"You guess, girl, please. Russell still treating you like a queen?" Toni asked, patting Regina's hand. "You're so damned lucky," she said wistfully.

Regina smiled. She really didn't want to talk about her and Russell. "I got my first big assignment at the *News*," she said, perking up. "I have to interview the tenants of a housing project."

Victoria turned up her nose, remembering her own days in the projects. "And you're excited about that? Why?"

"For the same reason you get excited about what you do," Regina said, not up for any of Victoria's asides tonight, not after her mind-bending conversation with Russell about her job and the new baby.

Victoria arched a brow.

"I hear you, Gina," Antoinette said, pleased but surprised at Regina's unusual edgy tone.

"Say what you will," Victoria huffed. "We each have our own agenda. So let's be honest." She took another sip of her wine.

The atmosphere shifted. A sudden silence enveloped them, dropping like a final curtain. They all became overly involved with their menus, and an almost audible sigh of relief flowed around them when the waitress came to take their orders.

"I'll have another glass of iced tea with my meal," Regina said, handing over her menu.

"No daiquiri for you tonight?" Antoinette asked, knowing it was Regina's favorite.

"No. I'm not drinking tonight."

"Big day tomorrow?" Victoria asked.

"No . . ."

"So, what's the deal?" Victoria pressed. "Please don't tell me you're going to give up your one vice and make me feel totally decadent." She lit a cigarette.

"Um, I'm pregnant." Her gaze darted from one face to the other.

"Get out," Antoinette said, grinning broadly.

"Another one? So soon. Michele is barely two." Victoria frowned.

"According to statistics it's best to have children close together," Antoinette chimed in. "They can grow up together, and you have more time for yourself much earlier. That's how I want to do it."

"Well, it's not on my agenda anytime soon," Victoria grumbled. The evil chants of her sisters echoed in her head.

"I can't wait," Antoinette said, wishing it were her. "I know I'll make a good mother."

Regina sipped her water.

"Russell must be thrilled," Antoinette stated.

"What about that job of yours at the paper, and graduate school?" Victoria wanted to know. "I thought they were so important to you. How are you going to do

54

both with a new baby?"

"I'll work it out." She didn't know how, and the more she thought about it, the more overwhelming it became. Russell was adamant about her quitting both. He couldn't have been happier that nature stepped in and did what he'd failed to do with his behavior. She wanted to tell them what was really going on, how she felt, what was happening to her. But she was certain they would think she was making too much of it. And how could she ever explain the forces that bound her to him when she didn't understand them herself? They'd probably just tell her to lie back and enjoy it, and be happy he wasn't out with some other woman.

"Hey, Regina has a good man. I'm sure Russell is a great help. Right, Gina?"

Regina forced a smile. "Most of the time. He kind of leaves the running of the house to me." She took a breath, then leaned forward. "He wants me to quit working and stop going to school." She looked from one to the other, hoping to see understanding there.

They were quiet for a moment.

"So what's the problem?" Victoria suddenly asked, a bit perplexed. "How many men these days want their wives at home, or can afford it?"

"Not many, I can tell you that," Antoinette jumped in on her rescue horse. "I've seen three clients just this past week who say that their husbands are almost useless around the house. They have to work, take care of the kids, their husbands, and themselves. They're so burned out they're no good to anyone."

"Consider yourself lucky," Victoria said. "I mean, if you're really so gung-ho about school, take a correspondence course or something. And you can always freelance if you really want to be a writer."

"But I don't want to be tied to the house for the next two years. I like what I do. I like the interaction with people."

"Oh, Regina, enjoy it while you can," Victoria said. "Women would run in the street naked to be in your shoes."

Antoinette laughed at the image. "You know, you *are* lucky, Regina. Russell is a great guy. I mean, he must really love you to want to take care of your every need. Just relax; being out in this rat race is no picnic, believe me."

Their food arrived, and the topic shifted to the lack of great black actors in film after Antoinette mentioned the latest movie with Richard Pryor, and her tentative plans to visit her folks before the holiday.

Regina hung on to the fringes of the conversation, nodding and smiling in all the right places. Maybe she was wrong to feel the way she did. But she didn't think so. Who would believe her if she told them what her marriage was really like — that it wasn't Camelot in living color — that she wanted to run, not walk, away from her life as she knew it? But she couldn't — for too many reasons. Reasons that she couldn't explain, at least not yet. But one day she would. She had to. *Let's be honest,* she thought, recalling Victoria's earlier, telling remark. *Hmph.* If they were really honest, they'd probably never speak to each other again.

# PART TWO
## This Is Now

# CHAPTER FOUR

There was no reason to believe that it was any day other than a windy Friday afternoon in March. The sun rose at its appointed time. Traffic on FDR Drive crawled along at its usual snail's pace. The newsroom roared in its customary state of bedlam.

So what was the big deal? For as far as she could see, monkey business continued as usual. Nobody gave a damn. Who really cared that her whole life had just taken yet another three-hundred-and-sixty degree tailspin? A lousy card would have been nice — from somebody, anybody. After all, she'd only devoted the best years of her life to this thankless, pain-in-the-neck job.

She dropped her precious Rolodex into the brown cardboard box and cut a quick look at Conan, the barbarian security guard who watched her every move.

*Don't worry. The only thing worth taking out of this place is my sanity,* she shouted silently.

He stared at her, stone-faced, his thick-fingered hands laced across his wide girth. If she made a run for it, he'd never catch her, she thought in a crazy flash of heat-induced delirium. She imagined herself leaping tall desks in a single bound, dashing around cubicles, and knocking down all those holier-than-thou, bigoted, sexist male editors who always believed her place was at home with her two kids, not as a crime reporter for the award-winning *Daily News*. It didn't matter that her Associated Press Awards contributed to their coffers.

Still, a lousy bunch of flowers would have been decent. She sniffed and shoved a battered manila folder into the box, followed by the framed photo of her daughter Michele and her son Darren. *Well, guys,* she thought, glancing quickly at their smiling faces, *wait until you find out what Mama did.* Her stomach did a quick high-dive. Wait until *her* mother found out what she did. She shut her eyes a second and prayed for God's mercy.

One by one she removed the three plaques from the wall. *To Regina Everette for Outstanding Achievement in Journalism, Associated Press, 1999 . . . 1996 . . . 1994.*

She looked around. Nimble fingers flew across computer keys, tapping out the latest tragedy for human consumption. Phones rang incessantly with anonymous tips and tips for hire and piles of discarded text; stacks of newspapers and reporter's notebooks created minimountains of black-and-white debris, projecting the illusion of snowcapped mountains muddied by hiking boots. She loved and hated it at the same time — loved what she was capable of doing, but hated what the job had done to her.

For an instant she grappled with uncertainty and her eyes suddenly filled with doubt. What was she going to do? How was she going to take care of her children? What if everything blew up in her face?

She'd struggled with this moment for months, searching inside herself for the courage to put an end to the madness. Her moment had come today, when her boss called her into his office for her latest assignment.

"Everette, I want you downtown with the camera crew. Drop whatever you're doing."

"What's happening downtown?"

"Kid, about fifteen was found raped and strangled on the rooftop of the building she lived in. I need you to get over there, get me the pictures, and get an interview with the mother. That's key," Stuart emphasized with a wag of his tobacco-stained finger. "Then get interviews with the older sister and the neighbors. Find out what kind of reputation this kid had, any drug problems, arrests, what kind of home she came from. You know the drill."

Regina simply stood there, trying to breathe as her stomach rolled over and over. Already she could visualize the grief-stricken face of the child's mother, hear the wails of agony coming from behind the apartment door. And she knew she couldn't do it. She just couldn't.

"Stuart, I think maybe you should send someone else."

His bushy head of white hair snapped up. Lifeless gray eyes stared at her in confusion. "What did you say?"

Regina tugged in a breath. "I can't do it."

"Can't do it? Or won't?"

"Take your pick, Stuart. I just can't do it."

"You mind telling me why, Everette?"

"This isn't what I came into journalism for."

"So, what, you thought it was going to be a bunch of bullshit flower shows, cooking contests, and spelling bees? Christ,

Everette, this is the real world — and it stinks. Our job is to report just how bad."

Regina slowly shook her head.

Stuart's face turned a light shade of purple. The veins in his forehead began to throb. "You have two choices, Everette. . . ."

"No. I only have one. I'll get my things." She turned on her heel and returned to her desk and began packing her things. Her entire body shook with a mixture of fear and relief. When she went into journalism, starry-eyed and eager, it wasn't only to be a good journalist, but to prove to all the naysayers — her mother, Russell, Toni, Vicky, even the children — that Regina could do something on her own and be good at it. She had accomplished what she'd set out to do, so leaving — packing up her marbles and going home — shouldn't feel like failure, but somehow it did. They were right, and she was wrong. Her chest tightened with apprehension. She hadn't thought the scenario through this far, not really. It had always been just a story, an article idea in her head that never made it into print. But now it had — here she was, for all the world to see — a failure.

Yet underneath it all she knew she

couldn't take it anymore — the ungodly hours, the horror stories that grew more horrific by the day, the lack of support she received from many of her male colleagues who felt that she was taking up their space on the page. It didn't matter that her stories were good, well researched and well written. She was a woman, and not even one that they could be particularly attracted to, to help take away the sting of her presence. It was all surface. Superficial. No one ever bothered to see beyond her womanhood. What was really any different here from the way it was at home or with Toni and Vicky? Everyone saw what they wanted to see, believed what they wanted to believe. And nothing else mattered — least of all her. She drew in a breath. Still, was she making the right decision, cutting off her livelihood without a backup?

Regina gazed around the overcrowded, smoke-filled, sweat-drenched room that served as her second home, over hunched backs and balding heads, waiting for some sort of answer — a revelation, a hint. None came. *This is on you, girl,* she concluded, *to win or lose.*

Her entire career had been reduced to a brown grocery-store box. She tucked it

66

under her arm and grabbed her purse from the back of the chair, which had taken her two years to break in just right. Dropping her keys into the opened palm of Conan, Regina Everette completed her last byline.

Antoinette Devon sat across the desk from her last client of the day, a sixteen-year-old runaway who'd recently been placed in foster care. He was so angry, she thought, stealing a glance at the clock just beyond his head. They were all angry. Girls and boys. They were angry with their parents, their teachers, their friends, society, themselves. And the adult couples she counseled in her private practice were angry with each other. Some days she felt as if she was the one stabilizing force that stood between them and the growing turmoil in their lives.

At times she wasn't sure how much she helped, if at all. But she must try. Thank heavens her own family was intact, she mused, as the doo-rag wearing potential thug went on and on in a hip-hop, free-flowing lingo that would take more than Merriam-Webster to decipher, with each sentence punctuated by "you know what I'm sayin', yo."

*Not really*, she thought, feeling slightly

wicked. *But I'll listen anyway. I'll try anyway.* Someone had to. She really needed to get by the salon and have her dreads retwisted, she thought absently, momentarily tuning out the chatty hiphopper.

Toni checked the clock again. "Well, Richard, I'm glad we talked. This is good. You need to get your feelings out in the open." She flipped through her appointment book, looked up at him, and smiled her best social-worker smile. "Next Tuesday, at four?"

He slouched a bit farther down in his seat. "Yeah," he mumbled, then stood and bebopped out of the cluttered office. His three-sizes-too-big jeans hung off his narrow hips. She watched him until he was out of sight, and made a note. Next session she'd talk with him about appearances and how it would shape the world's view of him. She shut the case file.

Toni sat back and blew out a breath. *Whew.* Her day was finally over, and she could sure use a stiff drink.

"Mrs. Hunter, here are the loan applications that you need to review."

Victoria Hunter gazed up from her orderly desk, pressed "shut down" on her computer, and took the proffered files from her assistant.

"Thank you, Alyse. Would you take that stack of new-accounts files and have them processed?"

"Yes, Mrs. Hunter. Will you need anything else?"

"No, Alyse. Thank you. Have a good weekend."

"You, too, Mrs. Hunter."

Victoria liked being called Mrs. instead of the politically correct *Ms.* She had worked hard to secure her marriage and was immensely proud of the fact that she sported a five-carat diamond ring on the third finger of her left hand. She'd earned it. Just like she'd earned her way up the corporate rungs to the position of vice president at the bank, the only black female with the title.

All through school she was teased and taunted: "darkie," "chocolate syrup," "sun-dried raisin." They laughed at her hand-me-down clothes and her short, nappy hair. Even the teachers would pass her over for her fairer-skinned, straighter-haired classmates.

But she'd shown them all. No one dared think of her as the nappy-headed ink spot again. At least not to her face. She'd graduated at the top of her class in the Business School at Columbia University, landed a great job at the bank, and had a financial portfolio that would see her far beyond retirement. She purchased her stylish designer clothes from the best boutiques in New York. Had her short hair permed and trimmed regularly. She leased a new car every year, owned a house on Long Island, and a white husband. That last possession shocked people more than anything.

*Hmph.* She smiled to herself. She had the perfect life.

Victoria took her Gucci purse from the bottom desk drawer, then locked it. Taking a quick look around to be sure that everything was in tip-top order, she picked up her briefcase with her initials embossed in gold, flipped off the light, and shut the door behind her.

Another successful week was over.

The Shark Bar had a waiting list of twenty minutes for a table.

Regina never could understand why they always came there anyway, except that Vicky insisted that the Shark Bar was *the* place to be seen, and so much classier than some of the other name-brand clubs. And there was no debating with Vicky once she'd made up her mind. It was easier just to go along.

"Where are we on the list?" Toni quizzed. She wiggled her full hips onto the bar stool and wondered if her husband Charles was coming home tonight.

"Somewhere near the bottom," Victoria replied, taking a puff on her cigarette. At some point she was going to have to quit. Lately they'd been making her ill, she mused.

Regina remained quiet, picking at the peanuts in the wooden bowl. The longer they sat there, the longer it would be before they all got down and did their usual once-per-month, Friday-night thing — talk about themselves.

Toni would go on about her clients and how hard she tried to work with them, how hard it was to find answers to the myriad of problems they laid on her desk. She'd tell them they would never understand how taxing it was to be responsible for someone else's life and happiness day in and day out.

Then Victoria would chime in and boast about how many new corporate accounts she'd handled, how many snoozer meetings she'd had to sit in on, how much she anticipated her next bonus would be, and how Phillip, her great white trophy, was plan-

71

ning another "glorious" vacation and how she would be bored out of her wits but would go anyway.

At some point, they would turn to Regina and ask how her week went — if there were any breaking stories she could share, give them an inside scoop. And she would pick up her customary strawberry daiquiri and calmly announce, "I quit my job today."

"What did you say?" Toni asked. "I can hardly hear you." She looked expectantly at Regina. An old Ashford and Simpson favorite, "Ain't No Mountain High Enough," played in the background.

Regina could feel the color drain from her body. Had she actually spoken her thoughts out loud?

Victoria tore herself away from her reflection in the mirror behind the bar. "Hmm? What did I miss?"

"Nothing," Regina mumbled, visualizing the brown box of her life shoved into the trunk of her two-year-old Volvo.

"Oh." Toni peered over a few heads in front of her. "Thought you said something about quitting your job."

Victoria tossed her head back and laughed. "Now, we both know the last thing Gina would do is quit her job. She loves that place. All that sweat and cigar smoke — yuck. Besides, who would take care of the kids? Russell's child support damn sure isn't enough to cover all your expenses. Not with the children, a car, and an apartment to manage." She blew a cloud of smoke into the air.

Regina was suddenly shoved back in time to Our Lady of Victory, the Catholic grammar school she'd attended for eight years. She was staring at the feet of Sister Consilio and Sister Jean, terrified to look into their all-seeing, judgmental eyes. Their ominous black, floor-length dresses and white cardboard headbands with black veils that fanned around them when they walked were enough to terrify any little sinner into repenting, whether she was guilty or not.

That sensation, that feeling of guilt even when she'd done nothing wrong, had been ingrained into her over the years, became a part of who she was — her mother, then Russell fanned the flames. The feeling that she'd done some terrible thing, that her actions needed watching, was always there just beneath the surface, ready to leap out at the slightest provocation and make her confess. *Confess.* Like right now. Sister Toni and Sister Victoria waited.

73

"You *didn't* quit your job?" Toni stated more than asked, knowing that her straight-and-narrow friend would never do anything that radical. Divorcing Russell was some sort of glitch in Gina's thought processes, they'd concluded. As much as she claimed things were fine with her and the kids, Toni had to agree with Victoria. Having a husband to share the load was a hell of a lot better than not. A flash of her husband Charles flickered for a moment in her head. Inwardly she flinched. They didn't have to know. They would never know.

"Oh, don't be ridiculous, Toni. You know better than that," Victoria chimed in. "Not *our* Regina."

"Your table is ready, ladies."

Regina sighed in a moment of reprieve, but as she followed Toni and Victoria to their table, something inside jump-started, like an old car battery that got a boost. Everyone always expected her to follow the rules, not cause waves, to lead by example, be seen and not heard.

From the time she was little, her parents, especially her mother, put her on a pedestal, on display, a testament to their ideal of parental perfection.

When the other little girls were playing

double Dutch, tag, and dodgeball, she was taking piano lessons and etiquette and ballet classes. Her mother would trot her out at all the holiday parties and family gatherings as if she were a show horse.

"Isn't she simply lovely?" Millie would gush, tightening the pink satin ribbon on her ponytail. "Regina, sweetheart, play something for us. Play the new piece you learned." Millie turned to the expectant group of aunts, uncles, and cousins, who'd grown accustomed to these displays. "She learns so fast," she would say in a pride-filled hush. "Her instructor insists she's a genius."

Regina could feel herself shrink, diminish like a plant without sunshine. Panic gripped her. Her heart raced madly in her chest. She wanted to run screaming from the room, tell her mother how much she hated the piano and ballet lessons, learning how to hold a fork and enunciate her words, performing on command. But of course she couldn't. That would be rude, unacceptable. And she hadn't been taught to be either.

So she would suppress her tears, force her mind to go blank, and play, let her fingers glide across the keys, pound out her frustration, and everyone would applaud her brilliance, oblivious to her plea for freedom in every note, every perfect phrase, every curtsy.

Regina glanced impassively from one woman to the other, both projecting the perfect picture of beauty and success, and they, her friends, expected from her the same thing her parents, her teachers, her instructors, her husband, even her children did — perfection.

But she couldn't do it anymore. If she did, she was certain she'd snap. She didn't want to be like the woman in the story she'd covered, who'd purposely overdosed on sleeping pills because the pressure of having to keep up the illusion of success when she was no longer able had gotten to be too much for her, and all she wanted was some peace. No, she wouldn't become fodder for a sordid newspaper feature. She didn't want to knock on another unsuspecting mother's door and ask how she felt about her teen son being shot down by police in the street. She didn't want to arrive at another fire and hear the screams of parents whose children were trapped inside. Didn't want to have another fifteen-year-old kid die in her arms because the reporters arrived before the ambulance.

Toni signaled the waitress. "You guys

ready to order? Because I'm starved. I was so busy today with clients I didn't get to have lunch." She snapped her menu shut.

"I guess," Victoria ho-hummed, knowing she'd order her usual.

"I'm not hungry," Regina announced.

Toni and Victoria looked at her as if she'd grown a third eye.

"Not hungry! Girl, you're always hungry," Victoria said, laughing lightly. "I don't see how you stay in shape with the amount of food you consume and never exercise. I wish I had your metabolism. But I have to work out," she said with a toss of her head.

"Maybe I'm just not hungry," she snapped, thinking about her nonexistent income and the fact that if everything else in her life was in an upheaval, maybe her diet needed an overhaul, too.

"I have a teenage girl I'm counseling," Toni broke in, dipping a celery stick into the bleu cheese dressing. "She's enormous. I finally got her to see a nutritionist. Hopefully it will help. Her eating was brought on by depression and emotional deprivation from her parents. She ate to feel better. You, on the other hand, have it made."

"Gina just eats because it's there," Victoria barbed. "Oh, I'll have a wine spritzer to start," she said to the waitress. "And I'll have the blackened salmon salad." She handed over her menu.

"I'll have the grilled chicken with wild rice," Toni said, "and a rum and coke."

"And you, miss?"

"Just a small salad for me, thanks." Yes, she'd start with salad. And now that she had some free time, she'd finally sign up with a gym. Yeah, that's what she'd do. A makeover, one step at a time, she thought, feeling a bit edgy and off center. Her stomach was fluttering like crazy. She took a long swallow of water.

"Hmm. What's going on with you?" Toni asked. "You're in a strange place tonight."

Regina pulled in a lungful of air, looking from beneath her lashes at her friends. There was that damned fluttering again. "I did quit my job today." She took a sip of water.

Victoria's perfectly made up face visibly drooped. Toni's celery stick slipped from her fingers with a tiny plop into the dressing.

"What did you say?" Toni babbled.

"I quit. Walked out. Handed in my resignation."

"So you have a better job somewhere

else?" Sister Victoria asked, certain that was the case.

"No. I don't."

"What! Gina, are you crazy? What in the world are you going to do?" Sister Toni wailed.

"You know if you quit you don't get unemployment or anything," Victoria announced in a tone totally offended by the sheer stupidity of the situation.

"First, I'm not crazy. Second, I know what my options are."

"Fine. But you have two children to take care of," Toni insisted, certain that Regina had not factored them into her equation.

"I know I have two children," Regina responded in a flat monotone, struggling to keep a lid on her bubbling temper. "I know I have an apartment, a car, and bills to pay, and no health insurance." Her voice began to quake when she considered the sheer enormity of it all.

"How in the world are you going to manage, Regina? Michele will be ready for college in another year. Do you have a plan?" Victoria pressed.

"I will."

Toni and Victoria looked at each other in complete bewilderment.

Victoria leaned forward. "Listen, Gina,

I'm sure the job had its downside, but if I recall correctly, you were the one crying on our shoulders when you left Russell, wondering how you were going to make it. I told you then that you needed to rethink things and stay with him. Nothing could be that bad. And you two have kids together, for Christsake. Now look at you." She leaned back, her brows rising in a know-it-all attitude. "And whether you admit it or not, it was the biggest mistake you ever made. Now you're ready to make another one."

"How could you just up and quit your only form of livelihood without a backup?" Toni cut in, inwardly cringing at the memories of her own deprived childhood because of unemployed and illiterate parents. "That's something a flighty teenager would do, not a grown woman with responsibilities. It wouldn't cross my mind, one, to leave my husband, and two, to leave my job. Especially without something in the hole — another man and another job."

"You got that right. I worked too hard to get what I have, and I'll be damned if I'd just give it up on a whim," Victoria agreed. "Your mother is going to flip, and I truly don't want to have to go through another scene with her like I did after your divorce," she continued, as if this all were a personal attack on her.

"I think you're just going through an early midlife crisis thing, Gina," Toni stated with authority, emphasizing each point with her customary hand accompaniment. "You're going to be forty in a few weeks and it must be hitting you hard, throwing your hormones off. You know this happens to a lot of women, Gina," she ran on in her rapid-fire style. "I've treated so many women who have these . . . these false notions that turn their lives upside down, and then they regret it. And, of course, they turn to me for help. Maybe you should go to counseling or something, get some of your inner problems dealt with by a professional. I could recommend someone. This is just so unlike you."

"Exactly. You're the one who's always been on the straight and narrow. Damn, what *are* the kids going to say? Have you thought about them at all? You know, you haven't been the same person since you left Russell." Victoria shook her head sadly, as if she were dealing with an irresponsible child. No matter what her issues with Phillip, she'd be damned if she'd give it up. She'd never give anyone a reason to say, "I told you so."

They went on and on taking turns telling her how foolish she was, how irresponsible, how this was just another phase she was going through. Regina could feel the storm clouds building in her chest. She'd known these two women since college. They'd shared holidays, joys, sorrows, and too many a Friday night together. And she didn't know them. Neither did they know her. Maybe it wasn't only time to move away from a job that was killing her spirit, but from people who could care less about her as a person, who saw her only as the good girl from next door, the one who would never do anything to upset anyone, who totally underestimated her. It was painfully obvious that they took her behavior personally, that *she* was someone who needed fixing, not the situation. Just like when she finally left Russell. They couldn't believe that anything could be so terrible that she would give up her wonderful life. And her inability to move from behind the wall of her shame and tell them of her weakness, the control that her body often had over her actions, led them to believe that she was overreacting, being childish — foolish mostly.

Now this. Well, she couldn't sit back and take it anymore. She couldn't. If she did, she'd truly be no better than everyone expected her to be: silent, good-natured Regina, who went along to get along, who never thought things through, just acted on impulse like an irresponsible child who needed monitoring.

She placed her glass solidly down on the table and gripped it. Toni and Victoria jumped.

"You know something, not once did either of you ask me why. Not once did either of you ask what you could do. The first thing that came to your minds was, Regina's gone off the deep end again. Doesn't know what she's doing. Well, you know what, I may be the only one who does." She turned to Toni. "You, great savior of the downtrodden, you're so busy doling out advice you need to take a look in your own backyard. It's always easy to take over someone else's life when you've lost control of your own. And Ms. Vicky, high and mighty, your idea of success has nothing to do with being happy on the inside, only with what people can see on the outside. All appearances, all superficial. There's nothing there, Vicky. Nothing beneath the surface. You two claim to be my friends. When was the last time you were my friends when I needed someone?" She breathed hard to keep from shaking. "Since we're being so honest, since I need to be put in check, for once I'm doing what I need to do for me." She jabbed at her chest. "But I don't think either of you will ever have what it takes to do the same. You'd rather live in your make-believe worlds where everything is beautiful. But guess what? It isn't. Not until you both see it for what it is." She pushed back from the table and stood. "I'm not the one to feel sorry for. I feel sorry for both of you!"

She snatched up her purse from the table and walked off, leaving them both with their mouths agape.

And the farther away she walked, the closer she came to crossing the threshold, the more she knew that she had taken the next steps toward the rest of her life. She only hoped that Toni and Victoria would one day choose to do the same. But just where in the hell was she going?

# CHAPTER FIVE

Toni found a lone parking space on the corner of her quiet tree-lined street. The gentrified Harlem neighborhood had changed dramatically in the last year. The once boarded-up and abandoned brownstones were rehabbed and inhabited by white couples and their young children. Now, most black folks couldn't afford to live in a neighborhood where once upon a time you couldn't give the buildings away.

For several moments, Toni sat in her car, staring sightlessly at a young man walking his dog, a woman emptying her garbage, a young couple strolling hand in hand. Her own backyard. Regina's words echoed in her head, stirring up realities she didn't want to see. It *was* easier to solve everyone else's issues, find answers to their problems, and feel appreciated and victorious because of all her hard work. Make their lives better because hers had spun out of control and she hadn't seen it coming — didn't want to, because if she did, she'd have to admit that she'd failed. And she couldn't do that. How could Regina have known?

She turned on the radio, lowered the window, and lit a cigarette. She blew a cloud of smoke into the balmy night air, then watched it slowly vanish. She looked across the street. The lights in her house were off. She only wished it was dark because her family was tucked away in sleep. *What a joke.* There was no telling where her husband Charles was, and her fifteen-year-old son Steven could be any number of places. Anywhere but in the home she'd built for them. All for them.

Toni blew out another cloud of smoke. Funny, that was what her life had become, her real life — a meaningless smoke screen. But it wasn't always this way. Not always. At some point she'd been happy, truly happy, with the world at her feet and a man who adored her and she him. Now all the lights were out and there was no one home. And there was nothing in her manuals to tell her how to fix what had turned her life upside down.

Victoria stood under the beat of the shower, scrubbing her ebony body with a loofah sponge, the better to get rid of dull, dry skin. She turned her head away from the hot spray of water, mindful of getting her hair wet, even though she'd covered her head with a silk scarf and a plastic shower cap. Her next appointment was the following Wednesday. She had to keep her hair together until then. She scrubbed a bit harder, almost as if she wished she could wash some of the color away. She'd tried when she was little, scrubbed so hard her skin would become sore and tender to the touch.

She turned her back to the water, letting the spray slide down her spine. Regina had one hell of a nerve saying the things she did. Who did she think she was anyway? She was the one without a husband and a job. What did Regina know about what went on in Victoria's head, her life? Regina had no idea what she'd had to deal with all her life. Appearances. "You're damned right," she muttered. Without them, what did you have? *You don't have shit. Simple as that.* The whole world was built on appearances. She could testify to that in court. *You're judged by what people see. The hell with what's inside.* Regina only wished she had Victoria's life. Maybe Toni was rattled by her tirade, but she knew where it was coming from — fear and jealousy. She'd made another stupid mistake and wanted to take it out on them. Well, she had another thing coming if she believed for a New York minute that anything she said applied to her. Because it didn't. Never could. She wouldn't let it.

Victoria turned off the water and wrapped her long dancer's body — which she worked diligently to maintain — in a thick, white terry-cloth towel.

When she entered her bedroom, which was straight out of a designer's catalog, Phillip was already in their four-poster bed reading an accounting manual, his shock of silky onyx hair dropping casually over his thick brows. His pale, broad shoulders and thatch of black chest hair peeked out above the sheet that covered his slightly rounding stomach and long legs. When had she stopped loving him? she thought suddenly, the notion like a sharp stab in her heart.

Had she ever, or was he simply the trophy she'd leaped the hurdles to win? Phillip symbolized her achievement — in the flesh. He represented everything she'd been led to believe she couldn't have, wasn't worthy of. He validated her blackness. A wave of incredible sadness rolled through her stomach.

Phillip looked up over the edge of his wireless glasses, his brilliant blue eyes magnified. He smiled, that same smile he'd given her the first day they'd met at a banking conference nearly five years earlier.

He covered his mouth and yawned. "Hey, sweetheart. I was trying to wait up for you." He flipped the floral-patterned satin designer sheet back and patted the empty space next to him.

Slowly Victoria dropped the towel and slipped between the sheets.

Phillip draped his arm around her shoulders and pulled her closer. "Hmm, you smell good." He exhaled and shut his eyes. "I was thinking maybe we could go to Vail next weekend, get some skiing in. What do you think?"

"Sure. Sounds fine," she mumbled.

"Good." He stroked her hair, and she wondered how often he thought about how different hers felt from that of the other women he'd known. "So how was your evening with the girls?" he asked over another yawn.

She heard Regina's accusations, saw the hurt, anger, and disappointment in her otherwise compliant eyes, thought about the words, then pushed them away. "Fine.

Just like always," she said quietly. "Nothing new."

When Regina came in, Michele and Darren were camped out in front of the television in the living room watching music videos, their favorite pastime. The volume was so loud they didn't even hear her come in. A half-eaten bowl of buttered popcorn sat on the floor between them.

She looked around at her small but neat apartment on the second floor of a private house in Brooklyn's Canarsie area. She could use some new curtains in the living room, she observed, and the wood floors could use a good coat of varnish. But overall she liked her space. And the kids did, too. She had thought it would be hard to get them adjusted to living in an apartment after growing up in a house all their lives. But after the divorce she'd decided not to shoulder that responsibility alone. She and Russell sold the house and put the money into a college fund for the kids. It was the one thing they'd been able to agree on.

Michele and Darren had adjusted just fine. Better than she'd expected, actually. They both had their own rooms and were able to stay in their same schools. The space was much smaller, but they were happy. The constant tension was gone; the shouting, slamming doors, tears, and arguing had stopped. They didn't have to cower in their rooms while their father berated their mother. The erosion of the marriage intensified after Darren's birth, when Regina insisted on returning to work. At first she worked from home while Russell was at the office, hiding her assignments when he returned. Anything to avoid an argument, the feelings of guilt that she was somehow shortchanging everyone by her selfishness, her need to savor a little part of the world for herself.

Then she grew bolder and started going into the newsroom twice per week, then three times. Russell seethed in silence for the most part, talking to her only if he had a complaint or could find something wrong with the house or the kids that he could then attribute to her being away from home — or when he wanted to make love.

But she pursued it, stuck with it. And it finally paid off.

In 1994, she was nominated and ultimately received her first Associated Press Award, one of the highest accolades in journalism. She was so excited and certain that this would finally prove to Russell that this wasn't just a lark, some inconsequential thing she did, but something of value.

When she came home from the office, bubbling over with joy, she couldn't wait for Russell to come in so she could share her news.

She prepared his favorite meal of grilled salmon steaks, wild rice, and tossed salad. She was just finishing up in the kitchen when he came in. She hurried to the front of the sprawling two-story Tudor home and greeted him in the foyer.

Her face was radiant. "Russell, guess what?"

He dropped his briefcase near the hall closet and shrugged out of his cream-colored cashmere coat. "Well, don't you look happy." He walked up to her and put his arms around her waist. Gently he kissed her, and she allowed herself to enjoy the moment, giving into the warm sensation of his mouth. "What is it, baby?" he murmured. He stroked her hip. "Are you pregnant again?"

She briskly shook her head. "No, nothing like that. I was nominated for the Associated Press Award."

The light in his eyes grew dim. A crease formed between his brows. "What?"

"The Associated Press Award for my story on the homeless crisis. They're having the big annual banquet next month and I just might win, Russell," she said, barely able to contain her joy.

He turned away, unimpressed, as if she'd just recited the alphabet. "Where are the kids?"

Her mouth dropped open, and she frowned in confusion. "The kids are upstairs. Did you hear what I said?"

"Yeah, I heard you." He walked past her and into the kitchen. He rooted around in the fridge and took out a can of beer, popped the top, and took a long swallow. "I'm going up to take a shower before dinner." He disappeared from the room and they never discussed it again.

She went to the awards banquet without him, without her kids, without her friends. She was too ashamed to tell anyone that her husband didn't think her night was important enough for him to attend.

Even now, three years after the divorce, sometimes without warning the old fears would creep up on her. It might be a look in a stranger's eyes, the smell of a certain cologne, the sound of keys jingling in someone's hand, and she would see Russell's face twisted in anger for what he believed was some infraction or another.

"Do I have to tell you everything, Regina? Can't you make a simple decision like what to fix for dinner without asking my opinion? Maybe if you paid as much attention to what I liked, paid attention to this house and your family and our needs, as much as you do to going back to that damned job, you could get something done!"

"Why is it so hard for you to understand that I need more than babies and cooking? What about something for me, Russell?"

"What about you, Gina? Don't I take care of you, pay the bills? Do I run around with other women? Don't I pay attention to the children? I give you everything you need, but that doesn't seem to be enough for you. I bust my ass taking care of my family. You should do the same. Your job is your family. First, last, period. I don't need a wife like my mother," he said with disgust. "She wanted a career, too. It took her out of the house and away from what was really important: my father and me." His face creased in pain. "When we got married" — he pointed a finger of accusation in her face — "you said you wanted to be a wife and the mother of my children. And that's what I gave you. That should be enough for you. And I don't want to hear anything else. I've put up with enough."

She felt herself shrink, just like when her mother would make her perform for the family. She felt guilt for wanting something of her own, for thinking her own thoughts, just as she did standing before the nuns when she questioned the mysteries of faith. So she said nothing. Remained the good, obedient girl. Kept the turmoil and rebellion inside day after day, year after year, until one day Russell came home to an empty house. She and the children were gone.

She wasn't quite sure what became the final turning point for her — if it was simply the accumulation of years of feeling unfulfilled, or that night on the beach.

They'd had a small dinner party at their house in Brooklyn Heights.

Toni arrived tucked under Charles's arm, and Vicky was proudly draped all over her new husband, Phillip. Toni and Charles's son Steven immediately went in search of Michele and Darren, who were in the basement, playing video games.

"Everything looks beautiful as always," Toni complimented, sidling up to Regina in the kitchen. "You're our own Martha Stewart."

Regina didn't comment.

"Can I help with something?"

Regina spun toward her friend. "Toni . . . I can't stand it anymore."

Toni frowned in confusion. "Stand what?"

"This house, this half life, my marriage." Her voice caught and she drew air in through her nose as she pressed her lips together to keep them from trembling.

"Gina, come on, it can't be that bad." She placed a comforting hand on Regina's shoulder. "The kids are doing great, you have a good husband, financial security. What's wrong?"

"All of it," she blurted out. "Russell treats me like some sort of possession — an empty vessel that can be filled only by him. The kids . . ." She exhaled and pressed her palm to her forehead. "All I am to them is the cook, the chauffeur, the laundress. They treat me the same way they see their father treat me — as a nonentity with no opinion, no decision-making power." Tears of frustration rolled down her cheeks. She quickly wiped them away.

"Gina," Toni said in her best social-worker voice. "Marriages go through changes."

Regina straightened, shook her head

tightly. "This isn't about changes. It's about all the time. All the time. Day in and out. Every day. Do you hear what I'm saying?"

"There you two are." Russell pushed through the swinging door of the kitchen, crossed the space in that assured, take-charge way of his, and kissed her forehead, then pushed a tendril of her hair away from her face. "We're all waiting for you, babe," he said in a voice so close and personal that it made Toni blush.

"I'll be out in a minute," Regina said stiffly. "I was just finishing the stuffed clams."

Russell reached into the tray and plucked one of the delicate morsels from the doily-laced server and popped it into his mouth. His eyes closed in what almost resembled ecstasy.

"Babe, you've done it again. Delicious." He turned shining eyes on Antoinette. "I'm a lucky man." He beamed. "Gina is the best." He turned to his wife and duplicated his first kiss. "Anything ready to take inside? We don't want to keep them waiting too long," he added in the patronizing way of his that reminded her that she was remiss without actually saying it.

Regina tugged on her bottom lip. "You

can take the platter of hors d'oeuvres and dip inside to get them started."

He looked behind him on the wooden island counter at the array of food that Regina had spent hours preparing. "How 'bout the shrimp cocktail?"

"Sure, that's fine."

Russell picked up the tray and headed for the swinging door.

For a hot minute, Regina wished someone would push from the other side. She needed some comic relief to ease the tightness in her chest.

"Don't take too long," he repeated and pushed through the door — unhampered.

*So much for wishful thinking.*

Toni watched the tense expression on Regina's face and the inhibited body language she'd displayed when Russell came near her. Then totally in contrast was Russell, who was open, demonstrative, and affectionate. She could tell by the way he responded to Regina, the way he could barely keep his hands and body away from her, that he truly loved her — wanted her.

She knew the look. Charles used to look at her like that, with the same heat, the same desire flowing from him. But it was like she said earlier — marriages changed shape as they took on more years. You simply had to adjust yourself to the new fit.

Antoinette stole a glance at Regina, whose back was turned to her. Maybe Regina was frigid! Damn, that was enough to make anybody tense and crazy. *Hmm.* Would Regina want to even tell her something that personal about her sex life? Did she want to hear it? It was one thing to listen to clients — strangers. It was a different issue when it was your dear friend. There were some things that didn't necessarily need to be shared.

"Gina," Antoinette finally uttered. She click-clicked across the gleaming floors, absently wondering how Gina managed to keep them glowing like that. "I think you and Russ just need to talk, maybe get away for a weekend — to a spa to really relax. The kids could stay with me and Charles. You know Steven would love the company."

"I . . . don't know. It'll take more than a weekend." She shook her head wearily.

"Think about it, hon. A change in atmosphere can lead to a change in attitude," she said with authority.

"I'll think about it," Regina mumbled halfheartedly, realizing that it was pointless to pursue this topic with Toni, who believed that everything could be fixed. The truth was, some things remained permanently damaged.

The evening progressed uneventfully, with casual small talk about politics, sports, finances, and the incredible heat wave. Through it all, Regina refilled drinks, offered more food, took plates away, and refilled trays — playing the good hostess to the hilt.

"How about a drive out to the beach?" Victoria suggested as the evening began to wind down.

"Sounds good to me," Phillip seconded, looking to the men for additional confirmation.

"Sure, why not?" Charles chimed in.

"What about the kids?" Gina asked.

"They'll be fine right here," Russell said. "You worry too much, babe." He dropped an arm around her shoulder. Regina forced a half smile.

The beach at Jacob Riis Park was beautiful that steamy August night. The heavens were clear and the final bands of a blazing orange sun still burned across the horizon. All along the beach couples dotted the white sand or sat along the boardwalk. In the distance, stretched out along the calm water, the white masts of private boats could be seen.

The three couples parked, then made their way, laughing and talking, toward the water. For a while Regina forgot herself, let the unease that gripped her ebb away with the gentle pull of the water.

Victoria, impeccably dressed in a flowing, multilayered lime green skirt of gauze, slipped out of her strappy sandals and ran giggling toward the breaking waves with Phillip close on her heels.

Regina had never before seen the very practical, sometimes cynical, almost staid Victoria actually seem carefree, near childlike in her enjoyment. She glanced at Toni and Charles, who were strolling together — close, but not touching, speaking in hushed tones as they moved almost in unison along the shore.

Russell pulled in a deep breath of ocean-washed air. "You did a great job tonight, hon," he offered. "You really did."

"Thanks."

He slid his hands into the pockets of his slacks and stood facing the water. In that moment, seeing Russell there, set against the backdrop of nature at its finest, he was the man she'd married, the one she'd fallen in love with, given herself to for the first time. He was the one she believed would rescue her from herself, be her partner, share her joys, help her bloom. She couldn't blame him for the way he was. She'd allowed him to treat her the way he did. Her fears, her guilts, her insecurities about her self-worth made her an easy candidate for someone as strong-willed and single-minded as Russell Everette. What would it take to set her free from this inexplicable hold he had on her?

"Russell," she said tentatively, her soft voice a whisper in the night air.

"Hmmm?" He took her hand. "You know I love you, Gina," he said out of the blue. "I know I'm not an easy man to live with." He turned to her, looked into her upturned face. "But I only want the best for you. You know that."

"But, Russell —"

"No, please listen. Sometimes we're so wrapped up in ourselves, we fail to see the needs in others."

Her body tensed.

"And that's what happened with you, Gina. Things outside of our home, outside of us, became more important. I gave in, let you do what you felt you needed to, but . . . I can't let it continue. It's destroying our family."

"So everything that's wrong with our marriage is my fault. Is that what you're telling me?" The nerve beneath her right eye began to tic.

"Regina, this isn't about blame. This is about making things right," he said in that same "you're an idiot and I'm not" voice.

"I'm unhappy, Russell. I've been unhappy for a long time — at least twelve of the fourteen years we've been together. And you haven't even noticed."

He stared at her as if she'd lost her mind, because obviously she had. Suddenly he broke out in laughter, the deep rumble dancing across the ocean's waves. "Don't be ridiculous," he said, pulling himself together. "What do you have to be unhappy about? I give you everything any woman could want. We have a beautiful house, two cars, great kids, money in the bank, and the sex between us is just as good as — if not better than — when we met." He moved closer. "Even after all of this time." He lowered his head and attempted to kiss her. She turned at the last second and he caught her cheek.

Russell reared back, glaring at her. "What's with you? I can't kiss my own wife?"

"You haven't heard anything I've said."

"I heard you — and I answered you. Your feelings are totally ridiculous. They're not based on anything that makes sense."

God, how that hurt. It was more painful than any emotional slap she'd ever endured. And it was at that moment she realized her marriage was over, dead, simply waiting to be buried. And all her wishful hopes that tomorrow would make it better were completely stamped out. And she felt terribly alone.

In the early hours of that morning, as Russell made love to her body, she found refuge for her tattered spirit in a tight, inaccessible corner, where he couldn't hurt her ever again.

Michele got up to replenish their bowl and saw her mother standing in the doorway. Her face, so much like her father's sharp West Indian features, lit up.

"Hi, Ma."

Regina blinked, took a breath, and focused on her daughter and the present. "Hi, sweetie." Regina put her purse down on the table in the foyer, the tightness in her chest slowly easing.

Michele crossed the room and kissed her mother's cheek. "You're home early. Didn't expect you so soon."

"Short night. Hello, Darren."

Darren's eyes were glued to the screen. He raised his hand in a short wave. Regina smiled and shook her head.

"I need to talk to both of you," Regina said when Michele returned from the kitchen. She came into the living room and sat on the couch, took the remote control from the coffee table, and clicked off the television.

"Aw, man. I've been waiting all night for that video," Darren spouted, his once adolescent lankiness taking on the lean tautness of the man he would soon become.

"I'm sure it will be on again." She took a breath. "I, uh, quit my job today," she blurted out before she could change her mind.

Michele's hand stopped midway between the bowl and her mouth. "Quit? Why?"

Darren's head snapped in his mother's direction. His sullen expression was replaced with one of surprise.

"I couldn't take it anymore."

"But I thought you liked your job," Michele said, confusion raising the pitch of her voice.

"I do. Well, I did." She swallowed. "I've been thinking about this for a while, but I realized this morning after my boss wanted to send me out to another rape scene that I couldn't do it. Not anymore. I just couldn't. Of course, he thought I was just having a momentary lapse in female judgment. But I wasn't. And I'm tired of always being treated like I don't have a brain in my head simply because I'm a woman, no matter how good my work is. I can't do it anymore." There, she'd said it.

Her children simply stared at her blankly, trying to process the information and the impact it would have on their lives.

*What about new clothes and sneakers?* Darren thought.

*How will I get the car she promised for graduation?* Michele worried. She'd bragged about it to all her friends. Now they'd think she was lying.

"What are we going to do?" Michele asked.

Regina folded her hands in her lap. Her children needed to know that everything was going to be all right. They needed to be assured that their mother could take care of them. And she would. Without anyone's help, but on her own. And without anyone's permission. She tried to swallow over the knot in her throat. A hot wave of apprehension swept through her. She didn't have a clue what to tell her children.

# CHAPTER SIX

Just as she thought. Empty.

Toni flipped on the hall light, bathing the expansive ground floor in a soft white glow. The parquet floors gleamed, reflecting the smoked glass-and-chrome accessories. Floor-to-ceiling windows topped off with stained glass took up one wall, offering a picturesque view of the deck they'd had built in the back — actually that *she'd* had built in the back. At the time she had thought it would be great in the summer. The three of them could enjoy the deck on hot evenings, and even barbecue. It had been four years since its addition to the house. If the deck was used once as a family, that was a lot.

She crossed the room, her clicking heels the only sound of welcome in the silent, four-story brownstone.

When she and Charles had first married, he was content living in a one bedroom apartment in Brooklyn. However, she had bigger plans in mind for them. She wouldn't live the life her parents had, five bodies squeezed together in three little ramshackle rooms, breathing each other's air, sweat, and misery day in and day out. She wanted a house to live and grow in. And she wanted to live in Manhattan, the heart and soul of New York City, far away from the wretched memories of Algiers, Louisiana, and all it represented: poverty, illiteracy, and hopelessness.

Over Charles's protests she found a realtor, and the hunt for the perfect house began.

It took Toni six months to find the house she wanted, the one where she would build her life and raise her family.

"Charles, baby." She had rushed into the house ready to burst with excitement. "Charles!"

"In here."

Toni entered the bedroom that often reminded her of the tiny space she'd shared with her sisters Lynn, Ann Marie, and Gloria most of her life, and finally their multitude of children. It had one closet and a narrow window that faced the brick wall of the apartment building next door. She'd tried every design trick in the book to give the unwelcoming box some life and vitality, from painting Charles's dull forest green walls an eggshell white to give it the illusion of space, to adding colorful African and abstract art to the uneven walls. Caftans and throw pillows dotted the living space that doubled as a dining room. But no matter what she did the apartment would always be two boxy rooms with a lot of stuff.

She felt as if she were suffocating.

Charles was changing out of his chauffeur's uniform. His back faced her as she walked in. Smooth bronze skin coated taut muscles that he spent hours in the gym maintaining. His shoulders were wide, tapering down to a narrow waist and buns to die for. There was nothing about Charles Devon that didn't catch and hold the attention; the boyish grin and tiny gap in his front teeth, the thick, sweeping brows over dark, deep-set eyes and curling lashes. There was something about Charles, an innocence almost, that made you want to reach out, wrap him in your arms, and take care of him.

There was nothing obviously weak or vulnerable about Charles, just a carefree, naive way of moving through his days as if nothing were of great importance.

And that was what drew Toni to Charles, her need to nurture, fix, and care for another person, and her belief that Charles fit her idea of who he was and how she could make him better. Charles became another one of her projects.

The first time she'd seen him he was in an after-work bar in the West Village in Manhattan. He was alone, nursing a glass of Scotch, lightly bobbing his head to Kirk Whalum's saxophone remake of "Going in Circles."

It wasn't her way to introduce herself to a strange man. It was the first time she'd ever walked into a bar alone without the intention of meeting her friends. Everything about that first meeting was new and different.

"Hi."

Charles turned his head slowly toward her, a soft smile tugging the corners of his mouth. The room was smoky, the music mellow, the voices loud and raunchy. But when he looked at her, everything but Charles faded into the background.

His heavily lidded eyes rolled over her once, and a short shudder pulsed between her thighs and rippled up to her chest. He didn't respond, simply looked at her with a soft, inquisitive expression on his face, as though he were waiting for a question he wasn't sure he could or should answer.

Toni swallowed down the sudden dryness in her throat. "Mind if I sit down?" She indicated the vacant stool with a tip of her head.

"No." He put his glass on the counter.

"My name is Toni." What was she doing?

"Charles. Devon." He picked up his drink and drained it. "Can I buy you something?"

"Just a Coke would be fine. Thanks." She put her briefcase between her feet and folded her hands atop the counter, wishing she had a cigarette.

She noticed Charles looking down at her hands. *Totally ringless and totally free,* she thought as he moved a breath closer.

"Just getting off work?"

"I was visiting a client."

His brows knitted. "What kind of client?"

Toni laughed when the reason for his suspicious expression registered in her head. "Nothing quite that interesting," she assured him. "I'm a social worker. I have a family about a block from here that I check on once a month."

"Oh." The tiny lines around his eyes eased. "You do that a lot — visit clients?"

Toni settled into her seat. "It depends on

the client and what their needs are. Most of them come to my office."

"Where's that?"

"Sojourner Truth Health Center on Lenox Avenue."

"Long way from home making house calls."

The warm breath of his voice slid under the folds of her cotton blouse, gliding across her flesh in a slow, circular dance. For a moment she stumbled and lost her way when she fell into the penetrating darkness of his eyes and felt the goose bumps rise across her belly.

The bartender placed her drink in front of her, cutting off the current.

Toni blinked and the room cleared. "It's not too bad," she finally muttered in response.

"As long as you like what you do, that's what counts."

She sipped her soda and suddenly wished she'd ordered something stronger.

"What about you?"

Charles shrugged casually. "I drive for a limo company."

Somebody turned out the lights, let the curtain fall before the last act, flipped the switch. *A glorified cabdriver! Oh, damn.* She signaled the bartender.

"Could I have a rum and Coke, please?"
She collected her thoughts, then cleared
her throat. "You, uh, must meet a lot of interesting people."

He laughed, and she realized she really
liked the sound of it, the deep, sincere
richness of it. *Why a limo driver, Lord?*

"Sure. All the time." He angled his body
toward her, and she noticed the dimple in
his left cheek. "But I guess it depends on
who you consider interesting."

"Oh, I don't know . . . celebrities, sports
figures . . ."

"Hmm. You think they're interesting?"

The steady ground of her usual self-
assurance shifted right, then left. Her drink
arrived. She took a quick swallow and the
movement settled. "Sure. Don't you?"

"No."

Toni waited for an explanation, something to indicate why he felt that way, but
nothing came. Just a one-word answer that
hung in the air between them, creating a
hot longing for more.

Charles toyed with his refill. "You live in
the city?"

"Yes." She could play, too.

"Need a ride home?"

He was good at this game. "If it's not out
of your way."

He gazed at her from the corner of his eye. "Depends on where it is. Doesn't it?"

She pushed back a smile. "Barclay Street. About ten minutes from here."

He dug in his back pocket and took out his wallet, pulled out a twenty and a ten, and put them on the counter. "Ready?" He stood and walked toward the door, not bothering to look back, certain, somehow, that she would follow.

Toni hesitated a minute, thought about all the headlines in the papers and the horror stories on the television, tried to recall if she'd ever seen his face in the post office or a milk carton.

She snatched up her briefcase and followed him out.

He was leaning against a black Lincoln Town Car, standard fare for shuttling who's who around the city. His black jacket was hooked on his finger, draped across his white-shirted shoulder.

For all the bravado, there was a vulnerability in his expression, an uncertainty that softened his eyes and the tautness of his body. A silent language from a past she wanted to learn about.

How many times had she seen that look on the faces of the wounded souls she tried to heal? Her heart surged, then settled.

Slowly she approached. He opened the back door.

Momentarily taken aback, she slid onto the lush black leather seat; the scent of its newness and a hint of cigarette smoke mingled like slow dancers on a crowded floor.

The glass partition that separated them whirred downward.

He looked at her through the rearview mirror. "Hope you don't mind sitting in the back. Never know when I might pass another driver or one of the bosses."

"Are you still on duty?"

"On call."

"Oh." She settled against the cushions.

"Help yourself to a drink if you like. Just press the silver button."

She did. A minibar slid out, filled with tiny bottles of liquor, water, and cans of Coke and seltzer. A cellophane-wrapped bowl contained sliced lemons and limes on ice. She thought about fixing herself a drink just for the hell of it, then changed her mind. She needed her head to be clear. Just in case.

"Music?"

Her head snapped up. "Sure."

"Prelude to a Kiss," by Sarah Vaughan, floated like a spring breeze around her.

They rode together in silence, the sound of music covering the distance between them.

She wanted to question him, the way she did with her clients, delve into his background, seek out his hopes and dreams, have him reveal his deepest thoughts. But the music and his back stopped her, held her in place with a firm hand.

Before she had time to push the urge away, they were turning onto her street.

"What's the address?"

She was feeling like one of *his* clients.

"Eight-twenty-two."

He pulled to a stop, hurried around to the passenger side, and opened her door. She almost expected him to bow. Gingerly she got out, hesitated when she stood inches away from him, waited for some signal.

He stared back at her, his expression questioning. "Something wrong?" He looked behind him at the address, then back at her.

"No. Nothing's wrong." She pulled in a breath. "Do you always offer to bring strange women home?"

"Not if I think they're strange." He grinned at her, and she felt that shift again. "Is that what you are, Toni — strange?"

"Not that I've been told lately."

"Exactly as I thought."

She glanced away, then at him. The sun was setting behind the rows of buildings, casting everything in its path in a gentle orange glow. It reflected off his eyes, making them dance with pinpoints of light. She could hear the thunder of words in the distance, approaching, drawing closer, signaling the storm. She wanted to stop them, keep them at bay, but the clouds opened and the torrent fell. "You . . . want to come in for a minute? That is, if you don't have to . . . pick someone up."

"Yes."

Those one-word answers again. "Yes, you'd like to come in, or yes you have to pick someone up?"

"Both. But I have some time." He pressed a button on the tiny black box in his hand and a soft beep locked the doors. He followed her along the short walk and down the three steps to her basement apartment.

Everything about that first night was surreal, full of all the things she'd told her young female clients to steer clear of: from talking to a strange man in a bar, to riding in his car, bringing him home, and sleeping with him.

But those early days were full of spontaneous, carefree moments — risks. Charles brought out the little girl in her, made her lose track of reality, responsibility. He was like a kid without a care, and sometimes he made her feel the same way. Sometimes.

As the days moved from lazy summer to curl-up-by-the-fire winter, Charles and Toni settled into the rhythm of being a couple. Or at least Toni did. She took him to meet her friends and family, who thought, "He's darling." She took him shopping for clothes she thought would bring out the best in him. She circled job notices for executives and left them on his kitchen table, because of course he had to want more than to be a driver all his life. She told him about luxury apartments in midtown Manhattan, bought artwork for his tiny apartment. Asked him to marry her when she found herself pregnant with their son, because she knew he wouldn't think marriage was necessary. For all his sexiness, his insatiable appetite in bed, good looks, boyish charm, and clever turns of phrase, he was a boy in a man's body. A man six years younger than she, who might leave her any day if she didn't keep up, didn't help him grow up. And she convinced herself that she could. She would expand his horizons, help him up the corporate ladder to success. Because she loved him. Loved him more than she ever thought she could love another human being. And whatever it took to keep him she would do. Even when it meant forgetting her birth-control pills.

Now she had the gorgeous, sexy husband and a baby on the way. All she needed was *the* house and her life would be complete. The facade would remain intact.

"I figured you'd find one sooner or later," he said, stepping into a pair of sweatpants. He tugged on the strings, then faced her. "So where have you decided we'll be living?"

His question was empty as an abandoned building, stirring up dust and debris and things hidden in the dark.

She tilted up her chin. "It's a brownstone. Four stories, in Harlem. It needs some work, but it's magnificent. Just what we need."

"Really." He put on his sneakers and picked up his gym bag.

"Is that all you have to say?" The baby kicked in her stomach.

He stopped on his way to the door. "There's nothing for me to say, Toni. It's what you want, isn't it?"

The baby kicked again. "It's what we want. What we need." She covered her stomach with her hands. "We can't stay here."

"I guess we can't." He opened the door and walked out, closing it quietly behind him.

So here she was, fourteen years later, with a husband, a son, a solid career, and a beautiful home that she spent all her money making more beautiful — and she was completely alone.

Her own backyard.

# CHAPTER SEVEN

Getting through that first weekend was easy. It was Saturday, then Sunday. She didn't have to actually face the fact that she had no-where to go. Finding things to do around the house wasn't a problem. There were always dishes to wash, clothes for the machine, food to prepare, sweeping, dusting.

But then Monday rolled around, too soon as far as Regina was concerned, and she wasn't prepared for the overwhelming sensation of paralysis.

"Ma, can I have five dollars?" Michele asked, "we're going to get pizza after school."

"Me, too," Darren echoed.

"You ain't comin' with me," Michele made perfectly clear.

"I don't need you. I got my own friends," her brother tossed back.

"You wish," Michele mumbled.

"Cut it out, both of you. I don't want to hear it," Regina shouted, something she rarely did.

Michele and Darren snapped back in surprise, quickly putting a lid on their bickering.

Regina looked from one sheepish face to the other and was just about to apologize for yelling, then changed her mind. *I'm tired of apologizing.*

She pushed herself up from the table and went in search of her purse, her slippers making that slap-swish sound across the floor. Checking her wallet, she found two fifties, a twenty, a ten, two fives, and an assortment of singles. She plucked out the two fives and slap-swished back to the kitchen. She handed one each to her children.

"Thanks, Ma," they mumbled.

Regina nodded absently. "Hurry up before you're late for school."

Michele looked at her for a moment, almost as if she were going to say something but then changed her mind.

"Ma, can I still get my Jordans next weekend? You promised," Darren reminded her.

*That was before your mother quit her job,* she thought. A wave of panic rolled through her stomach. "We'll see," she said almost to herself. At some point she was seriously going to have to go over her expenses and her assets. But she couldn't bring herself to do it. Not yet. She did have her two-weeks-salary check coming and some vacation time due her, but that wouldn't last very long.

The kids said their good-byes and Regina was left alone. After some minor straightening up around the apartment and with nothing left to do, Regina found herself curled up on her bed.

What had she done? Toni's and Vicky's reprimands echoed in her head. For all her bravado a few days ago, suddenly things didn't seem so cut-and-dried. An uncertain future loomed in front of her and she had no concrete plan in mind. And it seemed the harder she tried to focus the muddier the picture became.

Regina closed her eyes and curled up tighter. This was the same sinking sensation she had felt when she had finally got the nerve to leave Russell.

It was about two months after the incident at the beach. She'd come home from a grueling day covering a fire in a row of houses in Harlem. The wails of the distraught family members were still ringing in her ears, raising the hair on her arms. The acrid smell of smoke clung to her clothing and stung her nostrils. Every sinew in her body ached, but more than that she was mentally and emotionally spent. Visions of injured children, bodies being removed by the ambulances, hordes of people gawking at the horror, still ran in a constant stream across her consciousness. What she needed more than anything at that moment was to talk it out, expel it from her system, feel protected and safe.

She'd just kicked off her shoes and was about to take a long, hot shower when Russell walked into the bedroom.

"Hi, Russ." She slipped on her robe over her undergarments.

Russell barely acknowledged her presence. "What's that smell. Is something burning?"

"I had to cover a fire today. It was . . . horrible," she uttered, exhaustion weighing down her voice.

Russell pulled his tie from around his neck and tossed it across the bed. "So you had to bring the stench of it into the house?" he snapped.

Regina's body coiled in tension. She felt the slow simmer as Russell's gaze landed on her. His expression hardened, and she knew that the boiling over was inevitable. She couldn't take it, not tonight, not after the day of destruction she'd been witness to.

Regina fastened the belt on her robe and walked toward the bathroom.

"Don't walk away from me when I'm talking to you, Regina."

Something deep inside of her snapped. She had a flash of the nuns commanding her to come to the front of the class and recite the opening passages of the Constitution for having spoken out of turn. And her failure to do that, as her classmates snickered at her plight, was a half-hour detention. She saw her mother in front of a roomful of people telling her to play something to entertain her guests. She saw Russell standing on the shores of the beach telling her that her feelings were ridiculous. She hated that helpless feeling of being put on display, a light being shone on her missteps for all to see and judge, her feelings held up for ridicule. Suddenly all the reprimands, the feelings of shame, resentment, and insecurities, the calls to perform on demand, to be seen and not heard, bubbled to the surface, spilling out between them like molten lava, daring them to cross it.

Regina spun toward him, fury burning in her eyes. "Don't you ever tell me what to do again, Russell," she ground out in a hiss that sounded like water hitting a hot skillet. "I'm not a child. I'm not an employee of yours." Her voice rose to a point of hysteria. "I'm sick of you treating me as if nothing I think, nothing I feel or do matters." Her breath came in short, staccato bursts. "I'm sick of your badgering bullshit. I'm a grown woman and I don't need you or anyone telling me where I can go, what I can do, and when I can leave a goddamn room!"

For an instant he simply stared at her in wide-eyed disbelief. He cocked his head to the side. "What did you say to me?"

Regina took long, deep breaths. "You heard me, Russell. I'm tired of you and everyone else telling me what to do. I know you don't give a damn about my feelings, or what I go through from one day to the next. You made that perfectly clear that night on the beach. But I'm not dealing with it anymore."

"Not dealing with it. Listen to you. Are you hearing yourself?"

"No, are you hearing me?" Her body literally vibrated with anger. "If you can't respect me . . . then . . . we don't need to be together." Her head began to pound the instant the words left her lips.

The edges of Russell's mouth trembled. His nostrils flared in and out as he sucked in air. "What the hell is going on around here? You have that two-bit piece of job and so now you think you . . . don't need to be with me, that we don't need to be together. Is that what I'm hearing, after all we've been through together?" His eyes clenched as if he were in terrible pain. "We have two kids, a home, a life, Regina. What have I done but ask a simple question — that's all. A simple question and look where you're taking this." He crossed the room and stood close enough to her that it forced her to look up at him. "I've had a rough day at the office," he said, his voice dropping down to that place in the center of her stomach.

Her pulse raced.

Russell's expression softened. He ran his hand along her waist, then across her hip.

Regina backed up. He caught her around the waist and pulled her closer.

"Where are you going?" he said in a hot whisper. He lowered his head.

"No, Russell. No."

He ignored her, kissed her long and hard, cutting off her protest, holding her tightly enough that she could feel every inch of him. Russell loosened the belt of

127

her robe with one hand, and held her in place with the other.

Regina's first urge was to scream; for the first time she clearly understood the true meaning of being violated. But she knew her cries would bring the children, and that she couldn't bear.

But as Russell moved slowly and firm within her, his voice burning in her ear how much he loved her, how his life would be nothing without her, and her body instinctively responded, she knew in her heart and soul that she could not live with herself another day if she allowed him to do this to her ever again.

"Don't leave me, Gina," he groaned into her ear, as she experienced the first wave of release. "I'm nothing without you." His body tensed as if shocked before he pressed his full weight onto her.

Even while her traitorous body continued to grip and release him, and a shudder rampaged through her, she stared up at the ceiling and swore tonight was the end.

The following morning, Regina prepared breakfast as usual, then kissed Russell and the kids good-bye. As soon as the house was empty she called her office and told her boss she was ill, and maybe she truly was, she thought as she went from her bedroom to the kids' rooms collecting all of the clothes she thought they'd need. She used every available suitcase, backpack, and laundry bag. She gathered their video games and anything else she thought was essential.

Wet with perspiration, Regina sat down on the couch. She shook all over. That first rush of adrenaline began to dissipate and doubt began to creep in. She looked around her at the rows of suitcases and bags. *Gina. I'm nothing without you.* She heard the words in her ears, felt his hands on her body, and suddenly she screamed, from the pit of her being she screamed — hollered out the hurt, the humiliation, the anger, and frustration that had been locked inside her for years, until her throat was raw and her eyes red and swollen.

Wiping away her tears, Regina took long gulps of air, pushed herself up from the couch, and went to the phone.

"Ms. Devon," Antoinette answered on the first ring.

"Toni, it's me, Gina."

"Hey, girl, whatsup?"

"I . . . need your help, Toni."

"Sure . . ."

"I'm leaving Russell."

"Say what?"

"Today. Right now. And I need to know if I can put some of our things at your house until me and the kids get settled."

"Gina, slow down. What happened?"

"The same thing that's been happening," she said, feeling the anxiety begin to build. "Can I or not?"

Toni jerked her head back from the phone. "Well, I guess you can put the stuff in the basement. But Gina, listen, have you thought this thing through? What about the kids, all of your things? What in heaven's name did the man do?"

Regina felt his hands, heard the hot whispers of his loving words. "Are you going to help me or not?" she nearly shouted, trembling all over. "Michele and Darren will be here by five and I want us to be gone before Russell comes home."

"Gina," Toni breathed, trying to find the words to get her friend to listen to reason. "Women don't just up and leave their husband of fourteen years for no good reason, especially when there are children involved. Listen, we need to talk." She got up from her desk and closed her office door. "Did he hit you?"

"No."

"Did he threaten to physically hurt you in any way?"

130

"No. Toni, are you going to help me or play Jeopardy?"

Antoinette blew out a breath. "Fine. What . . . How is this going to work?"

"I'll put everything in the car and bring it to your house. Can you meet me there during your lunch break?"

Antoinette checked her appointment schedule. "I have a client at two-thirty. I'll have to leave in a few to be back in time."

Regina felt tears of relief burn her eyes. "Thanks, Toni," she whispered. "I'll be there."

Antoinette slowly replaced the receiver. Regina was leaving Russell. She thought back to the night of the dinner party and how upset Regina had been. She'd attributed it to her being tired, maybe even a little PMS. But this . . . She checked her watch. She needed to leave. It should take Regina about forty-five minutes to get to her house from Queens. She picked up the phone, flipped through her Rolodex, and found Victoria's office number.

Regina's heart beat violently in her chest. Every car sound she heard made her jump, certain that it was Russell. She had to be out of there before he came home. She knew what would happen if she didn't.

When she pulled up in front of Antoinette's brownstone, she was surprised to see Victoria's BMW parked out front. She'd recognize the vanity plates — VICKY — anywhere. The instant she shut off the engine, Toni and Vicky emerged from the parlor-floor door. They descended the concrete steps in unison.

"Girl, what are you doing?" was the first thing out of Victoria's mouth.

"Gina, I really don't think you've thought this through," Antoinette added.

Regina held up her hand, her palm facing them. "We can run through the list of dos and don'ts some other time. Are you two going to help me or not?"

"Well, you know we're not going to let you just stay in the street," Antoinette said, heading for the car.

"And where are you going to stay?" Victoria asked.

Regina pulled a laundry bag from the back seat.

"I haven't figured that out yet."

Antoinette and Victoria looked at each other askance with an "I told you she was crazy" look in their eyes.

Regina and the kids wound up staying with Toni and Charles for two weeks. And watching the dynamics between them was quite revealing. It was clear who was in charge of that household, and she felt an overwhelming empathy, a bond almost with Charles. She spent the next two weeks with Vicky and Phillip before finally locating her current apartment, not too far from her old neighborhood.

Russell called her at work every day. At first he was furious, demanding that she come home. Then his demands became pleas and promises. He'd tell her how much he missed her and the kids; how could she hurt him like this; what had he done? He sent her flowers and cards. And day by day, Regina swore she would unravel. It took all she had to hold herself together, get up every morning, and find her way to work. His relentlessness was like water beating, drip by drip, on a rock, wearing her down. Between Russell and her mother's badgering, she was certain she'd go crazy.

One day she came outside for lunch and he was parked in front of the *Daily News* building. She turned to go back inside and became trapped by employees exiting the building. She felt a firm hand on her shoulder.

"Regina."

She pushed through the revolving doors.

Russell came in behind her, matching her step for step. "I want to talk to you, Regina."

"Leave me alone, Russell." She hurried toward the elevator.

"You're making me crazy, Gina. This whole thing is crazy. Come home; whatever it is we can work it out. Your mother's been calling every day. She's worried out of her mind about you and the kids. So am I, G. Please talk to me."

She wouldn't let him do this to her: first pile on the guilt, then coat it with sugar to make it easier for her to swallow.

"Baby, come on."

He was right up on her now. She could feel the heat of his body. She pressed the button for the elevator.

She turned to face him. "I've filed for divorce, Russell. You should be getting something in the mail."

The elevator door opened and she stepped inside. When she faced front, before the doors closed, she saw him as she'd never seen him before — true pain, misery, and loss shimmered in the pools of water that filled his eyes.

Her heart slammed in her chest, and a deep sadness fell over her. The doors slid shut.

Regina was surprised to find tears on her cheeks as she pushed the last vestiges of that day to the back of her mind. It still hurt, she realized, sitting up in bed. Even after three years the questions of right and wrong still lingered. She supposed there was no easy way to forget fourteen years of living with someone, and though you might love them, staying with them would destroy you. How did you choose?

Sighing deeply, she wiped her eyes. She had done what she had to do, she told herself. And one day the emptiness would be filled. But now there were other issues to face, and she must begin somewhere. But as hard as she tried, it was nearly three weeks after she quit her job before she could pull herself together to face the inevitable — her family's financial survival. Her wake-up call came from her daughter.

She could still hear Michele's accusing voice. "When are you going to get out of your robe? You don't even get dressed anymore, and you treat me and Darren like we're not even here!" After trying more than once to get her mother to answer her question, Michele just glared at her mother, then turned and stomped out of the house, slamming the door behind her.

Regina could still hear the hurt and confusion in Michele's voice as she forced herself out of bed. She crossed the room to the area she'd sectioned off as her little office. It was equipped with a computer, fax machine, and printer, tools that came in handy during her days as a journalist. Her stomach fluttered. She opened her file drawer and pulled out the folder that contained her financial information: bank statements, IRA, and the stock portfolio that she'd set up with her job.

Item by item she went through her assets, and her pulse began to race. She couldn't believe what she was seeing. She actually had money and plenty of it. She added the numbers again. There it was, more than eighty thousand dollars between her savings, her IRA, and the matching investment plan she had with the *News*. She had yet to tally the total of her stock investment.

Regina stared at the numbers. Sure, she'd been frugal over the years, routinely putting her money aside and never touching it again, especially since Russell insisted that he could take care of all the bills and didn't need her money. How ironic. But she never realized just how well the irony paid off. For the most part she and the kids lived off her paycheck and the support money that Russell sent. She began to giggle; then full-out laughter filled her neat bedroom.

They were going to make it, she realized. There was plenty to tide her over until she decided what to do.

She plopped down spread-eagled on the bed, a smile beaming across her face. What to do first? she mused. Well, she had time, that was for sure, and she certainly had some money. Then it dawned on her, clear as crystal. That night in the restaurant she had decided on a salad simply because she was worried about money and it had triggered another thought. It resurfaced now. She'd work on herself, inside and out. And when she was ready for the next step, whatever that might be, she'd take it.

# CHAPTER EIGHT

Every morning for two hours, after the kids were off to school, Regina went to the neighborhood gym to work out, something she hadn't done since . . . well, she really didn't know. At first it was a good way to get out of the house, keep her mind and body occupied. But in the three weeks that she'd been going and working with the nutritionist, she'd lost five pounds, had begun to firm up her hips and thighs, and was finally seeing that little pouch begin to disappear. She felt good, full of energy. Her mind and body were in sync, operating at capacity. Her skin even began to look better — clearer, brighter, and the breakouts had stopped altogether.

And as spring slowly made way for summer, the days growing longer and warmer, Regina knew her time of the carefree life needed to come to a close. As much as she enjoyed her newfound freedom and her emerging new self, there were still those pinpricks of guilt that made her feel that she was wasting valuable time.

But while she'd been toning her body, she'd been thinking as well, and a plan for her future began to materialize. She knew it might be a long shot, but the more she thought about it, did her research, and visualized her plan, the more she began to believe it was possible. And without the distraction of having anyone tell her how silly and ridiculous her idea was, it was easier for her to begin the process.

Regina waited on the worn brown leather couch of the real estate office. Six gray metal desks were lined up on either side of the aisle, three left and three right. Mr. Harris, the man she'd come to see, sat at the last desk on the right-hand side. He'd helped her once before, and she hoped he would again. A secretary with burgundy hair chatted nonstop on the phone, not looking up.

The bell over the door chimed, and a stout woman with three noisy children behind her bustled through the door. She ushered them to several available seats and warned them to behave in a thick West Indian accent.

Regina turned her attention back to the magazine she wasn't actually reading. It had been nearly two months since she'd quit her job, she mused, barely scanning an Internet article on stock trading. That long since she'd last seen Toni or Vicki.

Too many times she'd thought of calling them, apologizing for the things she'd said. But just as quickly, the desire fizzled like a soda gone flat. Her birthday had come and gone, and for the first time in years she celebrated it without them. They sent cards, but no calls, no visits, no surprise party like the one they'd given her for her thirty-fifth birthday.

Now she'd turned forty, a milestone in her life, and she'd had no one to share it with. Even her kids had parties and dates — other things to do. The funny thing was, she didn't feel bad about it at all. Maybe she was alone, but she wasn't lonely. She was too busy getting used to the new Regina.

She'd skillfully avoided her mother during the past weeks, fending off her multitude of phone calls with excuses of being very tired and not able to talk long. But she knew she couldn't hold her off much longer. Thank heavens she'd established years ago that there were to be no calls to her job unless it was life or death, or worse.

Regina opened another magazine, flipped through the pages without seeing the words, closed it, and picked up another. She crossed her legs and rocked her foot, looked down the aisle at Mr. Harris. He was still on the phone.

One of the three children, a little boy with the cutest round face and mischievous brown eyes, jumped up and went tearing down the narrow aisle like a shot. That must have been the signal for the other two to cut loose as well. The girl, who was possibly no more than four, with big white satin ribbons on her pinky-length braids, did a series of somersaults followed by her younger brother, who toddled off at a pretty fast clip with a bottle dangling from his mouth.

The secretary dropped the phone in horror, while the mother shouted, yelled, and attempted to corral them back to their seats, which only agitated them all the more, as they erupted into hysterical giggles and ran beneath desks and chairs.

If it wasn't so funny, it could be sad, Regina observed, suppressing a smile as she watched the melee over the top of a *Black Enterprise* magazine. Thank goodness Michele and Darren were never like that. They had their moments, but they never acted up in public. That was definitely not tolerated. Although she was much more lenient than her parents had ever been, there was still that streak of discipline in her veins cultivated from years of piano lessons, dance lessons, curfews, being at the top of all her classes, stern looks from the nuns, and threats of burning in hell. And with a budding teenage son, who in another year would tower over her, it was essential to maintain that strict parental control. It was tough enough in the world for young black men; compound that with moving into manhood without a father in the home and that wicked combination of statistics added up to trouble. Not to mention the countless teen girls who looked for the love of a man — usually the substitute for a missing dad — in the amorous arms of eager young boys.

She wanted the best for her son, for both her children, and for that to happen, the strength had to come from within. They must see her as the person they could depend on, admire, and respect.

Regina took a deep breath, thinking again about her recent decisions. That moment of doubt, that tingle of indecision still wanted to claim her, whisper in her ear at night, tap her on the shoulder when she let down her guard and cause her to stumble. But now there was no turning back, and she wouldn't return to her old ways even if she could.

The hush of silence lured her away from her musings. Looking around, she realized that the harried mother had collected her brood, containing them under a stern, watchful eye.

"Ms. Everette, Mr. Harris is free," the frazzled secretary finally informed her.

Regina swallowed, steadied her heart, and moved toward the back of the office.

Mr. Harris, robust by anyone's standards, stood upon her approach and extended a pudgy, pink hand.

"Sorry for the wait, Ms. Everette," he immediately apologized, leaving her hand damp from his grasp.

The urge to wipe her palm along the side of her shirt was so overwhelming that she balled her hand into a fist to control the desire. Regina gave him a tight smile and sat down, subtly using the side of the cushioned chair to wipe away the dampness.

Mr. Harris linked his fingers beneath his chin and smiled benevolently. "As you know, the market is very tight right now, Ms. Everette . . ."

*Here we go.* She battled to keep her disappointment from showing.

". . . especially for these types of ventures. Perhaps if . . . you had a partner. . . ."

Her stomach suddenly felt like a lead weight. "What are you trying to say, Mr. Harris — that I didn't get the financing because I'm a woman, I don't have a man signing on the dotted line? What? What is it? That I'm black?" She didn't realize until that moment just how badly she wanted this and how easily it could not happen.

Mr. Harris cleared his throat, his face turning red. "What I'm trying to say is that for the amount you were approved for, I was unable to secure the Manhattan location you wanted. However," he rushed on, flipping open a manila folder, "I was able to find something in Fort Greene. Not exactly what you want, but I think it's worth taking a look at. The neighborhood has gone through a complete renaissance."

Regina frowned in momentary confusion. *Ouch.* His words slowly began to register. She'd just made a complete ass of herself. She still had a chance. But Fort Greene! Renaissance? She'd heard horror stories about that area of Brooklyn all her life. She'd been threatened upon pain of

144

death, by her mother, never to set foot in that questionable part of the borough. All she knew about the place was drugs, shoot-outs, boarded-up buildings, and crime from A to Z. She looked across at Mr. Harris's expectant face. Her mother would have a fit. Regina smiled as her excitement mounted.

"Do I apologize now or after you take me to see it?" she asked over a mouthful of humble pie.

He smiled. "Why don't we just chalk it up to experience? I can take you over right now, if you like. Judge it for yourself."

Regina stood. "Then let's go. But I'm sorry anyway."

Regina walked through the wide-open space, carefully inspecting what was once a local bodega in the now up-and-coming upscale black neighborhood. The wooden shelves were still intact and sturdy, along with the glass counter cases that had prob-ably once held the standard cold cuts — eggs on one side, and a multitude of candy and cough drops on the other.

"The place has two sizable storerooms in the back," Mr. Harris offered as he fol-lowed Regina up and down the aisles. "I thought one of them might work perfectly for the café you were proposing, and the other could be used as an office," he added, using all the artillery at his disposal to make the sale.

Bill Harris had been working with Regina for about a month, and previously when she was in search of her apartment. When she first walked into his office and plopped down at his desk, she made it clear in no uncertain terms what she wanted. Which was rare for most of his clients, especially, he was sorry to say, women. Generally people came in with an idea, very vague at that, about what they wanted, where they wanted it, and how much they were willing to spend to get it, which made his job even more difficult. Regina Everette was just the opposite. He could tell from their conversation that her desire to own a business was well thought out. She knew exactly what she wanted and how she would accomplish it. His wife, June, always said he was too soft and got too personally involved with his clients. But closing a deal with a satisfied client was what kept her living in the grand style to which she'd grown accustomed, he reminded her. Besides, Regina Everette was a nice lady, with a good head on her shoulders. He had no doubt that left to her own devices she would have eventually found something on her own, with or without help. If he could make the process easier, then so be it.

As Regina strolled through, she imagined the rows of books for browsing. She'd certainly want to stock classic black movies, greeting cards, and perhaps a select supply of Afrocentric clothing.

She already had a list of vendors whom she'd contacted and had received estimates for the merchandise she'd seen in their catalogs. Lushena's and Culture Plus, the black book distributors, agreed to provide her with her book orders whenever she was ready. Regina tugged in a deep breath. She could do this, she realized, a rush of excitement tingling her limbs. No matter what anyone said. This was for her. She could feel it. Her only regret was that she had no one with whom to share her joy. But that was okay, too.

She spun toward Mr. Harris, a beaming smile on her face, her dimples flashing. "Would you show me the back now? I'd like to see how much work needs to be done. Then we can talk contracts."

Bill Harris led the way to the back, unlocking the door and thanking his stars for clients like Regina Everette.

★ ★ ★

As Toni pulled up in front of the single-family home on Brookwood Drive, she had a moment of doubt. She shouldn't be doing this. She knew it was wrong. But she'd gotten past the point of caring. Guilt had become the air that she breathed. It had been months since Charles touched her, or even looked at her as if he cared — that was when he was around, which was rarer and rarer these days.

Sure, she put up a good front for Victoria and Regina, but she was lonely, incredibly lonely. Sometimes it would hit her so hard, it became a physical pain, which she covered with light chatter, trips to the salon, and listening to other people's troubles.

When she'd met Alan Pierce three months earlier at the clinic, he was coming to her for therapy. Funny how the rules of the game had changed. Now she was going to him to have her aches soothed, her troubles momentarily forgotten.

She gazed up at the curtain-covered windows, curtains she and Alan had purchased together on one of their clandestine Saturday-afternoon jaunts.

"If you're so unhappy, Toni, why do you stay with him?" Alan had asked as they'd browsed through fabric.

"It's not that simple, Alan. There's my son to think about. I don't want him growing up in a house without a father. I've seen what that can do to kids. I won't have it happen to mine. If I have to be unhappy, that's one thing. But I won't have my son paying for any of my mistakes."

"Are you saying that marrying Charles was a mistake?" he asked in that tone she used on her own patients.

She cut her eyes at his profile and caught the stern set of his strong jaw, traced his smooth salt-and-pepper hairline, the fullness of his lips that had given her countless hours of pleasure, the thick black bows over deep-set eyes and a sharp nose that clearly defined his American Indian ancestry. What would have happened if she'd met Alan twenty years earlier, didn't walk into that bar that afternoon, hadn't decided to stop taking her birth-control pills; would they have made it? Or would they still both be doing what they were doing right that minute — only with other people?

"When I married Charles . . . I loved him. I wanted to make his life better. I thought I could."

"You didn't answer my question, Toni.

Do you think marrying Charles was a mistake?" He stopped walking and turned to her, his hazel eyes boring into hers.

"I don't know," she said softly. "I really don't know, Alan, and that's the simple truth."

Alan pursed his lips, gazed at her pensively for a moment, then continued down the aisle.

They never discussed his question again, but it hovered in the back of Toni's mind waiting to be answered. She knew once she was ready and able to answer that question, everything in her life would change. For better or worse, she couldn't be sure, but she knew it would. Would Alan be a part of that change? At this turbulent stage of her life it wasn't a risk she was willing to take. Not when he was all that she had.

Toni took her purse from the passenger seat, attached the Club to the steering wheel of the midnight blue Volvo, and got out of the car. She took a key from her purse and opened the front door, shutting it softly behind her. It was almost like coming home. Almost.

"Alan!" she called out, heading up the stairs to the bedroom they shared.

By the time Victoria was finished with

her exam and returned to the waiting room, the small group of women had thinned considerably. She was one of three remaining in the posh doctor's office on Park Avenue. She chose a seat facing the entrance door and crossed her long legs, smoothing the barely-there lines in her fitted skirt.

She'd selected Dr. Roberta Rowenstein years ago when she'd first made vice president at the bank. No more parade of clinic doctors for her, she'd decided. From what she could tell from her regular biannual visits, she was the only black woman who frequented the trendy suite of doctors' offices. That made her feel good. Another indication that she'd made it. Absently she checked her diamond ring, admiring the sparkle against her dark skin. Of course the service was above reproach, she mused. Instead of a lone water fountain spewing warm water, there were chilled bottles of Evian; orange, apple, and mango juices; a choice of international coffees; and salt-free snack crackers.

The latest magazines from health and fitness to finance were strategically placed on the gleaming wood tables. Plush imported area rugs covered the parquet floors. Relaxing music from some unseen source floated through the air. There were no wild, unruly children running and screaming and darting around tables. Just an assortment of highly fashionable, obviously wealthy women who expected the best and could pay for it. And she was right there with them. Exactly where she belonged — whether they liked it or not. She pulled out her compact and checked her makeup.

"Mrs. Hunter, the doctor will see you now," the nurse-receptionist informed her in a practiced hush.

Victoria snapped her compact shut, gathered her things, and opened the side door that led down the corridor to Dr. Rowenstein's office. She checked her watch. She'd been there for under an hour. Who could ask for better service?

She probably just needed some vitamins to boost her energy level, she concluded as she approached the door with the gold-leaf lettering. She'd be sure to mention it to the doctor. She patted her close-cropped curls and tapped lightly on the door.

"Come in."

Victoria stepped inside, smiling brightly.

"Victoria, please sit down." Dr. Rowenstein slid off her glasses and quickly read Victoria's chart. She replaced her glasses and folded her hands atop the folder. "How old are you, Victoria?"

"Thirty-eight."

"Hmm. But you're in excellent health. That's what's important."

Victoria relaxed in her seat, pleased with the diagnosis. Maybe she was just working too hard and that was why she felt so tired lately. She'd convince Phillip to take her on a short vacation to one of the islands. She'd talk to him when she got home.

"You're going to need to be in good condition for this pregnancy. Especially considering your age and this being your first child."

Victoria snapped out of her musings, blinking rapidly. "What did you say?"

"You're about six to eight weeks into your pregnancy and I want to be sure that everything is okay." She paused and eyed Victoria. "Didn't you know? Most women do and just come to me for confirmation."

Victoria plastered a smile on her face and tried to focus. "Are you sure?"

"Without question. The urinalysis and my exam confirm it. Of course, I'd want to order some genetic counseling and tests because of your age."

Victoria stared at Roberta Rowenstein as

if she'd suddenly sprouted fins. She knew good and damned well she wasn't paying three hundred dollars per visit to have this crazy bitch tell her some shit about being pregnant! Hell, no. But she wouldn't act out. She wouldn't leap across the desk and slap that stupid grin off her face. She cleared her throat.

"I take the pill, Dr. Rowenstein. Religiously."

The doctor shrugged her broad shoulders. "It happens. It's rare but it happens. Consider yourself blessed, Victoria. Some women pray all their lives to have a child and can't." She wagged a thick finger. "It must be meant to be," she said in a stage whisper, nodding at her own wisdom. She began writing notes in the file while she talked. "I want you to see me in four weeks. My nurse will give you an appointment for the tests and some literature to read. And I'll give you a prescription for prenatal vitamins."

She was going to be sick, throw up all over her brand-new Versace suit if she didn't get out of that room. It was closing in on her, this startling revelation of the new life inside her; all of it seemed to be sucking up the air in the room.

"Here you are, dear." She handed three

squares of white paper to Victoria, who numbly took them and shoved them into her purse, the smile still set in stone on her face.

Roberta patted her hand. "You'll be fine. Once the idea settles and you tell your husband, you'll be thrilled. You'll see."

*Tell my husband! Phillip. Oh, God.* She gracefully stood.

"Four weeks," Roberta reminded her. "And stop by the desk on your way out to get your test dates."

Victoria turned without another word and left. When she looked up again, she was standing outside in front of the building. She didn't even remember getting on the elevator. Tears blurred her vision. Her heart and head pounded in unison. *Pregnant.*

"Shit!"

A gray-haired woman walking her poodle arched her brow in alarm, scooped up the dog, and gave Victoria a wide berth, as if she were afraid of catching something.

Victoria glared at her as she hurried down the street. Tears rolled down her cheeks. She needed to talk to Regina. She'd know what to do. She always did. But then she remembered she wasn't speaking to Regina, not after the nasty

155

things she'd said about her, all those lies.

She walked toward her Mercedes and got in, pulled her cell phone from her purse, and punched in Toni's number. It rang until the answering machine clicked on. Frustrated, she disconnected and tossed the phone back into her purse. It was just as well. She didn't need a counseling session from Toni, anyway. And until she decided how to handle this, the fewer people who knew about her business the better.

She tore away from the curb and headed home to Long Island.

Regina stared in awe at the contract in her hand. She'd done it, actually done it. She was now a full-fledged business-woman. It was definitely cause for celebration.

Automatically, she reached for the phone, then stopped. She had no one to call. A sensation of overwhelming sadness crept through her. Who could she tell? Who could she share her excitement with? At the moment, she realized how very small her world had become.

Back at the *Daily News*, she couldn't count any of the hard-nosed male reporters as friends, even if they had shared harrowing, on-the-job experiences and even a byline. In the end it was just a job, and she was never "one of the guys."

As for Toni and Vicky, it was clear where things stood with them. As long as she kept her opinions to herself and maintained the persona they'd carved out for her, they could all remain friends. But the instant she tested her wings and forced them to look truth in the face, the tables turned.

She held no grudges against them. If anything, she sorely missed the camaraderie they often shared, even if it was flawed. But if the fences between them could ever be crossed, they would have to make that move.

Regina sighed and ran her fingers through the twists of her hair, pleased with the progress her new look was taking. It was a big decision on her part to toss the perms in the garbage for good, and let her hair do its natural thing. It gave her a strange sense of freedom that was hard to explain to anyone beside Toni, who'd taken the plunge several years earlier. Victoria, who lived in makeup and beauty salons, thought they were both out of their minds.

"As long as there's a perm on the market to keep this mess on my head straight, I will be using it," she'd said without a blink one afternoon while on their way to Regina's mother's birthday party.

Regina firmly believed that Vicky's adamancy was more in relation to her need to assimilate with her white husband, his friends, and her coworkers. The sad reality was that no matter how expensive the clothing, how straight the hair, how highbrow the neighborhood, Victoria Bellows Hunter would always be black, plain and simple, and that fact scared the hell out of her.

Well, she did have a half bottle of wine in the fridge, Regina thought, steering away from the things she couldn't change. She deserved at least one toast, even if she had to do it herself. She pushed up from the table and was rummaging around in the cabinets for a decent glass when the doorbell rang.

Glancing at the clock above the stove, she saw it was only two o'clock, a little too early for the kids to be coming home from school, and no one knew she was home. Maybe the landlady had locked herself out. She went downstairs to the front door and stopped dead in her tracks when the face of her ex-husband Russell peered back at her through the glass.

# CHAPTER NINE

Regina's lean body blocked the partially open door. "What are you doing here, Russell?"

"I came to see about my children, whom you seem to be incapable of taking care of." He glowered down at her, with that same look that would always make her bow her head in shame.

Regina planted her hand on her hip and cocked her head to the side, taking in the tall, muscular man to whom she was once married. "You haven't seen fit to come around in nearly two years, Russell. You expect me to believe that you've suddenly had a flash of parental concern?"

For a moment, Russell Everette reared back slightly in surprise at her biting response. This wasn't *his* Regina — at least not the one he wanted to remember. Quickly collecting himself, he adjusted his navy blue suit jacket and stepped closer.

Regina could smell the Cool Water cologne wafting around her, threatening to cloud her thoughts.

"As long as I pay you money, I can come around whenever I want. Those are my kids. Where are they?"

"At school."

"I'll wait." He tried to brush pass her. She didn't budge.

"Wait in your car, Russell," she said in a cool monotone.

Russell's deep-set brown eyes glared down at her, his warm chocolate skin seeming to simmer with the inner heat of his rage. She watched a vein throb viciously in his temple.

"Your mother was right. You have lost your mind," he ground out between clenched teeth, looking for all the world as though he wanted to slam her into a wall.

"My mother! What does she have to do with this?"

"Do you want to discuss this in the street like two savages or are we going to talk inside?"

"There's nothing for us to talk about."

"You don't think the fact that you're no longer financially capable of taking care of the kids is reason to talk? Is that what you're saying?" he challenged, the power of his deep baritone rising with his ire. "I don't think the courts would agree with you, Regina."

Her chest tightened. "Courts? Financially capable? What are you talking about?" Her thoughts ran in a blur: Toni? Victoria? Someone at her job? Who would have said something?

"Your mother called me. She's worried sick about the kids."

"There's nothing for her to worry about, Russell."

"The kids don't think so. They were the ones who called their grandmother."

Her stomach suddenly seesawed. *The kids? Why?* She looked up into his eyes and stood before him naked, exposed, completely betrayed by the very ones she was working so hard to provide for. What could she say?

"So do you want us to discuss this now, or when they get home?" He smelled victory.

Reluctantly she stepped aside and watched him walk up the stairs and into her apartment as if he'd lived there all his life.

"When will I see you again?" Alan asked as from his supine position on the bed he watched Toni get into her clothes. His body still tingled from making love with her.

Toni kept her back to him as she buttoned her blouse. "I'm not sure when I can get away. I'll call you."

He chuckled derisively and stared up at the ceiling. "What is this really about, Toni? Am I just someone you screw when the need hits you or do you really care?"

She didn't want to go through this, not again. What could she tell him, that she was going to leave her husband and son and they could live happily ever after? How could she explain without sounding totally mercenary that being with him, even if only for a few hours, gave her what she needed?

Toni turned to face him, pulling her locks away from her face. "When we got into this, you knew my situation. I told you everything. You said it was fine with you, that you weren't ready for anything permanent."

"What if that's changed?"

Her heart thumped. "What are you saying?"

Alan sat up, the strong muscles of his chest tempting her to touch them again. "I'm saying that . . . I'm in love with you. I'm saying that I don't want to share you anymore. I can't. If you are as unhappy as you say you are with your husband, then leave. We could have a life together, Toni. We could make it work. I know we could. But this . . ." His sentence drifted off, but they both knew what he meant.

She lowered her head. When they'd met, he'd come to her for counseling after the death of his wife, Karen. Instinctively she'd wanted to help him, take away his pain. And session by session she'd allowed her professionalism to become subjugated by her own feelings of neediness. It was so easy to find comfort in each other, both filling the gaps that the loves of their lives had created. Now that he'd slowly begun to heal, it wasn't nurturing and comforting words that he needed; he wanted her — all of her. And as much as she hated to admit it, that was what began to destroy her marriage. When she was no longer needed as a savior, but as a woman, Charles began to drift away, stand on his own, require something of her she was unable to give — herself, the one thing she knew nothing about.

Toni took a breath. "Please don't do this, Alan."

"Do what, Toni?" He stood in all his bold and glorious nakedness. "Ask you to be honest with yourself, your husband, me? To make a decision, answer a question that doesn't come out of a textbook or journal, but from inside you? Is that asking too much?"

"What do you want me to say?" Her voice rose.

"Tell me what you feel, for once." He stepped closer, the scent of their sex filling her head.

"I'm afraid, okay. I'm lonely," she snapped, her perfect cinnamon features tightening in pain. "I don't know who I am or what I'm doing or if it makes a damned bit of difference." Her voice shook. "And when I'm with you none of that matters. Is that what you want to hear?" She wrapped her arms around her narrow waist and stared defiantly at him.

Alan gathered her in his arms. His voice was as soft as the pillow they'd slept on. "I don't think we need to see each other anymore, Toni. Not like this." He held her tighter. "I know what I want. And until you do, I can't keep sneaking around to see you like some underage kid. I won't keep sleeping with another man's wife." He tilted her chin up and looked down into her tear-filled eyes. "You need to decide what you want to do. I'll wait, but not forever, Toni. I can't."

He released her, walked into the bathroom, and turned on the shower. When he emerged she was sitting on the edge of the bed. She looked up.

"I'll work it out. Some way I will. Just . . . just don't give up on me."

Alan tied the belt around his robe. He didn't reply. He took her hand and pulled her up from the bed. Together they walked to the door, his arm around her waist, her head resting on his shoulder.

The one thing Charles enjoyed about his job was the flexibility it offered him. He knew Toni considered him only a glorified cabdriver, but the stretch limo was his, fully paid for, and he had a steady list of well-paying clients that at least adequately contributed to the household expenses. He knew he'd been saying for years that he was going to have a fleet of drivers and open up locations even outside of New York. But the truth was, he was content just the way things were. The problem was Toni. She always wanted more, more. She always thought he could do better, felt that he was selling himself short. Maybe he was, but it was his life and he was doing what he wanted with it. Something she never seemed to understand.

He had to admire Toni, though. She was strong and determined, a little ball of fire, and knew what she wanted out of life. It was what had attracted him to her from the first time they met. But she'd never let him be a man. It was as if she believed it was her responsibility to mold him, give him his values, and define his life. And year after year, he felt himself diminishing until he wasn't there anymore, just a shadow passing through the house. On the rare occasions when they did make love, he invariably felt as though she was doing him a favor. But he loved her anyway and hated himself because of it.

Charles checked the computerized map on his dashboard, one of his favorite gadgets. On the few occasions when he took his son Steven for an occasional spin, they tried all the tricks in the book to see if the map would give them the wrong information. So far it was technology 10, humans zip. He saw his turn coming up and made a smooth left.

Mr. and Mrs. Dixon were new clients, recommended to him by one of his regular customers. They had some sort of shindig to attend in midtown Manhattan and the husband apparently didn't want the hassle of driving the round-trip from New Jersey to New York. Especially if he got a few good shots under his belt. Charles couldn't blame him. It was the smart thing to do, and most of all it was good for his business.

Although it would be the same ninety-minute trip for him each way, he was being paid well for the service and his waiting time. Especially since this was a last-minute call. Maybe with this extra money he'd take Toni on a minivacation or something. Even if it was only for a weekend, as long as they could spend some time together, get to know each other again. And he wanted some time away from the house so that he could talk with her about Steven. He was worried about him. He'd grown increasingly sullen lately, barely coming out of his room when he was home, and Charles didn't care for his new crop of friends either.

For the most part, he left the analysis up to Toni, who would swear on a stack of Bibles that she could spot and sense trouble with Steven. "I would know if something was wrong. What do you think all those years of school and training were about?" she asked whenever he would question her about Steven's behavior. "Do you really think if I believed there was a problem, I'd just let it go and not do anything about it? Come on, Charles. Maybe it's easy for you to just go along with life and let things be, but I can't. If I see something wrong, I have to fix it."

Well, it was plain to a simple layman like himself that his infallible wife had lost her touch. And it was past time for him to step in.

He peered out of the tinted window, looking for the address on his trip sheet: 56 Brookwood Drive. He eased down the block until he located the house and pulled into a vacant spot right in front of the door. This was a nice neighborhood, he observed, a quiet, tree-lined block. There was a perfect blend of the suburb — private homes with a bit of land around them, and city life, with quaint shops, restaurants, supermarkets, and public transportation close at hand. It was a family neighborhood, the kind he would have chosen to raise Steven. Not in the heart of a murderous city that ate its residents for lunch. Just as he prepared to get out and ring the Dixons' bell, movement from three houses down caught his attention.

It was a woman pressed up close to a man in the doorway. His face was partially obscured, but Charles could make out the height and body structure. The woman tenderly stroked his cheek before he leaned down and kissed her long and slow. She stepped back, turned, and walked with the sensual stroll of a woman who'd just been thoroughly loved.

Charles experienced a sense of unreality mixed with anger and a pain he didn't know he could feel as he watched his wife drive away.

Regina stepped into the apartment and shut the door behind her. Russell was in the living room, picking up and putting down magazines and examining her knick-knacks and furniture as if it were all up for bids.

He hadn't changed much since the last time she'd seen him, perhaps a bit more gray at the temples. There was still that arrogant power that radiated out of him like shock waves, the smooth, controlled movements and perfect attire. On the surface, Russell Everette was a devastatingly handsome man with sex appeal to spare. But underneath he was cruel, cold, and mean — traits that served him well in the cutthroat world of investments, but they made him a lousy husband, father, and man.

"So what is this about, Russell?" Regina

said, weary of her recollections.

Russell plopped a magazine on the table-top and briefly glanced in Regina's direction.

"That's what you need to tell me." He squared his shoulders. "I called your job. They said you walked out one day and they haven't heard from you since."

Regina rolled her eyes. "That's a lie. I handed in my resignation and *then* I left. Let's just be clear," she said in disgust.

"Any way you look at it Regina, you're out of work."

She crossed the room, wishing she could make him disappear. "Not for long."

"What's that supposed to mean? You have another job lined up — I hope. Not that bookstore crap."

"It's really none of your business, Russell. Do I ask you where your money is coming from, what you do in your spare time? No. Give me the same respect — for once."

"Respect!" He laughed nastily. "What you've done is the exact same thing I've always said about you, Regina. You're flighty and irresponsible. All you think about is yourself. You still need someone to look after you and tell you what needs to be done."

"Get out, Russell."

"I'm not finished."

"Get out!"

He stalked across the room and stood in her face. He was literally seething with fury. "You listen to me," he said in a harsh whisper. "If I have to, I'll take those kids from you. No court in the world would allow them to stay with you — you're financially and mentally unstable."

"Just try it, Russell," she said in a hiss, her eyes narrowing to two slits. "I'll see you in hell before I let you take those kids and twist them into what you've become. Get out of my house. Now. Before I have you removed." She walked toward the phone and lifted the receiver from its base.

His mouth curved into a nasty smile. "This isn't over, Regina. Not by a long shot. Nobody talks to me like that — especially you." He pushed past her and walked out, leaving the door swinging on its hinges.

Regina stood in the center of the living room. Her entire body trembled. She shut her eyes. She knew if nothing else that Russell was as good as his word. If he got it in his head to take her to court, he'd do it, if for no other reason than to give her grief. He no more wanted the day-to-day responsibility of raising two teenagers than he wanted a flight to the moon. But if he felt he'd been slighted, that his manhood had been challenged, that she wasn't just going to roll over and play dead, he'd do whatever he felt was needed to make her life miserable.

Now more than ever her business had to succeed, and she couldn't allow anything or anyone to jeopardize that. She wouldn't let Russell or anyone else control her life again. And that included her mother.

She glanced at the clock. Her mother should be home from her afternoon bingo game at the center.

Regina snatched her purse and car keys from the table in the hall. It was long past the time that mother and daughter had a talk. Her mother and her meddling ways had consistently infiltrated her life, and now she was willing to use her last weakness against Regina — her children — just to have what she considered "the best for Regina." Even if she had to use the only other person in the world who could make her feel completely insignificant and incapable — Russell — to accomplish her ends.

That was the old Regina. It was time her mother recognized that. She pulled her Toyota out of its parking space and headed to Queens.

# CHAPTER TEN

Victoria mindlessly drove around Manhattan, by sheer force of will stopping at all the appropriate signs and lights. The last place she wanted to go right then was home. Not until she had her thoughts together and could look Phillip in the eye, get in bed with him, maybe make love with him, and pretend everything was fine.

It wasn't fine.

How could things be fine if she had a child growing inside of her — her and Phillip's child? Her life had been perfect until now. Instinctively she pressed her hand to her taut stomach.

*Abortion.* The ugly word kept rolling around in her head like a kicked beach ball, bouncing against the sides of her brain, causing her head to throb.

How could this have happened? She'd been so careful, taking her pill without fail — except that one night when they'd come back from one of Phillip's clients' party at the Plaza Hotel in New York.

They'd both been drinking, she more than Phillip. Especially after she'd overheard two of the wives discussing her like leftover chopped meat. They didn't notice that someone was in one of the stalls, or if they did, they didn't care.

"For the life of me, I can't figure out what Phillip Hunter sees in that black baboon he married," one woman said to the other.

Her companion chuckled. "You know what they say about them: all they want to do is screw and have babies. He probably had a bad case of jungle fever." She laughed at her own wit.

Suddenly Victoria was no longer a brilliant vice president at a prestigious bank, the wife of a successful accountant, with a house on Long Island and a summer home in St. Croix. She didn't take trips to Europe and have most of her clothes made or imported from Paris. She didn't have a bulging portfolio of moneymaking stocks and bonds, or lease a new car every year. No. She was none of those things. Today she was little black Vicky again, with the hair that would knot up into little peas at the back of her neck and temples no matter how hard her mother brushed or pressed and curled it. She was the girl with the face that always had to shine like new shoes because her mother swore by Vaseline summer, winter, and spring. She was the one who wore oversize clothes before they became fashionable because her mother shopped at the secondhand store at the church. She was the only girl in her graduating class who wasn't asked to the prom because none of the boys wanted to be teased about not being able to see their date when the lights went out on the dance floor.

"But did he have to marry her?" the woman was saying. "I sure hope he isn't foolish enough to have children. Can you just imagine — a half-breed. White skin with black features and kinky hair." She made a disgusted sound in her throat. "How awful would that be?"

"He should have stayed with Melissa."

"Now their children would have been something to look at."

Victoria heard the bathroom door close and she let the tears finally fall until she was totally empty inside. So she drank more than usual that night, needing something to dull the knife wounds and keep the smile of propriety plastered on her face.

At home that evening she made love to

Phillip with a wild, almost frenzied abandon; demanding more, harder, faster, deeper. Needing desperately to feel the touch of another, to assure herself that she was real — worthy of being loved — and not just some black thing — to be filled where her soul had been carved out — again. In the end she lay emotionless and spent in Phillip's arms as he told her how much he loved and adored her, while tears of pain and a shame he'd never understand slid silently down her cheeks.

For some reason she'd found herself telling Regina, spilling her guts out over a cup of tea several weeks later, while Regina's kids played a wild game of Nintendo in the next room.

She'd tried to put on a good face and totally dismiss it all as ignorance and jealousy on the women's part.

"But what about you, hon, how do you feel?" Regina asked gently.

Victoria's dark eyes lighted on Regina's composed face, and for the first time she noticed that Regina was locking her hair. How long had it been since she had actually paid her any real attention — really saw her and didn't take her for granted? Good old Gina. The realization made her uncomfortable. She shifted her teacup around in the saucer. "I feel like shit!" she finally spit, swearing she wasn't going to cry in front of Regina.

"Why, Vicky? Ask yourself why. Who are those women to you? Nothing. You have nothing to prove to them. They're nobody. What does their opinion matter?"

Victoria leaned suddenly forward, her eyes intent, her dark complexion heightened by her agitation. "Don't you see, I've worked hard to be what I am, to get as far away from that little girl in the projects as I could. Look at me. Do I look like the 'thing' they said?" she asked, her voice the plea of a child who needed to be assured that there was a Santa Claus.

"Vicky, in most circles, if you grew your hair down to your ass, faded your skin until you were just as white as a piece of parchment, and stuck blue contacts in your eyes, you'd still be the black bitch who stole a white man. What's important is who you are inside, the kind of person you are. Who you believe you are and can be. Not what's on the outside. What people see will never change."

Victoria was quiet for a moment, thinking about what Regina had said that day. She was probably right, but it didn't make the hurt go away. She was going to be accepted whether they wanted her or not. And she had all the accessories to prove it.

The blaring sound of a car horn snapped Victoria out of her recollections. She looked ahead. The light had turned green. Slowly she drove across the intersection, then made a sudden left turn, to the annoyance of the drivers behind her.

She was about ten minutes away from the gym. Maybe a good run around the track would help to clear her head.

*Abortion.*

Regina used her key to unlock her mother's door. For some reason, other than being practical, Millie insisted that Regina keep a key, "just in case you decide to come back home." *Not likely.*

She shut the door and went straight to the kitchen, her mother's favorite room in the house, certain she'd find her there. "Ma."

Millie turned from the stove, perfectly attired in a pearl gray suit, as though she were readying for a photo shoot instead of dinner. Her almond-toned face seemed to light up when she saw Regina.

She'd dyed her hair again, Regina immediately noticed, as the auburn highlights glistened in the light streaming in from the window. Millie was a petite woman, no more than five-foot-five with heels. She managed to keep her girlish figure with brisk daily walks, and her skin was still as smooth and wrinkle-free as Regina always remembered it.

"Regina." Millie wiped her hands on a black-and-white dish towel and crossed the black-and-white tiles to where Regina stood in the archway. She patted her daughter's cheek. "What a surprise." She looked beyond Regina out into the hallway. "Where are the children?"

"In school," she replied in a monotone.

"Why didn't you wait for them to get home and bring them with you? We could have had dinner together. You know how much I love to see them," she went on, oblivious to the tension on Regina's face.

"I wanted to see you alone so we could talk, Ma."

Millie's small brown eyes snapped for a moment, then relaxed. "Sure, sweetheart. Sit down."

Regina tugged in a breath, promising herself she wouldn't respond to her mother's patronizing tone. She pulled out one of the black velvet chairs from beneath the white lacquer table and sat down.

Millie poured herself a glass of iced tea

and offered some to Regina, who refused, and then sat down.

"What is it, dear?" Millie took a sip of her tea.

"Why did you call Russell? How could you have done something like that?"

"Something like what — ask my grandchildren's father, my son-in-law, to talk to you about this craziness of yours? Those children are worried sick about you, and quite frankly so am I. What in heaven's name is on your mind? I didn't raise you to be this irresponsible. Divorcing Russell was bad enough, and now this. I —"

"Do you know how you raised me, Ma? You raised me to be too scared to have an opinion, so I let everyone else have one for me. Too insecure to make decisions, choices on my own. But I'm not that person anymore."

"That's obvious."

Regina slammed her palm down on the table. "Are you hearing me? I want to live my own life without interference from you or Russell. This is my life, Ma. I can take care of my children without being told how and when!"

"How? How do you propose to take care of my grandchildren without a job? Since when have you become a businesswoman

— a bookstore owner at that," she added with blatant distaste. "They're a dime a dozen. When it fails, and it will, what will you do then? You have no experience, no —"

Regina abruptly stood. "Maybe once — once — you could have a little faith in me. Believe that I could do something that wasn't somehow orchestrated by you." She started to leave, immensely satisfied with the appalled look on her mother's face. "If you can't be supportive, be my mother, then stay out of my life. And another thing — Russell is no longer your son-in-law."

"Don't be a fool, Regina."

Regina spun to face her mother. "I promise you, Mother, I won't be the fool I have been."

Millie watched her only child walk out the door. All the hard work and devotion she'd given that girl, all the money she'd spent, the doors she'd opened — everything tossed out the window on some whim. Well, she wouldn't sit still for it. She just wouldn't.

Toni nervously paced the floor of her bedroom. If she'd been home, not with Alan, maybe this could have been avoided.

*Oh, God.* She couldn't do this alone. Where was Charles? She'd paged him almost an hour ago and he hadn't called back.

She had picked up the bedside phone to call him again when she heard his key in the lock. She ran downstairs just as he was coming through the door. In the instant that she saw him there, he was the strong, handsome man she'd met in the bar, the man who made her heart sing, made her believe in the carefree life, take risks, believe that anything was possible. Charles would make things all right.

He'd thought about not coming home, just driving until the car ran out of gas somewhere. But that was no better than running away, something he'd been doing for far too long.

"Charles!" She ran to him. "I got a call from the precinct. Steven's been arrested." Her words tumbled over each other. "They want us down there. I didn't know what to do."

At first he didn't understand what she was saying. It didn't make sense. Maybe it was some ploy of hers to keep him from dealing with her affair. But that was low, even for Toni. *Steven. Arrested.*

"Is he . . . okay?"

"I don't know. They didn't let me talk to him."

Tears ran down her face, and he could feel her body tremble. He had the over-powering desire to hold her, comfort her, and tell her everything would be all right, that he'd make it all right. But he couldn't bring himself to touch her, not knowing that she'd been in another man's bed.

"Come on. Steven needs us."

He'd deal with Toni and her lover later.

# CHAPTER ELEVEN

Phillip was in his study. It was his favorite room in the ten-room house. It was where he came to think and unwind. The warm brick walls and inlaid panels gave the huge room an almost country-home feel. Exposed wood rafters and a working fireplace added to the image. The hardwood floors were covered in spots with expensive fur rugs, with a massive maple-wood desk and a long gooseneck lamp in the center. The only things missing, Victoria often said, were the stuffed animal heads mounted on the walls. That always made him smile. Everything about Victoria made him smile, from the first moment he'd met her.

It was a banking conference at the Watergate Hotel in Washington, D.C. Bankers, brokers, accountants, and corporate CEOs from across the country were in attendance at the three-day seminar.

By the second day, Phillip had grown weary of the grandiose speeches and corporate mumbo-jumbo. He'd sneaked away to the hotel bar and was having a drink of Scotch when he saw Victoria walk in.

The first impression that came to mind was the pure regality of her, the way she entered a room as if she owned it, but was gracious enough to allow the lowly common man to bask in her glow. Yet there was a light of uncertainty in her eyes, as if for an instant she questioned her right to be there. It softened her somehow.

She was slender, with the legs and grace of a prima ballerina, and her short, perfectly cut hair capped her heart-shaped face, luminous doe-brown eyes, and lush and sensual lips that all the women he knew went to their plastic surgeons to acquire.

He watched her as she moved fluidly around the tables and bodies, blending in without disturbing the waters. That struck him most of all, intrigued him. And he wondered how anyone so incredibly beautiful and poised could have a moment's hesitation about her rightful place in the world.

She sat alone at a table near the door and ordered a white wine. She seemed content by herself, as if being alone was a common way of life for her. Most of his women friends traveled in pairs and rarely ventured out unaccompanied. This struck him, too, and he wondered if she wanted it that way, or if that was just the way things were.

Phillip watched her for a while as she raised and lowered the thin glass to her lips and gazed casually around at the people who moved in and out, many of them attendees from the seminar. None stopped at her table. No one said hello or acknowledged her in any way. And she seemed too self-contained and assured to care or notice, which finally compelled him to get up and go to her table.

Just as he neared it, she rose, left five one-dollar bills on the white linen covering, and headed for the door.

Phillip followed her out, walking several steps behind, when Victoria suddenly stopped, turned, and held him in place with an inquiring smile.

"If you'd come over a few minutes earlier we could have talked," she said calmly, as if they'd been in the middle of a conversation. "But I'm really exhausted." She tipped her head to the side and smiled fully, giving him a glimpse of beautiful white teeth. "Maybe we could meet tomorrow for lunch after the morning session."

Phillip blinked, completely disconcerted by her casual boldness, yet utterly fascinated. All of a sudden he'd developed a stutter he didn't know he possessed. "Uh, I, um — I think that would be great." He shoved his hands into his pockets, feeling like a complete idiot.

"See you then." She turned, continuing toward the elevators.

"Uh, my name is Phillip. Phillip Hunter."

Victoria stopped and turned back. Her dark eyes sparkled. "I know. It's on your name tag."

Phillip's eyes shifted down to the white plastic tag clipped to the lapel of his suit. When he looked up, she was gone. And he'd been enchanted with her ever since.

But nothing else between them ever came that easy again. From the moment they first ventured into the uncharted territory of being a couple, they were met with cool stares from strangers and skeptical raised brows. That was to be expected, they both realized. What was most difficult was the reaction of his family and his friends.

From the beginning, his family was adamantly against his relationship with Victoria. His friends, though not so vocal, shared their jaded opinions as well.

"Interracial relationships are nothing but trouble," his onetime best friend Marcus had said. "Just get the goods and move on."

"We won't have her in this family," his mother vehemently insisted in her strong Southern drawl. "They're fine for *friends* but not wives!"

"If you do this, Phillip, you'll be cut off," his father warned, cringing at the thought of what his associates at the country club would say.

It didn't matter that he loved her, that she was the first woman who made him feel good about himself, who didn't want him because of his money. If anything, it was Vicky who was cautious about their relationship.

"I won't come between you and your family, Phillip. That's too much to ask. I couldn't do it. I know how much they mean to you. Let this go. Walk away."

Her brown eyes had pleaded with him, but he could hear the hurt in her voice.

"Listen to me, Vicky; we love each other." He took her hand in his. "I don't give a damn what everyone else thinks or feels, only us. That's all that matters."

"Everything is so easy for you," she said

with the heaviness of reality in her voice. "So easy to just move through life, take what you want, be accepted wherever you go." She shook her head, paced restlessly in front of him. "It's never been that way for me. You don't have to worry about walking into a store and being followed simply because of the color of your skin. Or work harder than anyone else to prove you deserve the job. Turned down for a house or apartment because the block association doesn't want their property values to go down. Laughed at and teased by your own people because of how dark you are." She turned, her eyes burning into his. "Have you?"

He stared up at her, his deep-set blue eyes seeing the ingrained hurt that had been a part of her everyday existence, that had distorted the core of who she was. Yet it gave him insight into her aloofness, the invisible glass wall she kept around herself. If she couldn't be touched, she couldn't be hurt. And all he wanted to do was make that pain go away, smooth the road for her, protect her from the ugliness of the world, make her life a part of his. And he knew it would come with a price — one that he was willing to pay. His vows had not changed in all the years they were together.

189

Victoria was his world.

He released a long sigh and looked down at the note he'd written with the message from her doctor. It said that she needed to call right away about some tests. When he asked the nurse what tests, she, in her most professional manner, advised him to discuss it with his wife.

Phillip slowly laid down the message, and the unsettling sensation he'd experienced when he'd taken the call several hours earlier began to resurface. He didn't think he could bear it if anything happened to her, if something was wrong.

Maybe it was something simple, something routine, and he was worrying unnecessarily. But that thought still did not ease the knot of tension in his belly. If anything happened to Victoria it would be like losing a part of himself. He stared at the white square with his neat scrawl. *Tests.*

Charles stood beneath the scalding water of the shower, the steam coating the room, misting the mirrors, crystallizing his thoughts.

He scrubbed, lathered, held his face up to the spray, praying he could wash away the stench of the day.

Did Toni shower after she'd left that

man? he wondered, his mind leaning in a dangerous direction, countered only by the weight of his son's arrest, watching him being led out in cuffs into their custody.

His stomach lurched. Where had everything become so twisted, so far out of reach? When had he lost sight of what was right in front of him: his wife and her adulterous affair, his son's drug use, and his own surrender to circumstances?

During the tension-filled ride to the precinct, Charles barely listened to Toni's quiet sobs and run-on questions and commentary about *Why? How could this have happened? I give him everything; I'm always there for him, he knows he can talk to me.*

Funny, Charles thought as he steered the Jeep Cherokee around a stalled Volkswagen Jetta, there was no mention of him in that scenario, the role he played, and maybe that was the core of the problem. He had ceased to exist as husband and father — roles that he'd relinquished over time because it was easier that way. And because of that, he had been replaced in both of them.

Yet, for the first time in their fourteen years of marriage, Charles saw Toni weakened and humbled. Gone was the know-it-all, can-solve-the-world's-problems persona. In its place was a woman who was questioning herself, her ability, her chosen path. A woman frightened. And instead of being the one who took over with her credentials and self-righteousness, she'd stepped back, letting Charles weave them through the maze.

At first he felt so out of place, so out of character, that he lost his lines, like an actor who hadn't rehearsed for his close-up. However, bit by bit, as he dealt with one level of red tape after another, asking all the right questions, taking names and making calls, the role felt perfect for him, one that he should have starred in long ago. And his reward for it was the moment he set eyes on the terrified and shamed face of his son, Steven, as the boy walked into his arms and cried how sorry he was while Toni, for the very first time, stood aside in a supporting role.

Charles turned off the shower and wrapped the thick navy blue towel around his waist. Had it been any other time in their marriage, any other day, things between them could have dramatically changed — that one gesture on her part would have altered their course.

But it wasn't any other day, any other time.

Charles opened the door to the bath that led to the master bedroom. Toni was already in bed. The bedside lamp was turned low. She wasn't asleep. He could tell by the way she was breathing, something he'd learned over the years. Like the way she always talked with her hands, like a mime, he would tease her; the way she walked that brisk walk of hers even when she was bone tired; the way she smelled in the morning, always soft and alluring; the way her eyes sparkled with delight when she bought him endless surprise gifts or talked in that rapid-fire way of hers about her clients.

There were so many things he had come to know and love about her. That was what hurt him most of all.

He went to the dresser and pulled out a pair of black silk boxers, the pair she'd bought him for Valentine's Day last year. What had she purchased for her lover? he suddenly wondered, and his chest tightened.

Toni sat up in bed and watched his approach. He was still so incredibly handsome. He had the same sweet disposition as the day they met. Maybe that was the problem. Charles had never changed and didn't seem to want to — until tonight. Tonight she saw her husband in a way she'd never seen him before — a man in charge. And something inside her shifted.

Charles stopped at the foot of the bed, and his whole life seemed to tumble around in his head. His voice was flat and emotionless. "I saw you today — with whoever he is."

Toni's eyes widened in panic. "Charles —"

He held up his hand. "Don't. Don't give me the explanations," he said in the same flat voice that began to terrify Toni with its chill. "They don't really matter." He pulled in a breath and let it go. "After we work out whatever needs to be done with Steven, I'm leaving, Toni. Something I probably should have done a long time ago."

Toni's heart was racing so fast she couldn't breathe, couldn't think.

He left her there, her face marred by shock, shame, and something he'd never thought he'd see again — fear.

Charles thought he'd feel some sort of victory, relief, even elation. Instead, the only sensation he experienced swirling around inside him was an incredible sadness.

He spent the balance of the night in the guest room.

★ ★ ★

Phillip heard the front door open, then close, followed by the familiar rhythmic click of Victoria's heels. But tonight they sounded vaguely different, a bit slower, not as certain.

He rose from his desk chair and walked out into the front room, the message from the doctor clutched in his hand.

Victoria was standing near the foyer table, absently putting her keys in her purse.

"Hi, sweetheart. I was getting worried."

Victoria lifted her head and forced a smile. "I decided to go to the gym at the last minute." She shrugged and vaguely shook her head simultaneously. "Then a few of us went out for a light dinner." She crossed the short space between them and kissed him softly on the lips, before running her fingers through his thick, inky black hair. "I didn't mean to worry you. I should have called."

"Is everything all right?"

"Sure. Fine."

He watched the relaxed expression on her face. "Your doctor's office called." For an instant the nerve beneath her right eye flickered, then calmed.

"Oh, really. What about?"

Phillip handed her the note.

She briefly glanced at it, then folded it in half and turned away. "You know how Dr. Rowenstein is. She wants me to take some stress tests, cholesterol tests, mammogram, you name it." She laughed airily, keeping her back to him as she fiddled with her purse. "I was so glad to get out of there I just forgot to pick up my test dates."

Phillip slowly began to relax. He eased behind her and slid his arms around her waist. He kissed the back of her long neck. "If there was anything wrong you would tell me, right?" he whispered behind her ear.

"Of course." The lie slid over her lips as sweet as honey.

Later that night, as darkness shook off its velvet cape for a mantle of gold and brilliant orange, Phillip and Victoria lay locked in each other's embrace. Victoria's long dancer's legs wrapped around her husband's back while he moved deep within her, whispering words of love, and that ugly word kept shouting over them, drowning them out. *Abortion.* But how could she ever do it and Phillip not know? she worried, even as her body convulsed in release and he shuddered inside her.

There had to be a way, because Phillip

could never know that she'd destroyed the one thing he wanted most in the world, the one thing she could not ever give him. She hugged him tighter and sealed off her tears.

Parker Heywood strolled along Fulton Street, amazed at the metamorphosis his old neighborhood had undergone in the years that he'd been away. But he'd changed as well, he had to admit, from a onetime Afro-wearing revolutionary to a professor of art with dreadlocks down to his shoulders. Behind the lenses of his dark glasses, his mind's eye painted a new landscape. Where there were once burned-out buildings, an overabundance of liquor stores, and what passed for Chinese restaurants, now there stood antique shops, West Village–type coffee shops, hair salons specializing in natural styles, African and West Indian restaurants, and clothing boutiques.

He wove seamlesssly in and out of the eclectic blend of businesses, all black-owned, with the practiced eye of the artist he was, looking for a possible location to showcase some of his work.

His investment broker, in a casual conversation, had mentioned Fort Greene, or what was quickly becoming known as the "black mecca," as a possible site for his exhibits. But it was only now, during the tail end of the summer recess, that he could take the time away from teaching to check it out.

As he strolled down the prosperous avenue, he was struck by how at home he felt, how easily he blended in. He'd spent the last two years in Europe and Africa, perfecting his craft, studying the masters in the galleries, museums, and in the bushlands before returning to the States to teach a graduate class in art history at Parsons School of Design.

He stopped in front of one establishment, checking the name on the poster board that hung in the plate-glass window of the open door: *Regina's Place: Help Wanted.*

Workmen moved in and out carrying tools, cans of paint, and planks of wood. Parker stepped around one man who was sitting on a crate, guzzling a bottle of water, and walked inside.

Banging, hammering, and deep-throated orders reverberated throughout the high-ceilinged space. Parker walked farther inside, taking in the warmth of the burnished gold trim along the smooth cream-colored walls, the gleam of the varnished shelving,

198

and the brilliant, eye-catching African-print fabric in golds, blacks, and oranges that covered the large, circular ottomans and overstuffed lounge chairs. It gave the feel of someone's cozy living room or private study. He could almost see his work hanging on the walls, or encased in the glass cabinets.

"Can I help you with something?"

He hadn't even seen her when he came in, and suddenly she was standing right in front of him with the most amazing light brown eyes and inviting voice. There was a spot of white paint on her nose that only softened the serious expression on her face. She wiped her hands on her jeans, and Parker's eye trailed the soft curve of her hips and the strong line of her legs, right down to her sneakered feet — perfect, paintable.

He caught himself and returned to her face. "Uh, I was just taking a tour of the neighborhood and kind of wandered in." He gazed around. "Great-looking space. What is it going to be?"

"Hopefully a bookstore and a café, if these guys ever get finished — although not according to my family and friends," she added wryly.

Parker looked at her curiously. "Not finished, or not a bookstore?"

"Both."

His brows arched in curiosity.

She waved off his inquiring look. "It's not important."

"Is this . . . yours?"

She smiled proudly, her dimples hollowing her cheeks. "Yep. I'm Regina."

"Parker Heywood. I used to live around here. Grew up here, actually." He chuckled. "It has definitely changed."

"What made you come back?"

"Got a good tip from my financial adviser. I've been looking at offbeat locations to display my artwork."

"Really? What kind of art?"

He grinned. "A combination of modern, African, and me."

Regina was thoughtful for a moment, an idea churning around in her head. "Have you found anyplace yet?"

"Still looking."

She paused for a moment, then plunged ahead. "I don't know if this would interest you or not, but maybe you might want to think about showing some of your work here — as part of my grand opening."

"Wow." He pursed his lips and slowly nodded, looking around. "Maybe."

"Well, think about it. *I* think it would be

great." If Toni and Victoria or her mother were there, they would say, "There she goes again, acting and not thinking," she mused. *That's why they aren't here.*

"But you haven't seen my work," he said, surprised at the cut-to-the-chase attitude.

Regina stared him in the eye. "I've turned over a new leaf in my life, Mr. Heywood. I'm going by my instincts, my woman's intuition, these days, taking chances on things I would have never dreamed of. And today my instincts tell me your work will be fine." She crossed her arms and let out a breath of resolve.

Parker chuckled. "I like that. A quality that's much too rare. When are you planning to open?"

"In about six weeks. Why don't you stop back by and bring some of your pieces?"

"I'll do that. Say . . . in a couple of days?"

"Fine."

The noise hummed around them.

"I, uh, had better get back to work," Regina said softly.

Parker suddenly felt warm inside, something he hadn't felt in a long time. He swallowed. "Yeah, I'd better get going, too," he mumbled, although he had no destination in mind and felt as if he could just sit there for a while, discover what else she might be suddenly inspired to do.

Regina nodded. "So . . . I'll see you then." Her statement sounded more like a question and hung precariously in the air between them.

"Definitely. Uh, do you have a card? I'll give you a call when I'm on my way."

Regina fished in her pocket for a piece of paper, jotted down the number, and handed it to him.

"Thanks." He stuck out his hand and she slipped hers into it. "Take care."

"You, too," she said as she watched him walk toward the door.

He stopped in the doorway, his path blocked by a figure she couldn't quite see, his broad, muscular body shielding it from her.

Parker continued on his way, leaving Russell framed in the open doorway.

# CHAPTER TWELVE

Millie returned from her weekly hairdressing appointment totally shaken. She'd been going to Ms. Ellen's Beauty Parlor for a wash and set for a good twenty years. She'd seen every style under the sun come and go, from Afros and Afro-puffs to Jheri Curls, braids, weaves, and everything in between. But as far as she was concerned, a wash and set suited her just fine.

Over the years, she and Ellen had shared a host of Saturdays together. While Ellen held Millie under the warm, sudsy water and massaged her scalp, Millie would talk — about everything. She'd tell Ellen all about Regina and the wonderful things she was doing in all of her lessons. She'd confess about her husband, Robert, and his drinking, cry about the Friday nights when he didn't come home, and how she suffered in silence. She poured her heartbreak out to Ellen, who listened in stoic silence when Regina left Russell. She'd worked so hard to convince Regina to marry him, she complained. He was just what Regina needed, someone strong and forceful, who knew his mind, who had a solid future ahead of him and could provide for her and a family. Someone so unlike her father, who gradually let life consume him until the day he died.

And Ellen would listen, never offering any advice, simply letting Millie talk with a few well-placed *umms* and *hmms* in all the right places. And Millie would leave Ms. Ellen's Beauty Parlor feeling cleansed inside and out. That was just how Saturdays were between Millie and Ellen. Every Saturday except this one.

Millie'd gone there for her regular appointment and had settled comfortably at the sink. No sooner had Ellen turned on the water than Millie launched into her current dilemma with Regina.

"She's being totally unreasonable about this whole business, Ellen," Millie was lamenting. "What choice did I have but to call Russell? He was just as stunned as I was. After all, Michele and Darren are his children, too. Well, you would have thought I called the devil himself, the way she carried on. Told me to stay out of her life. Can you believe that?"

"I would have told you the same thing,"

Ellen stated simply, and kept massaging Millie's scalp.

Millie was so stunned by the sound of Ellen's voice, she lifted her head too fast and water splashed all over her face and ran down her neck and back.

Ellen grabbed a towel and patted her dry before holding her back under the water. "You need to do what she asks, Millie — for once. As long as I've known you, you've been running that girl's life, telling her where to go, what to do, how to dress, who to marry. You ever ask yourself why your husband Robert drank so much and stayed out at night? It was the only relief he could get, Millie. No man wants to be made to feel like less than a man. You were so busy managing his life and Regina's that you ran both of them away from you."

Millie was stunned into silence. She'd never heard Ellen string more than four words together at a time, and surely never offer an opinion.

"You don't know what you're talking about," she huffed. "If they didn't have me, what would they have done? I was their lifeline. I devoted my entire life to them, and look at the thanks I get. Now you're turning on me, too, my one friend," she whined, bordering on tears.

"Millie, up until today, I had a strict policy of staying out of other people's business. But I've known you too long to keep my mouth shut this time. Regina doesn't need you. She needs to do something on her own, by herself, what she wants. Leave her alone, Millie, or you'll lose her for good."

Millie was so distraught she'd run out of Ms. Ellen's Beauty Parlor with her hair soaking wet. Now it was a bushy mess, which was a clear indication to her of what her life had turned into.

Millie sipped her glass of iced tea and stared out the kitchen window. Regina was always so agreeable and easygoing. She was the one everyone turned to when they needed a shoulder because she was so levelheaded.

But something changed in Regina during the last few years. It began when she left Russell. How she could do that was anyone's guess. Every marriage had its problems. She had hers, but she dealt with them. That was what you did in a marriage. You took the good with the bad. But not Regina. So she'd turned into another statistic: a single black woman with kids.

Now this.

And she never cared for that job of Regina's at the newspaper either, dealing with all sorts of riffraff. That was not how she raised her child. She went along with it — though grudgingly — but complained bitterly to Russell, who agreed entirely. Regina needed to be at home, raising her children and taking care of her husband. And look what happened with that. She up and quit — on a whim — simply because she didn't like it anymore!

Now Regina believed she could be some sort of bookseller at the risk of her own children's financial security, their welfare. It was completely irresponsible. That was why Regina needed her mother's firm guidance.

Somebody must do something. Ellen's words echoed in her head. *Leave her alone. Regina doesn't need you.* Of course she did. She shook off Ellen's warning. Regina was her child, and who knew a child better than her own mother. Regina and those children needed her now more than ever; she was just too stubborn to realize it.

Russell walked around the workmen, mindful of his new suit, and headed toward the back. Regina hadn't budged.

"What are you doing here, Russell?" she asked the instant he stopped in front of her.

"I wanted to see this latest dream of yours for myself." He gazed around, grudgingly admiring the space and all the work going into it. Most of all, he had to admit this was a prime location and would probably do exceptionally well. The property value in this part of Brooklyn had skyrocketed. There were over one hundred and sixty black-owned businesses flourishing in this area. How did she pull it off? "You . . . did this all on your own?"

"Yes. You sound surprised, Russell, like you generally do when I have a thought that wasn't yours or my mother's." She folded her arms in front of her. "I have work to do."

He didn't flinch. "You really think this business of yours is going to work, don't you?"

"I know it will."

Russell looked her over, saw the determination in her light brown eyes, the set of her mouth. This was not the Regina he'd walked down the aisle with, spent all those years with.

When she'd left him and taken the kids, he was certain she would come crawling back, unable to make it on her own. But she never did, not once.

For so long he'd been used to a weak

woman who bowed to his will, did what he demanded, and asked nothing in return. At the time he believed it was what he wanted because he didn't want a flawed marriage like the one his parents had.

How could he have known that their marriage was the way they wanted it to be, that it didn't fall apart because his mother wanted a career, but because they no longer wanted each other.

He'd grown up believing that his father's unhappiness was all his mother's fault. He blamed her, and it wasn't until a little more than a year ago that his father told him what really happened — that it wasn't his mother's fault at all, but his own possessiveness that ultimately destroyed their marriage. By then, it was too late for him and Regina.

He'd spent the last year lonely and full of regret. Because underneath it all he'd admired Regina, took a sort of pride in her infrequent bursts of independence. And at the same time it frightened him, so he crushed it every time it would rear its head. How could he, the man of the family, tell her that he was afraid of losing her to her goals, to the rest of the world?

The call from Millie had been the key he'd been looking for, a way to insinuate himself back into her life, open the door again, try to explain. But he'd been so conditioned to being in control, to having everything and everyone the way he wanted — jumping to his commands — that he'd come at her like a boxer sparring for a fight. And she'd fought back.

Russell walked past her toward the back of the store, then stopped and turned. "You, uh, have all your finances straight? My company has a great accounting program for small businesses."

Regina's neck stiffened. Her eyes narrowed suspiciously. "My finances are fine — thanks."

Russell pressed his lips together and nodded. She was still as pretty to him now as the first day they'd met. Not a glamour-girl kind of pretty, but that quiet, classic pretty that got better with age. Even her complexion had cleared, and her body was sculpted and firm now. She'd been taking care of herself — without him, or in spite of him.

He cleared his throat and looked away, afraid that his eyes would betray him. "If, uh, you need any . . . help . . . with anything" — he swallowed — "give me a call, okay?" He quickly walked back down the aisle, past her, and out the door before she had the presence of mind to respond.

Regina stood there, dumbfounded by Russell's uncharacteristic behavior. Just days ago he was threatening to take the kids. Now he was offering his help. She briskly shook her head. She didn't trust him. He must be trying to lull her into a sense of security before he pulled another stunt, she concluded.

Well, she'd just be prepared.

# CHAPTER THIRTEEN

Regina was in her small but cheery candy-apple red-and-white kitchen, intent on preparing a midday snack before she tackled the stacks of inventory forms she needed to review, and begin writing the checks to the vendors for the goods received.

Duke, Miles, Trane, Billie, Sarah, Nancy, and Ella gathered around the table, slapping fives, playing, singing, and scatting, but mostly just keeping her company as they followed one another in and out of the small radio that sat in the window-sill.

She had the house to herself. Michele and Darren were off doing teenage things with their friends, and she didn't expect them back anytime soon. Which was fine. The atmosphere between the three of them was strained, at best, so these few hours of reprieve would do them all some good.

She filled out her first check to the book distributor on the account bearing her store's name: Regina's Place. She smiled with pride. It was really happening, finally coming together. All her sacrifice and hard work were paying off.

Without a doubt, there had been moments, long moments, when she questioned the wisdom of her decision. Suppose everyone was right and she was wrong? What did she really know about running a business, except what she'd read in books and listened to in seminars? There was nothing like life experience as the true test. The reality was, if this failed, she could lose everything, including her children if Russell decided to make good on his threat.

Russell. She couldn't figure him out. For a minute, back at the store, he almost seemed human — decent, like the man she thought she'd married, had been in love with once upon a time. It had taken her nearly a decade of those married years to accept the fact that she'd married a man with the same overbearing attributes of her mother — the very qualities she wanted to get away from.

She sighed. No point in revisiting the past. That episode of her life was behind her. Her only regret was that the people closest to her didn't understand her at all, or understand why what she was doing was so important.

Although she'd had a long talk with Michele and Darren and tried to explain things to them, their responses still remained skeptical and distant. The fact that their grandmother fed into their worst fears of abject poverty and loss of "designer world" privileges certainly didn't help any. But she'd made it perfectly clear to them that it was not their responsibility to go running off and carrying stories to their grandmother. Anything that went on in their household stayed in their household, unless they'd decided as a family to do otherwise.

Regina picked up a bill for a shipment of posters and thought of the man she'd met, Parker Heywood. It had been a long time since she'd been remotely attracted to a man. While she was married to Russell, although the marriage was rocky, it never occurred to her to cast her eye in another direction. After the divorce she was too battle-weary and scarred even to look in the direction of a man. Besides, her greatest concerns were her children and their healing process. During that time, the last thing she needed was to parade a new man in front of them. But it had been three years. Hard years, often lonely years, but time sufficiently began to cover the wounds that her marriage and divorce had inflicted.

But there was something about Parker Heywood that soundlessly and without effort peeked behind the wall she'd erected, and it disturbed her as much as it excited her to know that she could still feel something. She hadn't died inside.

She put the bill aside and wrote out the corresponding check. She didn't want to contemplate a relationship with anyone. She still had her own healing to do.

She shook her head in dismissal. Now she was letting her writer's imagination create a scenario that didn't exist. She had too many other things to occupy her attention and certainly didn't need a distraction like Parker Heywood. As a matter of fact, it was probably best that she quash the whole idea of exhibiting his work in the store.

The sound of the front door opening drew her attention. She heard the voices of Michele and Darren — her stomach clenched — and Russell.

Toni'd heard Charles's Jeep pull off before the sun rose. All during the torturous night she'd wanted to go to him, to try to explain. But she had been afraid, too afraid

215

of what he'd say and afraid of what she couldn't.

She'd paged him several times in the hours that he'd been gone, but he didn't call back. She wasn't sure if she'd expected him to or not.

What had she done? She crossed her bedroom floor and stared out of the window. A feeling of doom grabbed hold of her insides, escalating her heart, turning her stomach, heating then cooling her skin. But what could possibly be worse than what was already happening? Her entire life was falling apart and there was no one to blame but herself. Charles didn't deserve this — and now the trouble with Steven.

Her stomach lurched, and she pushed her fist to her mouth to stifle the sob that rushed up her throat.

Cars moved up and down her block, passed all the overpriced brownstones, pulling in and out of the few parking spaces. The upscale residents paraded down the tree-lined street, walking dogs, carrying home packages from gourmet supermarkets and specialty boutiques. She was a long way from Louisiana — a long way from home. As far away from the struggle to survive, the hopeless looks in her parents' eyes, the looks of submission in her sisters', as she could get. But at what cost? What did she really have? The illusion of success and happiness. And no matter how many degrees she earned, how much artwork and handcrafted furniture she brought into her home, it would not change the fact that it was all surface — things used to camouflage the ugliness, the truths underneath. It was long past time that she stopped pretending that ugliness didn't exist in her world. The guilt of leaving her family she had left behind still haunted her, so she tried to make it up to everyone she met, to do for them what she failed to do for that household in Algiers.

She wiped away her tears and left her bedroom in search of her son. She wasn't certain what she would say to him. It was always easier when it was someone else's problem, someone else's child. You could sit back and offer sage advice handed down from one professor and textbook to the next. You could mark the file "case closed" when everything turned out fine; marriages were reconciled, resources utilized; programs implemented. Or in the really tough cases, chalk it up as the one that got away, the one you couldn't save. And in both scenarios you tucked your emotions aside and moved on to the next case.

But here, today, in her own home, she couldn't simply walk away, telling Charles and Steven that their session was over. *Your own backyard.* Regina's words echoed again in her head. How right she had been. How clearly Regina had seen what she'd been too blind to. And in the quiet moment of reflection, she realized and accepted just how wise Regina truly was. Of the three of them, she was the only one who saw and accepted things for what they really were and was brave enough to do something about it. Could she say the same?

Toni stood in front of Steven's closed bedroom door. What would Regina say if this were Darren or Michele? she wondered as she raised her fist to knock.

Victoria had one of those nights that a bad day is made of. After she and Phillip made love, she lay curled on her side with her back to him, staring at the wall, silently crying.

He'd been so sweet and tender with her, his touch almost reverent as he fueled her body with his love and whispered his adoration.

During a weak moment, she almost believed it would be good and possible to have a child with Phillip, to tell him about the pregnancy. She knew how much he wanted a baby — a real family, he'd said. And she also knew part of it was to make up for the loss of his own family, who would have nothing to do with him — because of her.

Why couldn't she give him this one thing he asked for, the one thing she knew would bring him total joy?

*Nothing beneath the surface. All appearances, all superficial.* Regina's words still haunted her. The ring of truth still echoed in her head. But no one understood her fears, her insecurities, the inner torment that raged incessantly within her.

That last evening at the club, and now this unplanned pregnancy, had forced her to look beyond her reflection in the mirror, and she didn't like what she saw, but had no idea how to change it.

Now, alone in the kitchen, she stared at the hanging rack of sparkling copper pots and pans — more for decoration than use — in her high-tech kitchen, and absently took a sip of tea.

The doctor said she was about six weeks along. She didn't have much time. That much she did know.

Phillip's sudden kiss on her cheek caused

her to jump, sloshing some of her tea onto the Formica tabletop as a result.

Phillip chuckled. "Sorry, sweetie. I didn't mean to scare you." He pressed another kiss into her short curls and squeezed her shoulders. "You're pretty deep in thought. Anything wrong?" He walked over to the stove and turned on the jets beneath the teapot.

Victoria gazed at his bare back, the broad shoulders and defined muscles. He was still in pretty good shape for a man pushing forty-five. He didn't work out often, but he was very athletic, the outdoor type. He'd coerced her into enjoying it as well. Imagine, a girl from the projects skiing in Aspen, sailing around Martha's Vineyard, horseback riding in the Poconos, hiking in the Rocky Mountains.

Phillip opened a new world to her and eagerly welcomed her into it. Greedily she'd taken everything he'd offered, surrendered to his invitation to fantasy and adventure; but what had she given him in return?

She frowned as she began wiping up the small spill with a paper napkin, thinking she'd never been one to examine her behavior or question her motives. Until lately. Following her self-imposed ideals, she'd always done what she thought was best, what would reap the best rewards. Looking around at the trappings, all her possessions, even her job, the question now was: was this facade of affluence worth it?

Phillip sat opposite her, stirred two spoonfuls of sugar into the clear teacup, and took a tentative sip.

"What are your plans for today?"

"Nothing special. I thought I'd catch up on some reading."

Phillip nodded and took another sip of his tea. "I was hoping we could go out for dinner tonight. How about that new Japanese place in Chelsea? You like Japanese."

Suddenly what she really wanted was some collard greens seasoned with hot sauce and fatback, two juicy legs of fried chicken like her mother used to make, and a plate of peas and rice with brown gravy. She was tired of tiny plates of French and other exotic foods, most of which she couldn't name. Pasta, pasta, pasta, in all sorts of sauces, sautéed and tofu-ed. She'd become so conditioned to eating tiny portions of beautifully prepared and unpronounceable foods that the sudden urgency to find a plate of soul food totally caught her off guard.

"So what do you think, sweetie?" Phillip asked.

"Sure."

"You haven't been out with the girls in a while," he commented. "Everybody okay?"

Victoria gazed down into her cup. "Fine." The truth was, she had no idea how Toni and Regina were. Something had happened that night at the bar. Something more significant than Regina's announcement and accusations. Nothing had been the same since, and she missed it more than she'd ever admit.

"I'm going to change. I've got to run out for a while," Phillip said, rising from his seat. "I should be back around four."

Victoria glanced up, forced a smile, and nodded.

Phillip leaned down and placed a gentle kiss on her mouth. "You were wonderful last night," he whispered.

The phone rang. "I'll get it," Victoria said, disengaging the connection between them.

Phillip watched her walk away, the unease he'd felt the night before returning.

"Russell," Regina said on a breath. She looked from her daughter to her son and then back to her ex-husband.

"I was pulling up as the kids were coming in."

Regina arched a brow. That didn't explain what he was doing there — *again,* Regina thought. Russell smiled that boyish smile of his that used to make her heart race.

Michele and Darren were beaming as if Santa Claus had dropped down their chimney.

"Dad, let me show you my trophy from the basketball team," Darren announced with excitement.

Russell shoved his hands into his pockets and raised a questioning brow at Regina. She gave the barest nod of her head, and he followed Darren down the short hallway to his bedroom.

"I hope you don't mind, Ma," Michele said apologetically as soon as her father and brother were out of earshot. "He was just sitting outside in the car. I —"

"It's all right, hon. Don't worry about it."

"He . . . seems different," Michele said with a bit of hesitation.

Regina slanted her a look. "What do you mean?"

Michele shrugged. "I don't know exactly. Nicer, I guess." She sat down at the table and tucked her braids behind her ears. "Can I say something?"

"Of course."

"I . . . kind of miss him, you know."

Regina's heart ached. She looked at the sad expression on her daughter's face, realizing how deeply she loved her father. She'd always been his baby girl, but even she wasn't spared when Russell launched into one of his ranting tirades, leaving the entire household walking on eggshells. The remembrance of those turbulent times sent a shiver of dread up Regina's back. Then there were those wonderful, joyous times when Russell Everette could be the sweetest, most loving man imaginable. This was the man who had won her heart, whom she fantasized being with before their marriage. However, as the years passed, this warm, caring version of Russell rarely appeared. What was most disturbing about their relationship was that the stronger she attempted to become as a person and a woman, the angrier and meaner Russell became.

Many nights when Regina was alone in her bed, she wondered how she could have done things differently. Could she have saved their marriage? Could she have changed Russell into someone who truly honored the vows of matrimony? She was especially upset by how everything had worked out when she thought of Michelle and Darren not having a father in the house. What if her mother was right with her insistence that she should have stuck it out — through thick and thin, better or worse.

But things were different now. A woman had more options than back in the day. Now a woman didn't have to stay when the marriage went bad. It went further than that, because to remain would have slowly killed more than the marriage; she would have killed the essence of herself. The resulting damage might have been more than she could handle, deep in the soft tissue of her soul. She'd seen too many women stay too long and pay a high price for their commitment and loyalty. Something died inside them, and no man could ever penetrate their defenses again. Never to love again. That sacrifice was much too great.

"I know you miss him, sweetheart," Regina said finally. "I wish things could be different." She stroked Michele's hair. "Unfortunately, this is the way things are."

"Don't you miss him sometimes?"

Regina weighed her response. Michele was almost seventeen years old. Old enough to accept the truth. "Honey, your father and I had a lot of problems in the last few years. I think you know that." Michele lowered her head. "Things just didn't work out, and it became harder every day to make it work. So . . ." She released a long breath. "I had to make a choice, a very difficult one: stay, and have the problems your father and I were going through corrode the entire family, or leave and try to salvage what I could of myself and build a positive home for you and your brother."

Michele looked at her mother, her eyes wide and questioning. "If Daddy changed — if he stopped acting the way he used to — would you get back together with him?"

"Oh, Michele." She sighed gently. "I don't know. I really don't. Too many things have gone wrong, too many ugly words and deep hurts, honey."

Michele turned her lips to the side in contemplation. "You wouldn't mind if we spent time with him — me and Darren?"

"No. Of course not. I think it would be good for you and your brother. The way things have been with you all and your father hasn't been my doing, Michele. I want you to know that," she stated quite clearly. She was the one during the past three years who tried to encourage Russell to spend time with his children. Just because he no longer lived there and their marriage was over didn't mean that he magically stopped being their dad. He had made an effort for a while, but over time his visits became fewer and farther between, something Regina couldn't understand. Especially since she wasn't one of those ex-wives who gave their former spouses a hard time over visitation rights. But she supposed there was a lot she didn't understand about Russell — and now . . . well, it was too late.

Michele nodded her head. "Dad said we should try to be more understanding about your reasons for leaving your job and opening the store."

Regina blinked several times in confusion. Who was she talking about? Russell? "He said what?" she stammered.

"Daddy said you would never do anything that you didn't think was right, or that would hurt us, and that Grandma is just being Grandma — all hyped and freaked out as usual."

Regina was sure that at any minute Michele was going to burst out laughing and say, "Just kidding." But she didn't. Regina frowned. What was Russell up to? It wasn't like him to offer compliments or his support when it came to anything having to do with her.

"I owe you an apology for the way I've been actin'."

Regina stared at her daughter, dumbfounded and somewhat disappointed. Dumbfounded by her admission, and disappointed by how it came about. For all the explaining and cajoling — almost begging her children to understand and trust her — all it took was one conversation with Russell, and Michele was singing a different tune. In that instance, for all the good Russell might have done with his spiel, he did the one thing he was best at — making her feel insignificant.

"Thanks, apology accepted," Regina responded. She turned her attention back to her bills, not wanting Michele to see the pain in her eyes.

"Can I help with something?"

Regina kept her head lowered. "No. But thanks."

"I'm gonna see what Dad and Darren are doing."

"Fine," Regina mumbled over the tightness in her throat. She took a deep, chest-bursting gulp of air, let it steady her. She gazed toward the hallway, listening to the sounds of laughter and happy voices drifting toward her.

"Don't be fooled," she warned herself. "A zebra can't change its stripes." At least she didn't think so.

# CHAPTER FOURTEEN

Parker was in the room he'd designated as his studio in his two-bedroom apartment in SoHo, the heart of Manhattan's art district, south of City Hall and within walking distance of Chinatown. He was one of the few black artists in the area, but that was fine. He preferred to keep to himself.

He'd been up since dawn and was intent on the canvas, where he applied expressive washes of warm, muted colors to the background of his latest excursion into realism. There was no Degas, Pollock, or Monet in his work. He believed art should represent life as closely as possible, a true reminder of the splendor of nature and humanity.

Little by little, a portrait emerged as he added the fine details of Regina's face from memory. He wasn't quite sure why he'd begun painting her. But he hadn't been able to get her out of his mind since they'd met. And with everything in his life, if he was troubled or confused, he painted, which accounted for the hundreds of paintings he'd created during the last five years.

The canvases were a reflection of his life, with all of its varied moods and changes. Painting, for him, was a way of quieting the roar of pain inside — his one true outlet. Often the feel of the brush in his hand, the smell of the oils or acrylics, and the demands of the canvas stretched on the easel before him provided the only sure relief from the chaos of his life outside of the studio. It worked better than alcohol, drugs, or women. Most of his work was startling, provocative, and seething with a barely concealed rage. After years of struggling to keep a roof over his head, he truly knew the marginal existence of the suffering artist, and that was evident in his work.

But this rendering of Regina had a different feel to it. It was softer, accessible — things he hadn't conveyed in a very long time, and which rarely came across on canvas.

He mixed more paint to get the exact color of her light brown eyes, dipping his brush into the blended oils to see if the hue was just right. And suddenly she was looking back at him from the canvas, the allure and mystery of her gaze right there, justifying all of the effort he'd put into experimenting with light and tone. The shock of his achievement forced him to step back as if he'd been shoved in the chest.

There on the canvas was Regina, almost real enough to touch. The sensation of her being right in the room with him sent a surge of electricity through his body.

He dropped his brushes on the tray and turned away from her all-seeing eyes and tender mouth. He didn't want to feel again. It was easier to remain one step removed from emotion. That way nothing could hurt him. He couldn't go through that again. It wasn't worth it.

Parker turned back toward the portrait, removed it from the easel, and put it in a corner of his studio. It was finished, something that purged him in a sense. He'd painted, seen his soul's definition of Regina before him. Now it was out of his system, he concluded, and turned the painting away from him.

Charles knew he shouldn't be doing this, knew he shouldn't be there, even as he journeyed onto the street where he'd seen Toni and her lover. It was stupid and childish. But he wanted to see this man up close, maybe figure out what it was about him that attracted his wife.

He pulled the Jeep into a space across the street from the house where the tryst had occurred. His mind went on an uncontrollable rampage as he stared first at the closed front door and then at the windows. His Toni. How many times had she crossed that threshold? Did he love her? Did she love him? What happened between them when they came together for these illicit meetings?

His stomach rolled uneasily when he envisioned Toni in that man's burly arms, giving herself the way she'd done with him — calling his name, her eyes glistening with passion, her body arched in the throes of lust, her voice stilled by the waves of desire.

Charles squeezed his eyes shut and pressed his fingers to his forehead. Silent tears slid from his eyes, and his body rocked as he tried to hold on to his pain. He drew in a shuddering breath, glanced at the house one last time, and tore away from the curb. The answers weren't on the other side of that door; they were inside him and Toni.

"Where are you off to?" Phillip asked.

He watched Victoria change out of her silk lounging pajamas into her DKNY jogging suit in a soft lavender that did beautiful things to her skin, he thought.

"Just a few errands."

"Oh." He frowned momentarily. "I thought you said you were going to hang around the house?" He zipped up his jeans and slid a snakeskin belt through the loops. "You want me to drop you off somewhere?"

"No, thanks. I'll take my car." She quickly crossed the room and pecked him on the lips. "I'll see you around four."

She was out the door in the blink of an eye, and Phillip was suddenly suspicious of Victoria's uncharacteristic behavior.

Right after that phone call, she'd gotten very fidgety and seemed distracted. It was as if he were not even in the room. When he asked her about the call, she waved it off, saying it was nothing important.

He wasn't in the habit of questioning Victoria. He never had been. But now something was going on: first the strange phone call from the doctor's office the day before and now a phone call that sent her racing out of the house like a shot.

It wasn't like Victoria to be evasive and secretive. That's what concerned him most. She'd tell him the truth even if it would hurt. At least that was the way it had been.

Phillip was certain that his wife was hiding something, and he didn't like the feeling it gave him — especially about her.

For the most part, Vicky was all he had. When he made the decision to marry her, his family followed through on their threats to cut him off. He hadn't seen or spoken to his large family in more than five years.

Some days it was more painful than others, especially around the holidays. He still called his parents for their birthdays, but he never got beyond the answering machine or the housekeeper. They wouldn't take his calls. He never told Vicky. He didn't want her to feel that it was in any way her fault. So without that big family to lavish his love on, he poured everything into his relationship with his wife. All that concerned him was seeing her happy, meeting her needs, giving her everything she wanted. Seeing her happy helped to fill some of the emotional holes inside him.

Phillip trotted down the steps to the ground floor. He took his blue sports jacket from the coatrack in the hall and slung it over his shoulder.

Tonight, during dinner, they would talk, really talk. He would tell her how concerned he was, remind her how important she was to him. And tell her he thought it was about time they had a child before it was too late.

It felt good being with his kids again and knowing that Regina was in the next room, Russell thought as he listened to a poem that Michele was reading to him. This was what was missing from his life, and he had no idea how to get it back.

Since the divorce, it was as if a part of him had been cut off, cut out. And it was easier just to stay away, not to be reminded of what he no longer had. But how could he ever explain that without sounding weak?

He'd been a bastard to Regina. He'd treated her as though she were a helpless idiot without a concrete thought in her head and needed him to look after her, guide her. It took her leaving him to make him realize just who needed who. He needed Regina more than he would have ever imagined. And whatever it took, however long it took, he'd find a way to make her believe that he'd never stopped loving her and that he wanted to be a part of her life again. Somehow. He had to find a way.

"Excuse me for a minute, sweetie. I need to talk to your mom." He got up off the bed and walked out into the kitchen, his heart racing as if he'd been running a mile.

Regina briefly glanced up from what she was doing, then returned to writing checks. "Ready to go?" she mumbled.

"Just about."

"Hmmm."

"Gina . . ."

Her eyes snapped up. Russell hadn't called her Gina since the early days of their marriage.

"I know this will seem out of the blue, but I . . . was wondering . . . if you're not busy one night this week . . . I was hoping we could talk." He swallowed hard. "Maybe over dinner or something."

Regina stared at him as if he'd suddenly turned green. "About . . . what?"

Russell took a deep breath and looked straight into her eyes. "About us, the kids, everything. There's a lot I need to tell you, Gina. Things I want you to know." He inhaled again. "You have my number. Call me when you decide."

He headed for the door, then stopped. "Tell the kids good-bye for me, okay?" His voice hitched. "I can't."

Regina sat there in complete shock, staring at the closed door. If this was some sort of act by him, it was a damned good one. But her journalistic instincts told her it wasn't. And if it wasn't an act, it was something she was totally unprepared to deal with. And she didn't know if she wanted to, even if she could.

# CHAPTER FIFTEEN

Toni quietly closed Steven's bedroom door, shaken to her core by their conversation. Shaken not so much because of what was revealed, but rather by the pure simplicity of it all — the underlying cause for what had happened to her son, to the three of them. She'd expected every kind of explanation to justify her son's being arrested for drug possession, from it all being a setup by the police targeting black male youth to mistaken identity. When they'd come home from the precinct in the early hours of the morning, they'd been too exhausted, too angry, and too bewildered by it all to talk, agreeing that after some sleep and time to cool down would be better. Maybe she should have waited for Charles to return from wherever he'd gone, but she couldn't sit in the same house with Steven right down the hall and not know what happened.

What she'd painfully come to realize was that she didn't know her son at all. He wasn't the boy she'd imagined, had fixed in her head as the good-looking, above-average, well-mannered, well-adjusted teen, bursting into manhood. He was very much alone, struggling to find his way to fit in — at home, at school, with his friends. He'd said he felt like a ghost, existing, yet no one could see him. But dealing drugs made him feel important, noticed, respected, as much as he knew how wrong it was.

How could she not have seen what was happening to her child? How easy it was to be blind to the things right in front of you. To ignore it in the hope that it would go away. In truth, in sad truth, she had viewed her son through the same murky glass that she'd viewed her husband. There, but not there, needing to be led, but not heard. Now they were all paying for her mistakes, her self-righteousness.

Slowly she walked back down the carpeted hallway that was graced on either wall with original paintings and photographs by Gordon Parks. She'd spent hours at ICP and the Whitney Museum of Art trying to find just the right pieces during several exhibits. The thing was, once she'd gotten them home and hung, neither Charles nor Steven paid them any attention. It was a disease that had infected the entire family — ignoring what was right in front of them.

Toni lay across her bed and curled into a fetal position, wishing she could sink inside herself, shut the world out. But hadn't she been doing that all along? She'd shielded herself from Charles by being with Alan, which kept her from dealing with the real issues of her marriage, as if the affair would magically make what was wrong between her and Charles right. She hadn't seen what was happening to her son because she'd been too concerned with solving the problems of other people's children, other people's lives. Because to see what was going on inside her own home would be to recognize her own failures, to revisit, once again, the failure of the family she'd abandoned — something she had not been prepared to do.

Regina was so right. But Toni hadn't wanted to hear the truth, face it, and deal with it, so she had shut Regina out, too. Just as she'd done when Regina tried to tell her how unhappy she was in her marriage. She hadn't listened then, either. She hadn't been the friend Regina needed.

How could she begin to make things right again?

*Charles.* She shut her eyes. She'd had

such great hopes for him, for them. They were going to be the up-and-coming buppie couple that everyone would want to imitate. But while she continued to achieve, to strive, to ultimately grow in discontent, Charles remained the same: the same simple man with simple needs, simple wants. Who spent his life going with the flow, taking things as they came without causing a ripple in the water. Charles's very nature inadvertently brought out all of her protective, take-over instincts, the same way she handled her parents, her sisters and their children, her clients. So she and Charles fell into roles they couldn't shake; she the nurturer and protector and he the amenable recipient.

Except for last night at the precinct. There Charles suddenly matured, grew wiser, protective, assertive. For the first time in their marriage she actually felt secure and believed that Charles would take care of everything.

She realized when she woke that morning to find him gone that she not only wanted his return to the home they shared, but she wanted the man she'd seen last night to return. The man she'd always dreamed of, believed he could be. She wanted the man who could make everything all right, take care of her and Steven. How desperately she wanted to be taken care of. She'd been so accustomed to running things, handling things, making things happen, she didn't know just how good it felt to share the load and responsibility with someone else.

Now that she'd found him, he was lost to her, maybe forever. Her body shook as waves of sorrow and regret rocked through her petite frame. She *needed* for the first time in her life. She needed, and she had no one to turn to, no one to listen to what was in her heart, on her mind. And she had no one to blame but herself.

Victoria took the Long Island Expressway to the Grand Central Parkway. Her hands shook and she gripped the steering wheel tighter. Cars whizzed by her on the massive four-lane highway. Airplanes coming into and out of LaGuardia Airport roared overhead.

She reached for the radio and pressed the on button, hoping that some light FM would relieve the tension that coiled her body like a spring.

The clinic was located in the Lincoln Center area in Manhattan — very unobtrusive, so she didn't have to worry about protesters and picketers marching outside, she was assured by the receptionist when she'd called that morning about the "procedure." She'd been prepared to schedule an appointment until she was advised that she would have to participate in a mandatory counseling session with one of their staff before anything could be scheduled.

Then, to complicate matters, she'd been all ready to leave as soon as Phillip was gone for the day, as he was every Saturday, and the phone call came nearly giving her a heart attack. What if Phillip had answered instead of her? What if he'd gotten the message that her two o'clock appointment to discuss "termination" had to be moved to one o'clock?

She'd been a nervous wreck trying to think of some excuse to leave the house after she'd just finished telling Phillip she was going to relax and read. And each time she thought of the very idea that he could have gotten that call, she shivered. Explaining away two medically related calls in less than twenty-four hours would be hard for anyone to swallow.

Victoria eased into the right lane. She wished she had someone to go with her, someone to talk to. She should have called Toni, she thought, taking the exit onto the

Triborough Bridge. But they hadn't really spoken in weeks. And besides, she often wondered if Toni ever actually listened to anyone, or just waited for an opening in the conversation so she could jump in, afraid that if she didn't, the conversation might somehow shine a light on her, revealing things she didn't want anyone to see. And she was no better.

As much as she didn't want to admit it, she really wanted to talk to Regina, to tell her how desperately frightened she was about everything. Not just about this pregnancy and all it meant, but everything — the sham of her entire life. And deep in her soul she believed that Regina would understand — wouldn't judge, but would listen, and the advice she'd offer, if asked, would be from her heart, direct, with no strings attached, just as she'd always done — something that Victoria was beginning to realize that she missed, even if she pretended she didn't.

The clock on the dashboard showed 12:10. Victoria paid her toll, exited the Triborough at 125th Street, turned around, and went back the way she'd come.

Regina put away her paperwork and was

preparing dinner, her mind only marginally on the task at hand. By rote she washed four white potatoes, one each for herself and Michele and two for Darren, and put them, wrapped in foil, in the oven to bake. She cleaned and seasoned three T-bone steaks and effortlessly prepared the fixings for a tossed salad of spinach, tomatoes, and cucumbers. But her thoughts kept straying to Russell and his unsettling invitation.

It had been so long since they'd been cordial with each other that it came as a new experience for her to see him in a light she'd forgotten he could shine in. Charm was a trait that Russell wore like a well-made suit. It was what took him easily up the professional scale, and on the downside had blinded her to traits she hadn't seen until it was too late.

During the early days of their courtship, Russell Everette was the most attentive and considerate man she'd ever known. He made her feel as if she was the most important person in his life.

They'd met through a friend of her mother's, and Regina had been terribly reluctant to get involved with anyone her mother thought was perfect for her. But, conditioned just to go along and try to please, she gave in to her mother's constant haranguing and attempted to be cordial when she was introduced to Russell during one of her mother's ceaseless family-and-friends gatherings. But when Russell turned on the charm full blast she didn't know what hit her. She was taken by him, the sheer magnetism of the man.

He was self-assured and direct, knew what he wanted, the complete opposite of herself — someone whose entire existence hinged upon pleasing others and putting her own wants and desires on the back burner. He was just starting out in his field of investment banking, but he knew, even then, that his career was destined to take off.

"I intend to have my own firm one day — soon," he'd told her as they sat alone in her parents' living room while the rest of the guests roamed the house. "There's no way you can ever become wealthy or independent working for someone else. Education is great as a foundation, but what it teaches you is to be an employee, not an employer."

She thought about what he'd said for a moment. "That's probably true. But some people aren't cut out to run things and are content letting others take the responsibility," she said timidly, and knew she was speaking about herself.

Russell chuckled. "That wouldn't be me," he stated with confidence. Then his expression grew somber. "I watched my father struggle all his life, barely getting by at times, constantly at the mercy and whim of a supervisor." He slowly shook his head. "I promised myself I'd never let that happen to me."

And that was the way things had been between them from the very beginning: Russell determined and driven, and Regina pliant and agreeable. For her that role came easily. It was all she'd known, all she'd been trained to be. So she went along with Russell's dreams, his wishes, without question, without a fight.

But that very first conversation stuck with her, and like a seed, planted itself in her head and started to grow. It blossomed when she decided to go back to school for journalism, and the foundation of her marriage began to crack. The fissure widened when she took the job at the *Daily News*, and it progressively became impassable.

Russell morphed into a different person. He was no longer the loving man she'd married. Nothing she did was good enough. He ridiculed her accomplishments, ignored her achievements. The more independence and self-assurance she gained — the very things he prided himself on — the more difficult and belligerent he became.

How many nights had she lain next to him thinking that maybe she should give up her goals and save her marriage?

The breakup of a marriage was viewed as a failure by her family and a sin according to her Catholic upbringing. But what was the greater sin: to give up and give in, play the martyr, or walk away with some of her integrity intact and subject herself to ridicule from family and friends but save herself?

"Your husband and family come first, Regina," her mother would lecture. "You must be crazy to think about leaving a man like Russell," Vicky would comment. "Women would die to have a husband who wanted them to stay home," Toni would toss in.

It never occurred to any of them that they all had their own lives and careers. But they'd grown accustomed to Regina staying in the background, not causing waves, speaking when spoken to. No one knew how to deal with or accept this new Regina, who by her actions caused a disturbance in their patterned lives, upset their preconceived notions of who she was — and most of all, who she believed she had always been.

As much as the possibility of rekindling her relationship with Russell was intriguing, she was reluctant to take any steps that might lead her backward.

She'd set a new course for her life, and whoever wanted to come along for the ride was welcome, but this was her ship and she was the captain.

The opening of her store would soon be upon her. A part of her was incredibly thrilled and terribly frightened. What she wanted most of all was to be able to share her emotions, her fears, and her dreams with someone — her success.

Oddly enough, the one person whom she never thought would offer support was Russell. She'd hoped to have heard from Toni and Vicky by now, and had contemplated calling them time and again, letting bygones be just that. But it was obvious from their silence these past two months that they had no wish to let the past go and still thought of her as the one gone completely astray.

She sighed as she peeked in the oven and checked the steaks. Maybe one day things could be different between them, she thought. And then maybe not. It was a reality she'd come to accept.

"Ma!"

Regina cringed. "Yes, Michele." She sighed in exasperation and wished for the countless time that Michele wouldn't yell through the whole apartment every time the phone rang.

"It's Ms. Toni," Michele shouted again, in concert with the doorbell.

*Toni!* She couldn't have been more surprised than she was when she went downstairs to find Victoria on the other side of her door, her eyes red and tears threatening to ruin her makeup.

# CHAPTER SIXTEEN

Regina stepped aside to let Victoria in and followed her surprise guest up the stairs. She picked up the cordless phone in the kitchen while her gaze trailed the ghostlike Victoria as she took a seat at the table.

Regina cleared her throat. "Toni? Hi, um, I'm sorry to have . . . what's wrong?"

Toni tried to sound like her strong, in-control self and failed. Her voice trembled. "Everything's . . . coming apart, Gina."

Regina covered the mouthpiece. "It's Toni," she whispered to Vicky.

Victoria sniffed and looked away, her expression forlorn.

"Hi, Ms. Vicky," Michele and Darren chorused upon entering the kitchen.

Victoria forced a smile.

"Ma, can me and D go up to the park?" Michele asked on behalf of herself and her brother. "There's a basketball game."

Regina glared at her daughter's teenage rudeness. She knew how much Regina disliked being asked questions when she was on the phone. She alternated her attention between a sobbing Toni and a zombielike Victoria. And now she had this child up in her face, too. She glanced up at the clock hanging over the fridge.

"Hold on a sec, Toni." She covered the mouthpiece. "I want you both back in here by eleven."

A cry of "Ma" pierced the air.

"Eleven or don't go." She ignored the twisted expressions on their faces and turned her attention back to Toni as they marched off in a huff. "Toni, just calm down a minute so I can understand you. What happened to Steven?" Her eyes widened in shock and stayed there as Toni then told her about an affair with some guy named Alan, and Charles finding out about it.

"Damn," she muttered. *No wonder she sounded as if the world was ending.* "Listen, Toni, are you alone? Do you want me to come over there? Okay. Yeah, I understand. Can you come here? Will Steven be all right? Good, well as long as Charles is there. Maybe you should stay, Toni, and try to talk to Charles. . . . Oh, all right. I'll see you in about an hour, then. Um, Vicky's here. Yeah, I think it's time we all talked, too. See ya, hon. And drive safely."

Blown away by the latest developments, Regina hung up the phone thinking about Antoinette. She'd never, in all the years she'd known Toni, heard her sound like that. A shudder went through her. And then she looked at Victoria, who hadn't moved or uttered a word since she'd set foot in the door. Now she was a sight never to be forgotten. The very together, never-a-wrinkle Victoria Hunter didn't look picture-perfect.

"Toni's on her way," she said quietly so as not to startle her as she eased into a chair opposite Victoria. She clasped her hands in front of her and leaned tenuously forward. "What's wrong, Vicky?" she asked so softly it was almost a whisper.

Victoria's lips quivered, her eyes filled, and Regina watched her throat working up and down as if the words were stuck there and she was struggling to get them out.

"It's okay. You can tell me when you're ready." She reached across the table and patted Victoria's balled fists. "Can I get you anything?"

Victoria shook her head no.

Regina inhaled, releasing a confused breath. What in the world was going on? First Toni, now Victoria. She hadn't seen or spoken to either of these women in months, and now they were both on her doorstep, coming apart at the seams. But what was more ironic, they were turning to the very person they believed didn't have the sense she was born with. What was that about?

At least the kids were gone, she thought. So whatever was happening wouldn't have to be censored because they were in earshot. Her stomach dipped. As disappointed and as angry as she had been with both of her friends, she wouldn't wish them ill. She wasn't quite sure what she could do about whatever was wrong, but at least she could offer an ear.

The aroma of the steak and baked potatoes wafted through the kitchen. Regina excused herself from the table to check on dinner.

"I'm pregnant," Victoria uttered, and the fork in Regina's hand clattered inside the oven.

Regina stood frozen for a moment before slowly turning toward Victoria. Vicky's dark eyes were wide and plaintive. Her entire expression screamed distress. She'd never seen Victoria so unnerved. And why on earth would she be so totally miserable about one of the greatest miracles that could happen to a woman?

Slowly, Regina shut the oven door and returned to her chair. Maybe it wasn't Phillip's! Or maybe there was something wrong — with her or the baby. After all, she was a minute away from forty, herself.

Regina lifted her brow in gentle question, her expression open and patient, hoping to prompt Victoria into talking. It was a technique she used in many an interview when she wanted the person to continue to open up to her without posing questions at a delicate time.

"I haven't told Phillip," she mumbled, then sniffed loudly.

Regina took a napkin from the holder on the table and handed it to Victoria.

"Thanks." She wiped her eyes and nose. "I can't have this baby, Gina. I just can't."

"Do you want to tell me why?" she asked gently.

"I'm scared, Gina. Terrified."

Regina frowned in concern. "Of what?"

Victoria looked away, back into her past, to her childhood and the days of ridicule, the pain and loneliness she felt, the anger and vindictiveness — those times, those feelings she'd never truly shared with anyone. It all raced before her eyes like a bad B movie.

"I don't want any child, especially my

own, to go through what I did." She shook her head. "You don't know what it's like to feel ugly, Regina, inside and out. To be reminded of it every time you look in the mirror. I wake up every day with that same sense of shame, wondering when Phillip will see it, too."

Tears slid down her cheeks. She wiped them away, only for them to be quickly replaced.

"Everything you said that night is true."

Regina leaned forward, compelling Victoria to look at her. "Vicky, I may not know what you feel, but I know what it's like to have the devil of your own lack of self-worth haunt your every step. You can't beat it by running. It just follows your butt, looks you right in the face and howls with laughter. And pretending it's not there is no better, girl." She took a deep breath. "Look, I know I went off on you at the bar. Maybe I shouldn't have said what I did. I never meant to hurt you. I . . . I was just trying to make you understand that in the final analysis, when the lights go dim and the curtain goes up, it's what's inside." She pointed to her chest, then her temple. "That's what's going to withstand the test."

Vicky pressed her trembling lips together, then stared at Regina head-on. "Maybe I don't have anything inside, Gina. Ever think of that?"

"You can't mean that. What about Phillip? He has a role in this, too."

She vehemently shook her head. "He can't know. I won't tell him."

"Why won't you tell him, Vicky?" Regina prodded. "He loves you. That much I know for a fact."

"But do I love him? Did I ever?" she asked in a tortured voice. "I don't even know anymore. I've been so unsure about everything lately. Questioning myself, my motives, my beliefs." Slowly her gaze rose to settle on Regina's face. "No one has ever challenged me to look at who I was inside, Gina. Never. Until you did. All my life it was what people saw that mattered. So I tried to perfect it, make it look good, be the best at everything I did, get accepted to places that women looking like me didn't, and . . . marry Phillip."

Regina momentarily glanced away from the shame reflected in Victoria's eyes. She turned back. "Vicky, when I decided to leave Russell because he made me feel worthless, no one could understand why; no one could accept the fact that I just might know what was best for me. When I quit the *News* because the job was killing me, I had no support; all I had was my dream and what I knew was right for me." She paused for a moment. "I'm not going to give you some kitchen-table advice. I'm not going to pretend that I have the answers. I don't. All I can say is that you have to follow your heart and your conscience and be willing to deal with the consequences."

The doorbell rang.

Regina looked at Victoria for a moment. "That's Toni. You okay?"

Vicky nodded. "I'm going to go fix my face. I really don't want Toni to know. At least not yet. All right?"

"Sure." She pushed up from the table. "One thing, and I'm sorry but I have to say this. While you're thinking things through, think about what this would do to Phillip if you . . . you know — and he finds out."

Victoria flinched for a moment. She got up and went to the bathroom.

Regina pulled herself together and went downstairs to the door, not sure what she was going to find when she pulled it open.

"I know I don't have any business being here," Toni began instantly. "Especially after the things I said to you. I didn't call for your birthday. . . ." Her voice wobbled like a three-legged chair.

"Toni . . . please . . . it's fine. Really. Come on in."

Regina put her arm around Toni's shoulder and squeezed her gently as they walked up the steps. *Toni and some other man. Humph, humph, humph.*

"I didn't know what else to do but call you," Toni whimpered.

"It's cool," she reassured her again, and opened the door to the apartment.

Regina didn't immediately spot Victoria and hoped she wasn't going to stay holed up in the bathroom for the rest of the evening.

"Vicky still here?" Toni asked, taking a seat in the kitchen.

"Yeah. Unless she slipped out the back window or something." She crossed through what should have been a dining room but was used as a spare, all-purpose room instead, and into the living room. One day she was going to turn it into an extra bedroom, she pledged once again.

Victoria was standing in the living room staring out the window, her arms folded tightly beneath her breasts.

"Vicky. Toni's here."

Victoria spun around, her no-longer-than-ten-minutes-ago expression of devastation completely erased. Her makeup was perfect. There wasn't a hair out of place, and her serene, almost smug look had Regina thinking for a minute that the last hour with Ms. Cover Model was all in her head.

"Oh, great," Victoria said, full of cheer. "Let me go and say hi." She strutted across the room to where Regina stood, prepared to go past her, until Regina grabbed her arm.

"Are you all right?"

"Sure. Why?"

"Why?" Regina squawked, dumbfounded.

"Listen, forget everything I said. I was only tripping." She laughed lightly. "I'm over it. No big deal. Relax. Ms. Toni always-has-the-answers Devon sounds like she's the one with the problems," she said cattily. She started again toward the kitchen. Again Regina stopped her and looked her straight in the eye.

"Vicky, for once in your life drop the bullshit. Okay? Who you are inside couldn't possibly be as shallow as the person I'm looking at right now."

# CHAPTER SEVENTEEN

Regina, Toni, and Vicky had moved into the living room, each sipping tea, lemonade, or Coke.

Victoria was still smarting from the sting of Regina's comment. She thought Regina understood her, saw past the veils she draped around herself — but more important, understood her need to have them there.

Perhaps she did, Victoria thought, listening to Toni's unbelievable story of adultery, betrayal, and drugs — all the makings of a made-for-television movie. Maybe Regina was simply unwilling to let Victoria slip so easily behind her facade, not face herself. But to remove all of her protective layers would leave her open and vulnerable to all the hurts she'd spent her life trying to avoid.

Except for that short time in Regina's kitchen, when she momentarily lowered the wall, she'd never truly allowed anyone to see that part of her — not even Phillip

— that damaged, frightened part of her. She'd worked so hard to repair the injuries, patch up the scars, and put on a brave front, she wasn't sure if she could do anything else, be anyone else. But Regina believed she could.

Regina. Funny how it was Regina everyone always thought of as the soft one, the one who followed and never led, the one who sat quietly in the background. Although she'd always been the one to turn to in a crisis, it wasn't so much because they expected her to fix anything, but because she would patiently hear you out without making any comment in conflict with yours.

But this Regina was different, Victoria realized. This was an assured woman who was braver than either of them, brave enough to do what she wanted, what was in her heart, and didn't give a damn what anyone thought about it. Something Vicky had yet to be able to do herself.

"Do you have a lawyer?" Regina was asking Toni.

Toni nodded numbly. "Charles . . . took care of it. I couldn't believe how in control he was," she said with a bewildered look on her face. "He seemed to know exactly what to do, what to say." She gazed across at Regina, then at Victoria. "I'd never seen Charles like that. For the first time in our marriage I actually felt that he could handle things, you know?"

"Did you ever think that the reason Charles functions in your marriage like a houseguest is because you haven't allowed him to be any other way?" Victoria said in her better-than-thou tone.

Toni weakly rolled her eyes. She had a nerve analyzing her marriage when everyone in the room knew Victoria's marriage to Phillip was a big farce. Vicky no more loved that man than she did a pair of used Reeboks. But, hey, who was she to judge, especially with the fix she was in?

"Hey, I don't think any of us are in the best of shape to be crossing our eyes at anyone else," Regina stated, truly not wanting to get into one of those catfights with these two. "From where I'm sitting we all have issues that won't get solved bitching and taking our frustrations out on each other."

"What issue do you have, Gina?" Vicky asked. "Out of the three of us you're the one who seems to have her program together."

"Yeah, really," Toni seconded.

Regina leaned back into the cushion of

the couch and crossed her denim-clad legs. She couldn't remember the last time, if ever, that Toni or Vicky actually asked her anything real about herself, what she was going through or feeling. She almost didn't know what to say, until she looked at their rapt expressions and realized that they really did want to know.

She blew out a breath. "Well . . . to begin with, I'm starting a brand new business, a new phase of my life, and everything depends on it being successful. The thought that it might not be is terrifying." She went on to tell them of her fears, second thoughts, the reappearance of Russell and his change in attitude, and her mixed feelings about it. Then she dropped her other bombshell when she told them about Parker Heywood. And it wasn't so much the fact that Regina had met a man, which both of them secretly thought was long overdue, but the way she described him and the feelings that she'd experienced.

As they listened for those few moments, they were able to push their own troubles aside as Regina described how she felt when she met him. "That dizzying wave that runs through your stomach and makes you feel jittery all over," she was saying.

*Yeah,* Toni thought wistfully. *I remember*

*that feeling.* It seemed so long ago, but that was just how she felt about Charles the minute she saw him. He was everything she'd ever wanted: good-looking, funny, kind, had a gentle manner, and was an incredible lover. Where had things gone so wrong to land her in Alan's bed? God, what a fool she'd been. And now the trouble with Steven, too. As hard as it would be for her and Charles even to look at each other, they'd have to put their problems aside to help their son get through this. What she wouldn't give to turn the clock back and do this all over again — the right way.

"He was easy to talk to," Regina was saying. "After a few minutes, I felt like I'd known him a long time. I know it sounds sophomoric, but it's true. And he was sure of himself, but not in a smug, overbearing way. You know. He actually seemed impressed that I was striking out on my own, and not threatened by it. It's kind of nice," she said, smiling shyly.

That was one of the things that impressed Victoria about Phillip when they'd first met, she thought. There was that playful easiness, a to-hell-with-society attitude that he wore casually but securely. He was comfortable with himself — something she admired in him because she didn't know what it was like to be that way. And she knew he was a man of deep love and conviction when he was willing to give up his family, a life he'd always known, for her — a sacrifice that she wasn't certain she'd ever be able to repay.

"He sounds wonderful, Gina," Toni said.

"I hear a 'but' in there somewhere," Victoria astutely remarked, crossing her long legs.

Toni focused on Gina. "Problem?" She pushed one of her thick locks behind her ear.

"Sort of, or maybe it's not a problem at all. I don't know."

"What is it?" Victoria asked.

"This sounds really stupid. . . ."

"Believe me, it can't sound any stupider than whatever's fallen out of my mouth tonight," Toni blithely confessed. She reached for her glass of Coke from the coffee table between them.

"Well?" Victoria pressed.

"I don't really know if I want to get involved."

Toni and Victoria looked quizzically at each other, then simultaneously turned to Regina. "Why?" they chimed in unison.

"I knew you two wouldn't understand."

"I don't get it. You find what appears to be a great guy and you don't want to get involved?" Toni asked, the pitch of her voice rising with the incredulity of it all. "Do you know how many women are looking for a decent man?"

"When was the last time you were . . . with someone, Gina?" Victoria asked. "I mean, I don't think there's been anyone since Russell."

Regina glanced away. "I . . . just don't want to get involved. It's really hard to explain, okay?"

"Give yourself a chance, Regina," Toni said.

Regina sighed deeply. Parker was someone she was interested in. She had to admit that, but she also knew she had some real issues about her own sexual vulnerability that needed more time to heal. She wanted to take her time, be sure of the man she was with — that he not only cared for her, but respected her. Parker seemed like he could be that person. But she was willing to wait and see.

"I'll think about it, take one day at a time."

"At least keep yourself open to the possibilities, Gina," Toni said. "You deserve to be happy."

"Amen," Victoria chimed in.

Regina gazed from one to the other, and a warm feeling of camaraderie filled her. She couldn't remember there ever being a time when either of them jumped to her defense or were actually in her corner. Maybe they were both still in shock over their own situations and weren't thinking clearly. Or maybe, just maybe, their own crises had forced them to seek the humanity inside themselves.

"Thanks. Really. I'll just see what happens." She paused a minute. "My stuff is minor compared to what you two have to deal with." Her gaze shifted apologetically toward Victoria for the minor slip, but Toni didn't seem to notice.

The atmosphere suddenly shifted. Victoria abruptly stood up, saying she needed to use the bathroom. Toni looked everyplace but into Regina's eyes.

"I wish I did know what I was going to do," Toni said finally. "I mean, when Charles came in this afternoon he wouldn't even look at me. When I tried to get him to talk he just shut the door to the den in my face and refused to answer me. I —" She covered her face with her hands and began to cry.

Regina came around the coffee table and

put her arm around Toni. There was no point in giving her all the pat statements about "brighter days," "darkest before the dawn," "things are going to be just fine." She didn't know if any of them were true. What she could offer was her shoulder, an ear, and her friendship for as long as Toni wanted it. And she had a strong feeling in her stomach that Toni was going to need all the friends she could get in the months ahead. Victoria, on the other hand, was a completely different story. The wall around her heart was still so impenetrable. There were some cracks; she'd seen them earlier. But it would take a dismantling from the inside, something strong enough to break through, before Victoria would ever be truly whole, able to love herself without all of the camouflage. And Regina had no idea what that would take.

Victoria emerged from the bathroom, her expression unreadable. "Well, ladies, this has been an experience," she said, as if they'd only been discussing the weather for the past few hours. She checked her Rolex. "I guess I should get going."

Regina rose. "I'll walk you down."

"Take care, Toni. And . . . I hope everything works out for you. I mean that." She crossed the short space between them, leaned down, and kissed Toni's cheek, squeezed her shoulder affectionately, then turned to leave.

Regina stood in the downstairs doorway. "Are you going to be all right, Vicky?"

Victoria straightened, a determined expression on her face. "Of course. You worry too much. Go on back up and take care of our girl. She needs you. And Gina, thanks for not saying anything to Toni." She turned away before Regina could see her cheery facade begin to crumble. She had no idea what she was going to do, and she was far from all right.

# Chapter Eighteen

Toni's hand shook as she put her key in the door. She wasn't sure what she would find once she was inside. She pulled in a deep breath and shut the door behind her. She tilted her head, listening for sounds in the house. It was still, and she wondered if Charles had gone back out, preferring to roam the streets than have to look at her. But she was certain he wouldn't leave Steven alone. Which meant that he was in the house somewhere.

Slowly she entered and put her purse in the hall closet. Her beautiful home, she thought, looking around at the art, the expensive furnishings, and imported drapes. Once upon a time all those things were more important to her than anything. She believed that if she could make her surroundings beautiful, her life would be beautiful as well. If only she had paid attention to what was happening to her life, instead of only to the life-expectancy labels on her purchases.

She walked into the high-tech kitchen and poured a glass of water. She leaned against the counter, and Regina's most poignant question resurfaced to haunt her: *Why did you get involved with someone else?*

*Humph.* How often had she asked herself the same thing? She supposed it was because it was easy and she was needy, but more important, so was Alan. She could make him better, make him happy, make his life richer, because it seemed as if her husband and son didn't need her anymore. Her throat tightened. How stupid she'd been. She'd failed to see how much they did need her, but no longer in the way she was accustomed to giving. And now she'd lost everything.

"You're back."

Toni looked up. Charles was standing in the doorway leading to the backyard. There was an incredible sadness in his dark eyes that stabbed her more sharply than a knife.

"I . . . wasn't sure if you were here," she whispered.

"Would you prefer if I weren't?" he challenged, his tone growing hard.

"No."

He jammed his hands into his pockets, crossed the gleaming tiled floors, and

273

stood on the opposite side of the island facing her.

"I never thought I could feel this way, Antoinette. This hollowness deep in my gut." He swallowed, and she watched his Adam's apple bob up and down. "I've been so angry and hurt I haven't had the words to say what's been on my mind. All I knew was that I wanted to hurt you. Hurt you the way you've hurt me, this family." He chuckled derisively. "But then I'd be no different from you."

Toni lowered her head, shame rising up inside her like a tide rushing to shore.

"In all the years we've been together, no matter what was going on between us, even when I felt like I didn't matter, I never thought once about being with another woman. Was I happy these years?" He slowly shook his head. "No, not always. But that didn't matter, because I'd made vows to you that I believed were sacred. I believed that we were in this thing together and we'd work it out."

He turned away and began to pace the room as he spoke, needing, it seemed, to exorcise his soul. "When you turned up 'accidentally' pregnant, the last thing I wanted to do at that time in my life was get married. But I did it anyway, and you know why, Antoinette? Because I loved you. I still love you, and that's why this is killing me — slowly."

"Charles — I never meant to hurt you. Never."

He spun to face her, his expression twisted in rage. "Beep, wrong answer, Antoinette. You did hurt me. And it doesn't hurt any less because you didn't mean to." He stared at her, trying to see the truth in her eyes. "Just tell me why. Why did you do it?"

"It's . . . it's all so complicated. . . ."

"All we have left between us is time, Antoinette. . . ."

Victoria pulled her Mercedes into the two-car garage, cut the engine, and entered the house through the side door that opened onto the kitchen. She walked through the living room, which led to the staircase. She was an emotional wreck. And all she wanted right then was a hot bath and some peace and quiet so she could think.

She twisted the knob on the bedroom door and went in. Phillip was sitting up in bed watching television.

"Hi," Victoria mumbled, disappointed that she didn't have the house to herself.

"I thought we had plans," Phillip said, putting his glasses aside.

Victoria squeezed her eyes shut and arched her head back. "Oh, God, Phil, I'm so sorry. I completely forgot."

"Where were you, Vicky?"

His tone escalated the beat of her heart. "I had some things to do. Like I told you. The time —"

"Don't bullshit me, okay, Vicky? Where were you? You obviously weren't at the abortion clinic, because they called wondering why you didn't show up for your appointment. I guess I should be happy about that."

Her head spun, and the sudden sinking sensation in her stomach made her feel ill.

Phillip threw his legs over the side of the bed and stood. "So tell me, you were just going to kill our baby and never even tell me you were pregnant. Is that right, Vicky?"

The hurt in his voice was palpable.

She pressed her hands together. "Phillip . . . I —"

"Why? How could you?" His facial muscles twitched. "I thought we loved each other."

"I . . . we do, Phillip. It's just that —"

"Just what?" he boomed. "Just that you

276

didn't think of anyone but yourself. Where do I fit into all of this?" He slowly approached her. His voice dropped to a whisper. "A child with you is all I've ever wanted. You knew that."

Victoria sank onto her vanity chair. She lowered her head. How could she ever explain the turmoil raging inside her, the overwhelming feeling of being that little girl again whom everyone shunned? The fear that she had of bringing a child into the world who looked just like her, who would endure what she'd endured, grow up with the same burning insecurities that she did. The vicious comments of those two women in the bathroom that night still haunted her. *Half-breed.* He would never understand that. He couldn't. And that is what saddened her most — The thin line that divided them: color.

"I guess you have nothing to say." He turned his back to her, unwilling to allow her to see the anguish on his face. "I love you, Victoria," he uttered simply. "More than you will ever know. I gave up everything for that love. So I can't understand why you would want to get rid of a child conceived out of it. Perhaps I'm not supposed to understand. I can only pray that the reason you didn't show up for your appointment was because you had doubts about what you were doing. But the decision ultimately is yours. And I'm totally helpless in it. And whatever that decision is, it'll change both of us forever."

Victoria watched him walk out of the bedroom, and the soft sound of the door closing behind him felt like an explosion in her chest.

She sucked in air, refusing to cry even as her eyes clouded over. She turned toward the vanity mirror and stared at her reflection.

*Oh, what a night,* Regina mused, thinking of the old Dells classic as she picked at her dinner. It was all so incredible. She was still trying to process the revelations that were made. Toni having an affair and her son being arrested, Victoria pregnant and refusing to tell her husband, and Russell trying to ease his way back into her life. But what was most telling was that they had all found their way back to each other, and if only for a moment, dropped the pretenses and bared their souls.

No longer hungry, she picked up her plate and scraped the contents into the garbage. She wasn't certain where all of this would take them, but she knew that a turning point had come. Now it was a matter of choosing a direction, and whether the path would be walked alone or with the ones who were left standing once the dust had cleared.

The phone rang, and with the way things had been shaping up, Regina wasn't sure if she wanted to answer it. But the thought that it might be the kids spurred her out of her seat.

"Hello?"

"Good evening. I was trying to reach Regina Everette."

"Speaking."

"Hi, how are you? This is Parker Heywood. We met a few days ago."

Excitement and confusion jockeyed for position. She was thrilled that he'd called, but how did he get the number?

"Yes, I remember."

"I really wasn't sure if you'd still be at the store at this hour. I just took a chance."

"The store?"

"Yeah. This is the number to the store, right?"

She scrunched up her face. She'd given him her home number instead of the number to the shop. Freudian slip? "Oh, I'm sorry. I must have given you my home number." She chuckled nervously. "Guess

I'm not used to being a business owner yet."

"I'm sorry. I hope it's not a problem that I called."

"No. Not at all. Um, what can I do for you?"

"I was hoping it would be all right for me to stop by Monday afternoon . . . to show you some of my work."

"Monday," she repeated inanely. "Uh, sure. What time?"

"Say about four?"

"Four sounds fine."

"Good. So, uh, I'll see you then."

"Right. Monday."

"I didn't disturb you, did I?" he asked, not ready to let her go just yet.

"No. I was just finishing up a late dinner."

"Sounds quiet," he gently probed.

"Yes. It is, thank goodness." She laughed lightly. "My son and daughter are at a basketball game in the park."

"Oh, you have children."

She wasn't sure if that was disappointment or what in his voice. "Yes, Michele and Darren."

He was silent for a moment, waiting to see if she would add a significant other to the list. When she didn't, he continued with his less-than-subtle probe. "They must be pretty big to be out alone this time of night."

Regina smiled at his tactic. "They're both in their teens. My daughter graduates next June. And her brother is right behind her, or at least he thinks he is."

Parker chuckled. "And she probably wants you and your husband to buy her a car for graduation. Isn't that what all kids want these days?"

*He's really good,* she thought, amused. She leaned against the counter and wrapped one arm around her waist. "I'm divorced."

"Oh, sorry to hear that."

"Are you really?" she said, feeling suddenly bold.

Parker grinned sheepishly. "Well, to be truthful, not really."

Regina felt hot all over. "What about you, Mr. Parker — where's your significant other?"

"Don't have one. I mean I did once, but . . . well, that was a while ago."

She detected the hint of hesitation, of a memory that still stung.

"This may seem totally out of place, and you can hang up on me if you want, but since it appears, or so I think, that both of us are . . . unattached, maybe we could turn my visit on Monday into a quick bite after work." He held his breath.

"I'd like that," she said without missing a beat.

"Great. Great," he repeated, relief rushing through him. "So, uh, I'll see you Monday."

"I'm looking forward to it."

"So am I."

# CHAPTER NINETEEN

The late-September evening was deceptive in both temperature and mood. Its still coolness portrayed a false illusion of serenity. But the atmosphere between Toni and Charles was anything but serene or tranquil.

Charles was seated in one of the green-and-white-striped lawn chairs on the deck, Toni on the other. In the distance, the hum of cars moving along the black-tarred streets and the faint sounds of Saturday-night laughter filtered through the night.

How ironic, Toni thought, that the one time they actually used the deck was not in the form of family unity, but on the eve of a confrontation possibly bringing their partnership to its conclusion.

"I'm listening," Charles said, staring out into the blackness.

"I'm not sure where to begin, or how," Toni stammered. "It wasn't anything I . . . intended to do."

"You said that already." He cut his eyes sourly in her direction and waited to hear something new, some fresh explanation or novel excuse for her infidelity.

Toni lowered her gaze. "I let everything get away from me," she began. "I never told you about how things really were back home, what I ran away from." She drew in a breath and took him back to her days in the two-bedroom shack, the poverty, the filth, the feeling of being controlled by her environment and society, of the powerlessness to change anyone or anything. "I had bigger dreams than my mom or dad, my sisters. They had no problem being statistics, with leaving things just the way they were. And there was nothing I could do to change them, so I left the first chance I got. And I swore to myself that I would never feel helpless or inadequate again. I'd never be at anyone's mercy again. I gave in to a desire to help others, to change everything and everyone I could. Maybe it was to ease the guilt I felt at leaving them behind, or maybe it was to give to others those things my family refused to accept from me. So I came to New York, finished school, and got my degree, and then I met you." Her throat tightened.

Charles slowly rose, looking out toward the early blanket of stars scattered across the heavens.

"I guess I became a project of yours, too."

"Not consciously. No. Everything I did or tried to do was because I loved you and wanted the absolute best for you."

"Really? How does wanting the best for me connect with your sleeping with another man? Was that supposed to further your cause?"

"You stopped needing me," she whispered hoarsely.

Charles turned to face her. "Stopped needing you? How could you possibly think that?"

"Day by day, you seemed to grow away from me, moving into your own world, not really caring what choices I made, what decisions I faced — about anything. I started feeling like I was in the marriage alone, and you seemed content with the way things were. You started going out more and more. And when you were here, I still felt alone. What I slowly began to realize was that you were going through your life, your days, without me."

"Toni, you were always the one in control, the one who directed the course of our lives — about everything. You never let me be involved. Never. You always knew what was best for everyone. You didn't ask my opinion, just took it for granted that I would agree. And maybe part of all this is my fault, because I let it happen. I turned my life over to you, gave up without a fight. But you know why? Because deep down inside, I trusted you. I loved you, so I surrendered to your whims. Yet there was a part of me that resented it. Resented the fact that I felt so unnecessary in your life — insignificant in this marriage. So I stopped participating. What I needed from you was your respect. I needed for you to treat me like a man, not your child, not some damn social-work case."

"All I ever wanted to do was to take care of you, take care of Steven. Give you all the things I never gave . . . them."

"So I guess this . . . guy makes you feel . . . needed again."

Toni's stomach knotted. "I . . . I thought so."

"Do you love him, Toni?"

"He . . . was getting over a divorce."

"You didn't answer me."

"I . . . think I was in love with the idea of being needed again, having the power to make a difference in someone's life," she said weakly. "I thought I could help him deal with his pain. I felt he needed me."

"So sleeping with him, giving your body

to him, made you feel needed — by some stranger?" He started breathing hard, his voice severe and tight with emotion. "It didn't matter that what you were doing would risk our marriage, our family. Were your needs that great?"

She flinched as if she'd been hit. Listening to him, hearing both the disappointment and suffering in his words, made her realize how shallow and selfish she had been. She deserved his disdain and much more. It seemed as if he was trying to restrain his hurt from becoming unmanly tears or behavior that he would regret in the morning.

"All I ever wanted, Toni, was your happiness, from the beginning. Maybe I wasn't all you thought I could be, but it's who I am. I would give anything to go back, change things, make things different if it would have kept us from being in this place, right here, right now. I would if I could. But I can't. And now we all have to live with that." He stared at her for a long moment, the woman he'd loved, then turned and walked away.

Victoria sat alone in her bedroom, torn by indecision. A part of her knew it was irrational, maybe wrong to feel the way she did, but she couldn't help it. Who she was, how she felt, and what she believed were ingrained in her. She could no more change the realities of her life than she could alter the color of her skin.

Still, there was Phillip to consider, with his feelings and needs. From the moment they'd met, he had done everything in his power to erase the lines that separated them, and when he couldn't, he removed the two of them from the forces that would keep them apart, whether it was his family, his friends, or strangers on the street. He protected her, shielded her from the harsh slights and small minds of the world. In his eyes she was beautiful, desirable. And he'd spent the five years of their life together working to make her believe it as well. He truly believed in the love that warmed his heart every time he saw her.

But there were times when his love was not enough, times when black men hissed or made foul comments about them as a couple or when black women cut their eyes in complete disgust at them. On those occasions, she felt terribly vulnerable, emotionally naked, and oddly like a traitor to her kind. Although she falsely prided herself on rising above the trappings of skin color and class, that climb did nothing to lessen the psychological urge in her to still be counted, in some way, as a part of her tribe. Her people.

Two weeks ago, she was alone in one of the more upscale clothing stores downtown, looking for a sweater for Phillip. The entire outing was ruined by three store security guards who followed her around, acting like she was going to steal or rob someone. She had never been so humiliated in her life, but she couldn't tell Phillip about any of this. He wouldn't understand.

In truth, there was nothing he could do, nothing he could ever do. Change had to come from her. That much she understood. But she was terrified. Terrified to come from behind the sturdy wall she erected as protection from the forces that threatened to reduce her to the hurt, pitiful, and lonely little girl she had once been. Nothing could take her back to that dreadful place.

This baby, this child she carried inside her body was a representation of love, or at least it should be. And this is where her greatest doubt and turmoil rested.

She knew she respected Phillip. She knew that she felt protected and secure with him. She was grateful to him. But she also knew that her underlying reason for initially cultivating a relationship with Phillip was to prove to herself and to everyone that she could move fluidly in a white world, be accepted. She could laugh in the black faces of those who taunted her. She could ride on the crest of his white shoulders and feel validated and adored. However, that was not real love.

Yet she could not deny that she cared for him, deeply, probably as much as she could care for anyone — any man. He made her smile, made her feel good. He made her feel loved. But a child . . . How could she possibly take the risk of bringing a child into this world of hate and ignorance? What could she give this child — who would need more love simply because of the nature of their genes — to make it strong enough to survive the cruelty of the world, when she didn't know how to love herself?

Distracted by the confusion in her life, Regina tried to stay focused on the work at hand. The construction team was finishing up their task of laying in fresh drywall and overhead beams in her store, and carrying away their tools. Soon she wouldn't have the annoyance of busy bodies, the maddening sounds of hammering and drilling, and on-the-spot decisions to make. She would soon be alone, facing an uncertain future in her place, with all the responsibility on her slender shoulders. And suddenly she was afraid. It was all up to her now.

Suddenly the years of being conditioned to believe that she was less than, not up to, not capable of, froze her in place. For her entire life, all the decisions of her life had been made for her. She was considered helpless, only a weak female. And as much as she inwardly resented it, she understood, too, that it was easy. Easy to just go along, not cause a fuss, agree to agree.

Now it was all about to change. Suddenly, the determination that she felt, the spark of rebellion, wavered beneath her feet. What if she couldn't pull it off? What if she was the incompetent person everyone thought she was? God, this was a battle that always seemed to be going on inside her. It never ended. *I know I'm just as capable as anyone else;* I know it. But the inklings of doubt never ended. And now she was that little girl again, the shy, immature little girl who waited for the signal to act. Frozen by indecision and self-doubt. Waiting for Mommy and Daddy and the big boys to give her approval.

No one ever told her that she could. No one ever led her to believe that she was capable of doing more than what was put in front of her. Spontaneous, huh? Creative, huh? Just a worker bee waiting for orders. No one expected any more than that from Regina.

The discipline in school from the nuns taught her to be subservient, humble, insecure. The lessons from her mother only reinforced the servitude: do for others at the expense of yourself. Her husband ruled without question; her children petitioned for their wants and she gave, always believing that this was her role, even though a small voice inside her shouted to be free. Still, she gave, gave, gave until she felt that she could give no more.

Now she was free, standing on her own two feet. Or so she thought. But in truth, she had no experience with freedom. Perhaps small bouts of independence and rebellion when she would pretend to be sick so she wouldn't have to go to piano lessons or dance class. When she decided to go back to school, or leave her husband, or quit her job — they were all small victories in a way. Brief moments when the brainwashing didn't hold. But she'd been terrified. Terrified that those single acts of rebellion would crash and burn around her, vanish before her very eyes, and everything that had ever been said about who she was would be true. Everything validated by her own behavior.

How was she any better than Toni or Victoria, who lived in the empty lives they'd created?

Perhaps she should take solace in the fact that at least she did make the effort, took those small steps. Steps no one believed her capable of making. Steps no one expected her to take.

She drew in a long breath and looked around at the smooth wooden shelves, the gleaming glass cabinets, the boxes of books, magazines, and choice articles of clothing for sale, and decided then and there that she would let the fear that bound her, propel her. Because out of every fear she'd faced had come a change.

"I need your signature on this, Ms. Everette," the foreman said, pulling her away from the turn of her thoughts. He handed her a clipboard with a work-order completion form attached.

She blinked, smiled weakly, and signed on the line. "Thank you for everything. You all did a great job."

He dug in his pocket for a business card

and handed it to her. "You ever need anything, you give me a call."

"I will."

All too soon, she was alone.

# CHAPTER TWENTY

Parker felt as if he was interviewing for his first date instead of arriving at a business appointment to show the one thing he knew he was good at — his art.

His art was his salvation, the one thing that kept him sane during the erosion of his marriage. He used art as a place where he could submerge his battered soul, where he could transform his inner suffering into a marketable outer expression, where he could conceal his disappointment with love. With art, he placed the most wounded parts of himself aside and waited for a healing.

When he'd looked around at the home he'd cherished, the family he'd adored, and realized they were no more, he understood failure. His failure as a husband and father — as a man. He knew how little he really comprehended about sharing and communicating with those he said he loved.

His friends, the few he had, said he'd get over it. All he needed was to find a good woman to soothe the aches, take the sting away. But they never understood that his family was not just an extension of him; it *was* him — all that he was. And without them, he felt as if he, too, ceased to exist. He walked the earth like a zombie, with no joy or serenity. Wrapped in pain, he sometimes wondered how he was going to meet the next day, if there would be enough of him for another chance at intimacy. And love.

So he turned to the one thing he could do well — paint. He poured himself into his work, let the colors, the painful hours of standing, creating, consume him until he was too exhausted to think, to feel.

He turned the inward agony out onto the canvas, slashing and stroking in hard, deep sweeps of his brushes. Brilliant, dark, poignant, angry, genius — all the accolades were attached to his creations. His art took him to the shores of Europe — as much to study as to remove himself from the memories he'd tried to exorcise with his art.

When the offer to teach was presented to him, he accepted, finally realizing that no matter how far he ran, the hole in his heart would never be filled by distance. Still, he stumbled around in life, waiting for things to change, for an end to the series of bad events keeping his existence miserable. And then he met Regina.

He'd never believed in fairy tales, love at first sight, and June-moon-croon romance, in that thing that instantly clicked between two people. Even with Lynn, the woman he'd loved and married, that magic took time, flared for a while before it fizzled.

Yet from the moment he'd seen Regina, spoken with her, something inside of him shifted, warmed like cold hands being rubbed over the fire. And he hadn't been able to get her out of his mind.

It had been so long since he'd allowed himself to enjoy the pleasure of feeling. It took him by surprise to realize that his heart raced just a bit faster when her face came to mind, when he'd heard her voice on the phone, when she'd agreed to share a meal with him, when he gazed at the portrait he'd made of her. He didn't know what to do with any of it — the feelings, the uncertainty, the newness. But for reasons that were not yet clear to him, he wanted to take the chance. Just to see if he was truly capable of feeling again.

He drove past the store and onto the next block until he found a parking space. All too soon he was standing in front of the door. He could see her moving about inside with a quiet gracefulness — the arch of her neck, the line of her back, the curve of her legs, the slenderness of her fingers — totally unaware of how captivating she was. An artist's dream. He knocked on the glass.

When she turned to face him, her eyes and smile bloomed in instant light like the sun cresting on the horizon, and the sensation of coming home after a long journey filled him — startled him.

And suddenly Regina didn't feel so alone anymore.

Victoria stood in the doorway of her office, watching the activity in the bank slow as the final hours of business drew to a close. For once she dreaded the end of the day. A baby shower was planned for one of the clerks in her department, and everyone was expected to attend.

Barbara, the honoree, had been with the bank for a bit more than a year and had won the hearts of all of her coworkers, both male and female. They teased her when her once-thin figure finally showed signs of her pregnancy. But Barbara seemed to relish it, was thrilled when people said she glowed, and had no problem prancing proudly around with her growing belly. Her husband waited on her hand and foot, dropping her off at work and picking her up religiously, every day, often bringing flowers or other goodies. All the women oohed and aahed at how sweet they were together.

Absently, she pressed her hand against her stomach. How would Phillip behave when her once-svelte figure lost its shape and motherhood really took hold? Would he still stroke her, whisper loving words in her ear, remind her how beautiful he thought she was?

"Mrs. Hunter, we're getting ready to start," her assistant Alyse said cheerily as she hurried by the door with a tray full of snacks.

"I'll be right there," Victoria mumbled.

When she entered the conference room it was already filled with excited guests bubbling over about the beautiful decorations, the six-foot table full of food, the beautifully wrapped gifts, and, of course, the honored guest, Barbara.

Victoria took a breath, put on her best face, and stepped inside. All around her conversation flowed about love, marriage, and babies, babies, babies. How wonderful they were, how sweet, how they were miracles, how they changed lives.

"When I had my first one," a woman from the accounting department was saying, "I just couldn't stop looking at her. She was so tiny and helpless. And my husband, well, you couldn't get him out of the baby's room," she said, laughing.

"I know what you mean. I don't think my husband let me do one thing around the house during my entire pregnancy."

Victoria moved to the other side of the room, keeping her false smile in place, nodding to all the familiar faces. She picked up a paper plate and added some celery sticks and dip, then went to the bowl of peeled shrimp and added those as well, along with some cocktail sauce. The aroma of chicken fingers and honey mustard sauce drifted under her nose. Her stomach rolled violently and she suddenly felt light-headed. She grabbed the table to keep from falling, feeling her legs quickly lose their power.

"Are you all right, Mrs. Hunter?" Alyse was at her side, holding her by the elbow.

Victoria sucked in air and nodded weakly. "Yes . . . thanks, I'm fine." She closed her eyes momentarily to stop the room from spinning.

"Maybe you're next," Alyse whispered with a teasing smile, watching a line of sweat appear on the stricken woman's fore-head.

Victoria's heart slammed against her chest. "It's . . . just that I haven't eaten all day, that's all." By degrees, she pulled her-self together.

"You would make a great mother," Alyse chirped. "You already have everything you need: a wonderful husband, a fabulous job, benefits."

Victoria didn't reply, feeling a second wave of vertigo surge through her.

Alyse continued her assault of words, rambling and totally oblivious to the ex-pression of distress on Victoria's face. "And I know since you're so good with other people's investments that you have some of your own, especially with your husband being an accountant and all." She paused for breath. "Barbara is so lucky," Alyse said wistfully.

"Why is that?"

"My husband and I have been married for eight years. We've been trying to have a baby for years with no luck. It's the one thing missing in our lives." Her voice hitched. "I envy women who can have chil-dren. They have no idea how lucky they re-ally are."

Victoria looked at Alyse, really looked at

her. To the casual observer, she was the picture of the perfect white woman: silky blond hair, startling blue eyes, flawless figure, intelligent, with a successful husband — yet underneath all that perfection she was unhappy. She felt that with all she had there was still something missing from her life, from her marriage — a child.

"We thought about adopting," Alyse was saying as Victoria returned to the conversation. "But Bret refuses." Her eyes teared up. "I know how much having a child of our own means to him, how happy it would make him. And it's the one thing I can't give him."

*The one thing I can't give him.*

"Attention! Attention, everyone. Let's toast our guest of honor," one of the women announced, striking a spoon against a glass.

Alyse sniffed, picked up a napkin, and dabbed her eyes, then her nose. "I'm sorry," she whispered to Victoria. "I didn't mean to put all of that on you."

"Don't worry about it," Victoria whispered back. "It's all right."

Alyse nodded, excused herself, and moved to the center of the room.

For the next few minutes, one by one, all of Barbara's coworkers showered her with gifts, warm wishes for a healthy baby, happiness, and many more. A photo was taken of the fresh-faced expectant mother standing near the ceremonial cake, white icing with a small bare-bottomed infant on top, while everyone joked and sang. Barbara, smiling and sobbing, circled the room, thanking everyone for their kindness.

Victoria slipped out of the door as the heartfelt sentiments began to overwhelm her, and returned to her office. It was all too much: the baby talk, the gifts, and the Holy Order of Mothers, each recounting their first delivery. It was torture. She hurriedly gathered her things, tossed them in a Macy's department store bag, and headed out, with the sounds of joy and the promises of a bright future for a new life trailing her.

"Your client is here, Ms. Devon," Toni's secretary Christine said, peeking her head into Toni's office door.

Toni checked her appointment book for her two o'clock: Richard Cummings, her teenage foster-care client. She sighed. All day her thoughts had been in a jumble. She'd tried to put on a good face and push herself through the day by sheer force of will, but was barely making it. What she really felt like doing was screaming, screaming at the top of her lungs. All she could think about was Charles and Steven, her marriage, their talk, and the hurt she'd caused both of them. She had yet to talk with Alan and let him know what had happened — something she was not looking forward to doing.

God, how could she reasonably expect to change or make better someone else's life when hers was coming apart? What kind of helpful insight or advice could she possibly dispense in this state? Even Christine, her usually reserved secretary, had commented on her distracted behavior earlier in the day.

"You seem totally out of it today, Ms. Devon. Not your usual upbeat self. Is anything wrong?"

Toni pushed a smile across her mouth. "No. I'm fine. Just a little tired, I guess. Things are kind of crazy at home right now," she blurted out, and regretted it the instant she did. She didn't need her staff in her personal business.

Christine looked at her quizzically. "If you need to talk . . ."

"Thanks, but I'm fine. Really."

Christine raised a brow, then turned and left.

Toni went through the process of seeing her clients, five in total before lunch, and she couldn't remember a thing she'd said to any of them. What really caused her the greatest concern was when she was walking down the corridor and overheard two of the clinic nurses just ahead discussing the fact that three of Toni's clients had complained to the supervisor about her apparent uninterest in what they were saying.

"And she doesn't look well," one of the nurses said.

"I know. It's not like her to come in looking and acting as if she hasn't slept in days," her partner commented. "Maybe there's trouble on the home front."

*Trouble on the home front,* she thought miserably, turning the corner to return to her office. That was putting it lightly. Trouble with her life was more accurate.

"Ms. Devon," Christine said again. "Should I send him in?" She gazed at Toni strangely.

Toni snapped her head in Christine's direction, having totally tuned her out. She was coming apart. There were so many things on her mind. It was nearly impossible for her to focus. She swallowed nervously. "Sure, send him in."

She had to pull herself together. The last thing she needed was to be written up by her supervisor. All that held her together at the moment was her job, her interaction with her coworkers and clients. Without that, she probably wouldn't even leave the bed in the morning.

Moments later, Richard sauntered into her office, of course without knocking, and slouched into the available seat on the opposite side of her desk. He dressed in the customary hip-hop style of the day, with as many designer labels showing as possible. His overall appearance was not his usual best, most likely reflecting some type of temporary emotional crisis. Who knew what was going on in his life or head? Many clients, she knew, told her just what they wanted her to know, while others made up events as they went along. But a significant number used the sessions as a means to heal themselves or gain greater control over their lives.

Toni took a breath and leaned forward. "How are you today, Richard?" She reached for his file.

He shrugged in his customary fashion, keeping his eyes lowered. "Awright."

"How are things at home with your foster parents, Richard?"

He shrugged again and was silent for a moment. Then he looked up, stared into her eyes, and the anger and pain she saw there struck her like a slap. She wondered how much he would share with her. No aspiring gangsta would tell a female, even his shrink, all of his business. But today was different.

"They don't give a shit about me." His expression twisted into a grimace. "Nobody does. They never talk to me. Act like everything's cool just 'cause I got a place to sleep. But it ain't."

Her stomach lurched. "Do you . . . try talking to them?"

"What for? All they care about is a check. They never involve me in nothing, act like I'm a ghost or something."

*Ghost.* She heard her son's lament in this young man's words. How different were they, really? "But the Wilsons are good people, Richard," she forced herself to say. *So are Charles and I* she thought, her head spinning. "I really don't believe all they care about is a check," she said gently, straining to stay focused.

He stood abruptly, glaring at her. "What the fuck do you know, with your fancy office, your fine clothes? You probably got a family, people who really care about you.

You ain't never had it hard. You didn't wake up one day and find out that your folks didn't want you no more." His eyes filled with angry tears as he struggled not to cry. "I keep comin' here, listening to your bullshit about how things are gonna get better. When, huh, tell me when? You can't do nothin' for me with your fancy talk. Nobody can. I don't need words. Ain't nobody figured that out yet."

With that, he leered at her, then stormed out of the office, slamming the door behind him.

Toni was totally rocked. As she reached for a bottle of water nearby, her hands shook. Now she was losing her effectiveness on the job, losing her gift to read faces and emotions. She should have anticipated his torment by the way he entered the office, his posture, the set of his mouth, and the fire in his stare. Things were getting worse for Richard at home, and he lacked the words to fully express the extent of the turmoil there.

Within moments, Christine was standing in the doorway. "Ms. Devon, are you all right? I saw Richard tearing out of here and I couldn't help but overhear him."

"I'm . . . fine." She swallowed. "Thanks, Christine." She opened Richard's folder and stared at the pages in front of her. In a quick glance, she surveyed the accumulated psychological history on the youth but realized that the real causes of his angst were not there in those pages.

"Uh, Mr. Pierce is here. He doesn't have an appointment, but he said he needs to speak with you. He says it's important. What do you want me to do?"

*Alan, Lord, not today.* She didn't have the energy. The last thing she needed was another confrontation. But maybe it was best here at the office rather than someplace private. A controlled environment. At least here there wouldn't be a scene. At least, she hoped not.

"Just give me a minute; then you can send him in."

Christine nodded and pulled the door closed behind her.

Weary, Toni rested her head in her hands. For some reason, Richard's comments surfaced and rolled around in her head. She'd gone into social work because she believed she could help people, change lives, give something to others that she'd been unsuccessful in giving to her parents, her sisters. Her entire life had been driven by that goal. And it had cost her everything. So now what did she really have?

Today she felt like a complete failure.

The light tap on the door drew her attention. Lethargically, she lifted her head from her hands and gazed toward the door. She was emotionally spent. She didn't need this now. Why today, of all days? Alan was standing there, with Christine directly behind him. Toni nodded that it was all right for him to enter.

"Your work is . . . incredible," Regina said with a note of awe in her voice. Looking through a miniature handheld light box, she viewed the brilliantly colored slides of his work and instantly wondered why he wasn't exhibiting in some high-class gallery instead of thinking about tucking these treasures away in her little bookstore. At the time of her impetuous offer, she had no idea of the level and quality of his work. She assumed he was probably some struggling artist who needed a break.

She put the light box on the counter and looked at him with a newfound respect. "I would be honored to have your work here. But I don't think" — she gazed around at her almost finished space — "that Regina's Place will do it justice. You need to be out there . . . really out there, displaying in a recognized gallery."

Parker grinned sheepishly. "Naw." He shook his head, and his shoulder-length dreads moved sensuously around his shoulders. "That highbrow circuit isn't for me. I want to bring my stuff closer to the people, have them see what I do in places that they frequent. I want to be accessible. You know."

She nodded slowly, watching him as he put his tools of the trade away in a black leather duffel bag. "So do you paint full time, or what?"

"It seems that way. I teach art history at Parson's School of Design in about two weeks."

"Really? That's great. You seem like you would make a great teacher."

He angled his head to the side, curious about her comment. "Why would you say that?"

She glanced away for a moment, thinking back to her never-ending days in one class, one lesson or the other, and the myriad of teachers who'd instructed her. There were few who possessed both talent *and* personality. In her mind, Parker Heywood had both.

"Just a hunch," she said casually. "Call it woman's intuition."

He draped his bag across his shoulder, then leaned on the counter. "You said something like that when we met the first time. But to me, you don't seem to be a woman who lives by instincts alone," he joked, his dark eyes sparkling against the chestnut warmth of his skin.

"What type of woman do I appear to be?"

His eyes danced easily over her smooth, cinnamon-toned face, sank into the soft pillows of her dimples. "Like a woman who thinks things through. Makes wise choices. Doesn't take things for granted or at face value. Take this place, for example. It took a lot of work, preparation, and thought. This isn't something you jump into on a whim. Not everyone is up to that type of challenge. It takes a special kind of person to open themselves up to the risk."

Her face heated. No one, no one had ever said anything like that to her. Sure, she'd been complimented on things she'd done: performing in a recital, finishing at the top of her classes, receiving awards at the *News*. But no one had ever thought that what she needed was to feel that she was capable of making the decisions necessary to make her feel fulfilled in her life, and have the support of the people who professed to care about her.

Suddenly she felt a wave of sadness, realizing how much had been missing from her life for so long, and here, this near-perfect stranger summarized it all in a few sentences. She turned away and busied herself with unpacking a box.

Parker watched her for a minute, sensing that he'd hit some unseen nerve. Most people took compliments with a smile and subtle beckonings for more. Not Regina. If anything, she seemed strangely disturbed, almost as if she didn't know how to handle it, or as though it was something so foreign it was unrecognizable. But how could that be?

"Do you need some help with anything?"

"No, I'm fine, thanks," she said, keeping her back to him.

"Uh, did you get anyone to respond to the 'Help Wanted' sign?"

"Yes." She laughed lightly. "But no one who responded was anyone I would have actually work here. If you know what I mean."

He said nothing for a time, then stepped around her to lift another box onto the table. She smiled and opened it, inspecting its contents. As she emptied it, she felt his eyes on her, making her feel flustered. What did he want from her?

"So you're doing all this work by yourself?" he asked. "You'll be bone tired by the end of the day."

"Yes, I know." She continued to stack items from the box on the table.

"Do you ever get away from all this? What do you do for relaxation, for fun? All work, no play, you know."

Her long sigh let him know that he was again treading on dangerous ground. She didn't want to think about the times when she was not doing something in the shop. The idle times in her life were the hardest moments for her to endure, the hours when there was nothing to occupy her mind. She brooded too much, her mother always told her, when her quiet manner made everyone uneasy. Her parents, like everyone else, expected her to talk more, as if that were a sign of good emotional health. No one trusted people who didn't run their mouths all the time. Not her. Someone, she thought, should talk only when they had something worthwhile to say.

"What do you do with your leisure time?" she reversed the query. "Do you go out a lot?"

Parker smiled. "Sure. I try to catch all of the new shows at the major museums, even at the little ones. I love going to see performance artists downtown. And I'm a film buff, especially of foreign films. I love anything by Fellini, Kubrick, DeSica, Buñuel, Truffaut, and Lean. Foreign movies always seem to have so much more depth and sensitivity to them than commercial American movies."

"I don't know that much about foreign films," she admitted. "I like the old black-and-white movies from the thirties and forties. They always had something to say without being phony. Plus I love the old movie stars: Clark Gable, Gary Cooper, Carole Lombard, David Niven, Joan Crawford, Bette Davis, and Susan Hayward. I wish there were roles like those for our black actors and actresses today."

"Yeah, some of those old flicks are pretty cool," he replied. "Anyway, maybe we can go out and take in a film sometime."

"Maybe, sometime," she answered.

"How about this evening? You did sort of promise me when I called."

Regina smiled coyly, displaying a mischievous sparkle in her eyes. "I thought it was just to grab something to eat after I close up. This is starting to sound suspiciously like a date."

"Who's to say two hardworking adults can't have a friendly meal and enjoy a movie together — without tags, or strings — unless those two hardworking adults decide that's what they want?"

"These things often start out innocently enough, but then complications follow," she said. "I don't know if I'm ready for all of that. This is no reflection on you. It's me. I'm working through some stuff right now."

"Who says that a simple meal and a movie has to be so involved? Would you feel better if you paid your own way?" he teased, and Regina immediately felt silly for getting so serious.

She placed her hand on her right hip. "Okay. Dutch. You pick the movie; I'll pick the place to eat."

"I admire a woman who knows her own mind," he said, displaying again his disarming smile.

*Knows her own mind,* that was a switch. Regina felt her heart race, but she still had reservations, an unknown quantity that she couldn't explain. Yet she had to admit, even if not to Parker, that she wanted to explore these new options that he offered, an extension to her life. Maybe it was long past the time that she did everything alone. All she had to do to bring change to her life was to open up, take the risk, and invite new opportunities. She looked at Parker. Maybe opportunity had knocked.

# CHAPTER TWENTY-ONE

Alan stepped tentatively across the threshold and closed the door behind him. He stood above Toni, who remained in her chair, but turned to face him.

"How are you?" he asked.

"Why are you here, Alan?"

"I wanted to see you. Is that simple enough for you?"

She glanced away, not wanting a scene. "Now isn't the time."

He pulled up a chair and sat down, studied the pained expression on her face, the tension in her body. "What is it, Toni? It's not just my sudden appearance."

Her eyes pinned him. "He knows," she lashed out. "He saw us together." Her voice cracked with emotion. "And my son . . . Steven was arrested."

Alan was torn between which issue to address first. What he wanted to do was hold her, pull her into his arms and swear to her that everything would be all right. "Toni, I didn't know. I . . . what can I do?

How can I help?"

"There's nothing you can do, Alan," she responded with a hollowness in her voice that was frightening.

"How is your son?"

"It's all my fault," she said in a faraway voice. "I've been living my life in this fantasy world, believing I could save it, like what I said or thought made a damned bit of difference. It means nothing, Alan, nothing! Do you hear me?" she continued, almost on the verge of tears. "I can't even save my own son, my marriage, nothing." She looked across at him, still battling the growing feeling of sadness, her eyes misty. "I even convinced myself that I could make things better for you, better for myself by being with you. Toni Devon, savior of all mankind," she singsonged sarcastically. "And I've failed at all of it. Failed," she repeated, sounding beaten and conquered.

"Toni, don't do this to yourself. Don't," he whispered, stretching out his hand to cover hers.

She gazed down at their linked hands and the tears finally slid down her cheeks. Her slight body trembled. "I can't do this anymore."

"Do what, baby? What?"

"Any of this. This work, my life at home, me and you. I just can't do it. I can't even look at myself in the mirror. I'm disgusted by what I see."

Alan squeezed her hand tighter. "This isn't the Toni that I know — and love. This isn't the woman who walks into the projects at night because she has a client who needs her. This isn't the woman who's stood up in court to defend the rights of a child to live a life without abuse. This isn't the woman who made me believe I could feel again. Not the woman who, without question, loves her son — and her husband — no matter the mistakes that have been made," he added. "Sometimes in life, Toni, we get so caught up in just doing, we don't see what we've accomplished, the lives we've touched. We slow down and see the forest only when there's a fire."

Feeling her pain, he tugged in a breath and slowly released it. "This is your fire. You can either watch it burn and totally consume you and everything you love, or you can start hauling buckets of water to begin putting it out. There's gonna be damage when all the smoke clears, Toni, things — treasures — that can never be replaced. But you can always rebuild. Just don't wait until everything is destroyed and beyond salvation."

Slowly he rose, understanding that this would probably be the last time he'd ever see her, and the sudden searing pain of that realization stunned him with its intensity. His stomach rolled from the discomfort of the thought of the impending end of their time together.

"I know you, Toni Devon," he said gently, looking down into her eyes. "You'll make it through the ashes. And if you ever find that you need help with those buckets, I'll be there." He leaned down and placed a tender parting kiss on her forehead. "Just remember: you're not alone, ever. Goodbye."

Victoria knew it was rude to leave the party so early, especially without saying good-bye, especially since it was her department that was hosting the affair. But she couldn't take it anymore. All of the mushy talk. She didn't want to hear another thing about how wonderful, how cute, how enriching, how thrilling it was to have a child. She didn't want to listen to any more stories of herculean mothers who endured the agonizing pains of labor for untold hours only to beam with joy when they gazed down into the rosy faces of their infants.

Rosy faces. What did they know about being born without the approved rosy face, ruby lips, silky hair, and a guaranteed passport to the future? Nothing. That was what they knew. But she understood it first hand. And any child born of her and Phillip would have double the load to carry. It would also have to deal with the weight of being a biracial child in a world where society still tallied its citizens by ethnic group. Her child would fall into the netherworld of "other." Whatever that nonentity meant. And it wouldn't help that the father was white, especially if the child had the misfortune to look like her. But to take a life before it had a chance to begin . . . who was she to make that decision? *The only one who could.*

Victoria pulled into the driveway, shut off the Mercedes, then sat in the car for a few moments before going inside. She needed time to collect herself, to quiet the storm inside her. She hadn't seen Phillip's car, so she would have this respite to think things through — again — before he came home. She knew she was going to have to come to some decision. In this situation, even indecision was a decision, and she couldn't leave her fate to chance. It wasn't fair to Phillip to keep him dangling over something this monumental in their lives. At some point she must confront the pregnancy and him.

She looked down at her flat stomach. And it wasn't fair to the life growing inside of her.

Millie paced in agitation back and forth across her bedroom floor, her hair still a bushy mess, but she refused to go back to that woman's shop. She gripped the phone like a vise. "What do you mean, I should stay out of Regina's life?" she said shrilly into the phone, stunned by the turnaround of her son-in-law. He'd always supported her, always seen things her way. *They* knew what was best for Regina. Would everyone turn on her? She felt like Julius Caesar at the hands of his smiling conspirators.

"Ma, Regina is a grown woman. Give her some space. She knows what she's doing," Russell said as calmly as he could.

"I don't understand you, Russell. Those are your children, too."

"I know that. And I also know that Regina loves them, Ma, just as much as you or I do. No one needs to tell her that." He drew in a breath. "Regina and I have been divorced for three years. And never once in those three years has she ever come to me for anything, asked me about anything. And the kids are fine, more than fine. As sad as I am to say it, they seem happier now than they were when I lived with them. And that's my fault, because I made Regina's life a living hell. I deserve whatever I get."

"Russell," she cooed. "You don't know what you're saying. What did she say to you to get you so confused?" He was her last ally; she couldn't lose him, too.

"Nothing. It's what I saw. She actually opened a business, in a great neighborhood, with plenty of potential," he said with an almost reverent respect. "She's educated, talented, and has more courage than we've ever given her credit for. And I'm going to do everything in my power to win her back, if she'll have me — without your help, and without your input. You see, Ma, the funny thing is, we only believed Regina needed us, because *we* needed to — it made our lives more important. But all Regina ever needed was a chance to be Regina. We never saw her for the remarkable woman she is."

"I . . . I just don't understand," she whimpered. "She's all I have — her and those children. I did everything I could for her."

"If I could, I would go back and do it all over again — the right way, with Regina as my partner. But I can't. All I can do is try not to make the same mistakes again. And so should you."

Millie sat on the edge of her bed, staring at the phone, glancing around her beautiful but very empty home. She'd never felt so alone, so abandoned. Still, there was a part of her that would not let her believe that it was all her doing.

She sighed deeply. This was not how she'd imagined the later years in her life would be. She saw them filled with friends and family — and Millie as the matriarch. Now they'd all left her alone, and she couldn't understand why. A full, rich, productive life she'd ever wanted for all of them was the best.

When she was a little girl growing up in the south side of Chicago, she envied the girls dressed in the best clothes, heading off to piano and dance lessons, speaking properly, going to the right schools, catching the right man. She pored over the fashion magazines, listened to the great singers on the radio, watched performers on television, and she dreamed, dreamed that her life would be perfect and beautiful, just like theirs. She'd have everything they had and more.

She watched her mother struggle as a waitress to raise her and her two younger brothers alone after their father left them. Without complaint or bitterness, the woman went to work day in, day out, sick or well. And not once did she ever hear her mother bad-mouth her father. It hurt her deeply to see her mother come home too exhausted to even smile, to watch her brothers turn to dealing drugs and running numbers to make extra money, until they were replaced with numbers instead of names. And she swore that would never happen to her. She would find a man who loved her, who worked hard, who dedicated himself to his family. She was sure of it. And her children would have the best of everything no matter what it took. They would have the life she only imagined. She would never again let circumstance control her life or the people in it — she would. Because as long as she had control, she'd never have to worry about losing anything or anyone else she loved ever again.

When her mother died of pneumonia in that two-bedroom cold-water flat, Millie found herself alone at seventeen. All that remained was her determination to have the life she'd dreamed of. And when she met her husband, Robert, she was certain her dreams had finally come true.

Robert Prescott was five years her senior, the son of an Alabama hellfire-and-brimstone Baptist preacher with a highly respected church, a sizable congregation, and great influence in the community. He was handsome and educated, just starting out in the dry-cleaning business, and had fallen in love with the beautiful and fiery Millicent Bowen.

Oh, those early days of budding love were glorious. Robert and Millie did everything together, went everywhere together. Robert had dreams, small dreams at first, but Millie was certain they would grow, with her help. After all, she had been exposed to so much more of the world than her older mate.

They were married by the justice of the peace six months after they met, in the county clerk's office in downtown Chicago, even though Robert wanted a church wedding with all the trimmings. She laughed as she recalled how the justice had stumbled twice during the vows, but she didn't take that as a premonition of things to come.

"How do we expect to get your dry-cleaning business up and off the ground if we spend money on a big wedding, sugah?" she cooed to him before the city ceremony, kissing his warm brown cheek. "I'd love you just the same if we got married in a big church or in a mailbox," she teased. She never said that part of her reason was her shame in not having a respectable family or any real friends, but mainly it was because she never wanted to be poor again, to be alone again. And she wanted to be certain that not one dime was spent unless it was to make their life better. For Millie, better meant the wealth of social and job opportunities to be found in New York. So they moved, because it was Millie's desire, and Robert would do anything to keep his beautiful bride happy.

Things were good between them during the heady early years, when it seemed that they could do anything and all of their — or rather, her — dreams were still possible. Robert opened his first dry-cleaning shop, and then another. He owned three of them by the time Regina was ten. And Millie made sure that Regina would reap the benefits of that income after the bills were paid: Catholic school, dance and music lessons, a private tutor to keep her grades at the top of her class, the latest clothes so she would never have to feel ugly, and, of course, a weekly trip to Ms. Ellen's Beauty Parlor.

Yes, that was the life she'd dreamed of, struggled to achieve and maintain.

Millie sighed and a soft shudder shook her body. Where had things gone wrong? What had she done so terrible to turn everyone against her? It had never been her intention to cause anyone any harm. Still, things started slowly unraveling. Her once adoring and hardworking husband turned to drinking and nights with other women, becoming more emotionally distant from her and their young child. He seemed to prefer the company of others rather than being with her, as he'd always done. And, little by little, his lack of focus and consistent night crawling wrecked his empire of dry cleaners, and the once-prospering businesses began to fail, and he didn't seem to care.

"What are we supposed to do if we have no income, Robert?" she'd berated him one night after he'd stumbled in from an evening of drinking.

"You figure it out," he slurred, his bloodshot eyes burning into her. "I thought you had a plan. What do you need me for?"

"Why, Robert, why? Why are you doing

this to us? To yourself?"

Suddenly he laughed hysterically, as if she'd told the greatest joke. He wobbled momentarily but quickly recovered to right himself. He was a pitiful sight.

"Look at you; you're nothing but a drunken adulterer. Not the man I married," she wailed in frustration. "What will all of our friends say? What will they think?"

"I really don't care. I drink so I don't have to think," he mumbled. "And I sleep with other women to feel like a man. Something you seem to have forgotten how to do for me." He stumbled off into the bathroom and locked the door.

She listened to him splashing water on his face to sober up. This was not the way she'd envisioned their marriage, not like this. So what was she supposed to do now? A divorce? She wouldn't be humiliated by getting a divorce, having all of their private business made fodder for gossips and all those who never wished them well from the very first. No divorce, she decided then and there. With her newfound resolve, she stayed in a deteriorating marriage and suffered in martyred silence. They lived in a state of limbo, both feeding off of each other's weaknesses and disappointments.

To offset their dwindling income, Millie eventually took a job as a receptionist at an investment firm and moved her way up to administrative assistant. Every penny she made went to ensuring that Regina had everything she always did and more. She did nothing to shore Robert's faltering businesses, letting her husband face his own financial woes alone before the strain of it took its toll on him physically.

She told her few friends and Robert's extended family, by way of explanation of her change in lifestyle, that she was bored and needed some excitement in her life. The truth about their bad marriage was never spoken, especially after her husband's death from a sudden, massive heart attack.

It was because of her industry that the Prescott family maintained their status, Millie reasoned, and they should be grateful.

*Grateful!* This was gratitude, she thought mournfully, her gaze falling on the photograph of the three of them during happier times, before the drinking, the fighting, the women, the long silences, before they abandoned her, Robert by way of his heart attack and Regina by choice.

*Just leave her alone.* She could still hear Russell's admonishment, echoed by Ellen.

She was so afraid, afraid of letting go, certain that if she did she would again be that motherless seventeen-year-old girl in the cold-water flat in Chicago — alone.

Victoria stepped out of the shower, feeling only mildly refreshed. Usually the flood of hot water would relieve her of all tension, but now her head was still cloudy and her emotions were yet a tangled web.

She slipped on her robe and pulled the belt snugly around her waist and wondered how it would feel when the belt didn't fit all the way around.

She untied the belt, removed the robe, and surveyed her glistening, nude body in the full-length mirror that hung on the bathroom door. She envisioned her rounded belly, the full ripeness of her breasts, the high arch of her behind. And Phillip's strong, tender hands would stroke her taut skin, massage her swollen feet and tight back.

They would shop together for tiny clothes in a neutral green. But she preferred pink, she thought suddenly. A girl in pink. Yes. A perfect tea-brown little girl with wavy black hair and light brown eyes like Regina's, the kind that people paid for.

She'd be . . . a lawyer when she grew up,

Victoria decided. A tough one, and smart, too. Smarter than her colleagues. But she'd be so genuinely nice that no one would hate her for being so good at everything she did.

Phillip would spoil her. That much she knew for sure. And it would be okay with her. She'd heard that was what fathers did with little girls, and theirs would be no different.

And she would be so special and so perfect — just like those women's babies at the bank and in the movies and magazines — that nothing else would matter. Her little girl would change everything. Her little girl would make all her fears finally go away.

Victoria blinked, catching her reflection in the mirror again, and snatched herself back to reality. Slowly she replaced her robe, taking one last look before she tied the belt.

She turned off the light and walked out into the bedroom. She checked the bedside clock. It was almost seven. She'd been home for hours, daydreaming, and hadn't started dinner. Phillip would be coming in any minute. She hurried across the room and put on her slippers.

Not that Phillip was the type of husband

who expected a hot meal on the table when he came home. If anything, he was quite the opposite. He'd rather come in many nights and take her to dinner, or order out from one of the fancy restaurants in the neighborhood. "We both work too hard to have to worry about cooking, too," he would often say when she mildly protested.

But sometimes, like tonight, she wanted to fix his meal, to experience the intimate process of it — thinking about him with each step of preparation, until everything was just right. She wanted to do that for him.

Victoria smiled to herself, feeling surprisingly warm and happy for the first time in weeks, and headed downstairs. It was the last thing she remembered.

Regina checked to be sure that the back rooms were locked and the alarm was set. "Ready?" she asked Parker.

"Whenever you are."

They walked out into the balmy September night and strolled, for a time, in companionable silence. Many of the shops along the busy avenue were still open, their soft lights and enticing window displays dotting the street in a rainbow of colors.

"The restaurant is on the next block," Regina commented. "I think you'll like it."

Parker grinned. "I'm sure I will. I wholeheartedly trust your taste."

Regina glanced across at him. "And why is that? It could be a fast-food joint with greasy cheeseburgers and waiters with stained white T-shirts."

"If everything I've noticed about you is on the level, they're probably great greasy cheeseburgers."

Regina laughed. "You have faith, Mr. Heywood."

"Any woman who can do what you've done — by herself — and pull it off, is a woman I would put my faith in," he said, his voice taking on a note of seriousness.

Regina momentarily lowered her head, unsure how to respond, if at all. Compliments, at least compliments on her ability to make choices, were something foreign to her. Her first thought was that he was just running a line, making a play. But there was something in his voice that made her doubt that assumption. And she was suddenly fascinated by this new role of self-assured woman, by his perception of her. Her shoulders straightened with her new sense of pride, and she strolled with just a bit more dip in her step.

They came to a stop in front of Keur N' Deye, a traditional Senegalese bistro and one of Regina's favorites in the area.

"Mmm, African, huh?" He nodded slowly. "I told you I had faith." He opened the door and held it for her.

Seated beneath a brilliant portrait of the African horizon at sundown, Regina and Parker placed their orders and sipped lemon-flavored water.

"I spent two years in Africa," Parker commented as he took in the décor. It's an incredible place, magnificent and painful at the same time."

"I can imagine. What made you go?"

He breathed slowly, linked his long fingers together. "It was a couple of different reasons: to study, but mainly to get away."

The question itched her palm, like when she knew she was going to get money from some unknown source, or when she could sense a headline story from all the things a person *didn't* say. Unfortunately, she didn't think it was really any of her business.

Parker reached for his glass of water and took a long, thoughtful swallow. "When I went away," he began slowly, "all I could think about was putting as much distance between me and New York as possible. I guess I thought it would make things better," he added vaguely.

Oh, no, now this was too much. The suspense was killing her. She subtly pushed propriety aside with a slight shove of her elbow. "Why did you need to get away from New York, if you don't mind my asking?" But what she really thought was that if he didn't want her to ask, he wouldn't have brought it up. *Right?* That had been her one true experience as a journalist. People didn't lay things out there unless they wanted you to know about it. There was something in human nature that often compelled them to just open up and confess. She had a quick flash of the nuns and inwardly flinched.

Regina leaned a bit forward, removed all expression from her face, and looked directly at him. And suddenly she felt hot. Really hot. Her breasts tingled, and she adjusted her behind in the seat to still the pulse that erupted between her thighs.

Something in his eyes, the depth of his expression, the softness of his mouth, had reached inside her and touched her. She felt as if he were stroking her body with the featherlight touch of his gaze, and she shivered as if she stood before him naked and vulnerable. He rekindled feelings within her that she thought were no longer there.

She pushed those aside as well.

"Are you okay?" he asked gently.

Regina blinked in surprise and forced a smile. "Oh, yeah. I'm fine." *Humph, you can tell I haven't been out in a while,* she mused, embarrassed, but undoubtedly stirred by this assured but gentle man.

Parker cleared his throat. "I really don't talk about this much," he said, briefly looking at her and then at his entwined fingers.

Regina held up her hand. "Listen," she said softly, "it's none of my business, really. You don't have to say anything."

He stared right into her eyes and she felt that heated charge run through her body again. *Please don't let this be early menopause,* she silently prayed.

"I want to. I figure if there's any chance of us . . . seeing each other, I should be honest."

Her brows rose, but she didn't say anything, certain that she would blow it if she did. Did he really say "seeing each other"? She wasn't sure if she should be thrilled or insulted by his presumptuousness. But she'd be a liar if she denied that the mere possibility intrigued her.

"My wife ran off with my little girl."

# CHAPTER TWENTY-TWO

*Aw, damn, can't a girl get a break?* Regina silently screamed. She knew he was too good to be true: fine, talented, considerate, not a Mr. Macho. It was always something, she fumed, her mind running down the master list of relationship obstacles, with wife and kid right up there at the top. It was one hell of a hurdle.

Her eyes glazed over and she wasn't really listening until the word *divorce* pierced her mental fog.

She blinked, bringing Parker back into focus. What did he say about divorce? Maybe all wasn't lost after all. But if she cut in now and asked him to repeat himself, then he'd know she hadn't been paying attention. She pulled in a breath and concentrated on playing catch-up with the conversation.

"The last time I saw my daughter, Tracy, was eight years ago. She was only five. As bad as things had gotten between me and Lynn, they were my family. They kept me anchored in a way. When . . . they left . . . I felt like I was adrift, you know. Not knowing what to do, where to turn."

The waitress appeared with their plates of steamed vegetables, pita bread, and couscous.

Parker nodded his thanks and continued with his story. "The ink wasn't dry on the paper before she disappeared," he said bitterly, the dark cloud of his brows brewing over turbulent eyes. "She only did it because she knew how much it would hurt me. She knew it would rip my heart out."

"Have you tried to find them?"

Parker scooped up a forkful of food. "For three years I looked for them." He shoved the food into his mouth, chewed slowly. "No luck. Eventually I couldn't take it anymore. I gave up, had to get away before I lost my mind. I sold the house, put half the money in the bank, and went to Africa, then Europe."

"Your wife was the one who moved out of the house?" Regina asked, the idea just registering as she suddenly became suspicious of just how righteous he really was. Usually the woman stayed in the home, especially if there were children involved. When they were the ones to leave, it generally meant major husband trouble. What decent man, no matter how bad the marriage, would let a woman with a child go out into the street to fend for themselves — unless he was the cause for the exodus?

"She moved out prior to the divorce because she had someone waiting in the wings, her lover — the cop." He raised his glass to her in a mock salute and drank a long swallow of water.

"Oh, God, that must have been awful for you," she said with a combination of pain for him and relief for her.

"It still is at times. I got a raw deal with the judge, the whole system. It's a feeling of failure as a husband and father. That somehow I just wasn't capable, because if I was, I would have been able to keep my family together. I guess the worst part is possibly having my daughter think that I don't love her, that I abandoned her. It haunts me. I have no idea what Lynn may have told her."

"I'm so sorry. I can only imagine how you feel. I know how difficult it was for me before, during, and after my divorce."

"How did your kids take the divorce," he asked, moving the conversation away from his problems.

"They adjusted pretty well, thank goodness. Michele and Darren."

"Hmmm."

"Actually" — she toyed with her food — "you almost met my ex-husband. When you came to the shop the first time, you two practically ran into each other."

He frowned for a moment, trying to recall, and then a light in his eyes came on when the image of the well-tailored man came into focus. "You're kidding."

Regina slowly shook her head and smiled at the stricken expression on his face. "No. Fourteen years, to be exact. I've been divorced for three." She chewed on a piece of carrot.

"When I saw him coming to the store last week, I never made the connection. Wow. Small world," he muttered. He was thoughtful for a minute. "Is . . . that a problem for you?"

"Uh, no. There's nothing going on between Russell and me. Until recently I hadn't seen him in almost two years. We're just getting to a point where we can be civil with each other."

"Don't tell me that he's a deadbeat dad," he said, his voice taking on a sharp edge.

"No. Not totally. Financially, he sends his check like clockwork, calls periodically, but he just won't come to see the kids. The first time he saw them was just recently, the first in ages. To tell you the truth, I would have preferred if he'd kept his money and spent more time with them instead."

"For some men, as much as they want to see their children, sometimes it's more painful to be with them for a few hours than not at all. Those short visits are like tearing a piece of your heart out over and over again."

Regina was quiet for a moment, thinking about what Parker said, imagining how she would feel if she saw Michele and Darren only on weekends and holidays and then had to leave them. It would be torturous for her, given the depth of her feelings for her children.

Her expression softened. "I never thought about it like that. Maybe it is hard on him. I just took it to mean that he didn't care, or that he was angry with me and taking it out on them."

"Hey, there's a different reason for every man who's out there. That's just one of them, which a lot of women don't realize. Men are conditioned to be strong and not show emotion. A lot of times it's just hard for them — us — to express how we really feel."

The waitress returned, asked them if they wanted anything else, then left the check. They both reached for it at the same time.

"I know we agreed to do this dutch thing, but I'd really like to take care of this evening," Parker said. "No strings," he added quickly, and smiled.

Regina pursed her lips. "All right. If it'll make you feel better," she teased.

"I'll be able to sleep tonight."

"Never let it be said that I kept a man from a good night's sleep."

Parker's dark eyes grew suddenly intense. "I can easily imagine you keeping a man awake well into the night," he said, his voice dropping to an intimate tone.

Regina felt her face heat and she glanced away.

"I'm sorry, that was out of line. I —"

"It's just that it's . . . well, it's been a long time. . . ." Her sentence drifted off and she felt totally flustered and embarrassed.

"It's been a long time for me, too," he admitted.

Her gaze connected with his, and in that instant they both realized that they'd just turned another corner.

Phillip stayed later than usual at the office, something he rarely did, then decided to have a couple of drinks with some co-workers, another rarity for him. The truth was, he didn't want to go home. Just the idea of seeing Vicky and knowing she was carrying their child and that she was seriously considering getting rid of it was more than he could handle. He didn't want to pretend that it didn't matter to him, because it did. Maybe too much.

He was all for women's rights and their right to choose what to do with their own bodies, or at least he had been until it came to *his* wife and *his* child. What about his right to choose? What about his unborn child?

If only he could understand her fears, her doubts. Didn't she know how deeply he loved her, how much she meant to him? He would do anything for Victoria. And what scared him, what kept him in his office into the evening, then sent him to a local bar, was wrestling with the very notion that he loved her so much that he was willing to do whatever was necessary to keep her. Even if that meant giving up his child, making that supreme sacrifice.

He didn't think it was possible to love another human being so thoroughly, so completely. But he did.

Phillip sat in his car thinking of what he would say to her when he went inside, how he would explain what was in his heart.

Slowly he opened the car door and got out. He only wanted things to be right between them again, for them to be happy and not afraid to look each other in the eye. He missed his wife. He missed the closeness, the love, the intimacy.

When he stepped into the kitchen from the garage, the house was completely still. He'd seen Vicky's car in the driveway and knew she was home. Maybe she was asleep, he thought. He crossed through the kitchen and into the living room, and that was where he found her — unconscious, in a heap at the foot of the stairs. He rushed to her, kneeling by her body.

"What could I have done differently?" Toni asked her son Steven as they sat opposite each other at the kitchen table.

Steven shrugged in that same nonchalant way his father did sometimes. "I don't know, Ma. I wish I could say it was your fault or Dad's fault, but it ain't. This ain't about you."

"It isn't," she corrected him by force of habit.

He shrugged again. "I mean, I'm not

stupid. I knew what I was doing," he admitted, keeping his dark brown eyes focused on the table.

"Then why, Steven? I need to understand why. And I think you need to say it out loud so you'll understand, too."

They both heard the key turn in the door, and moments later Charles walked into the kitchen. He looked from one to the other.

"We were talking," Toni offered. "Why don't you sit down, too? It's been a long time since the three of us really talked." Her eyes begged him to accept the olive branch she offered.

Charles hesitated. He wasn't certain that if he stayed in the same room with Toni for any length of time he wouldn't be able to contain his anger and disappointment from his son. Steven didn't need to know the state of his parents' marriage. At least not while he already had so much to handle. But he also understood that to walk away, to offer an excuse, would hurt Steven more than it would hurt Toni. And the truth was, they hadn't talked in far too long.

With reservation, he pulled out a chair at the head of the table and sat down.

Toni released the breath of tension she'd

held and offered a short smile of thanks.

"What were you two talking about?" Charles asked, directing his question to his son.

Steven, almost the spitting image of his father, with his cool brown complexion, dancing eyes, and curly hair, looked shyly at his father. "Mom was just asking me to try to explain why I . . . did it."

"Do you know why, son? I mean really know?"

Steven shuffled his almost manly shoulders. He took a deep breath. "At first I wanted to believe it was because of you both, that you didn't understand me, didn't listen to me and stuff. And that's part of it, because nobody really pays me any attention, except when I do something wrong, like fail a class or come in too late. So long as I'm doing good, it's like I'm not really here."

Toni flinched, and Charles's face tightened. Maybe there was some truth in what he said. They had been preoccupied, too preoccupied, with the drama of their lives.

"But I've really been thinking these past few days . . . since it happened, and . . . well, it's not y'all's fault, not really." He heaved a sigh. "It's just that sometimes I feel like so much is expected of me, ya know. Like I have some ideal to live up to. Ma's got all these degrees. You got your own business. And I was just scared of failing at it. Scared of falling down and messin' up. Scared that I couldn't measure up. Scared that some way or the other you might figure out that I ain't this great kid you think I am. So I screwed up first. So that I wouldn't be perfect no more and you wouldn't expect so much from me." He sucked his teeth. "Man, it's just all mixed up," he mumbled.

"Son, everyone messes up," Charles said. "Especially teenagers. It's part of life. It's expected. We never expected you to be without faults, without slipups. What we do expect is for you to do the best you can, no more, no less. You'll be a grown man soon, and we won't be able to come to your aid, fix things and make them right. You'll have to do that yourself; it's part of being a man, an adult. And the decisions you make now will color the kind of man you'll be tomorrow."

"Steven," Toni added, "when your father and I give you the freedom you have to make choices, with your friends, the way you dress, the places you hang out, it's because we believe we've provided you with the foundation to make the right choices

349

— most of the time. But with the choices you make comes responsibility."

For a brief moment, she reflected on her own choices, the devastating ones she'd made over the past few months and the responsibility that came with them. How would she ever be able to explain to her son what she'd done, the decisions she'd made? What kind of example was she? What was happening between her and Charles couldn't be hidden from him forever. She wondered what the fallout would be from what she had done. How would it affect Steven?

He'd given up his right to choose, Charles thought. He'd simply held his hands up and let himself be robbed of his place within his family — robbed of his manhood. Or maybe he'd abdicated his position as husband and father. And that had been worse than choosing wrong. Yet here he was trying to explain to his son about being a man. How hypocritical was that?

Steven lowered his head. "I wasn't selling drugs," he said softly. "I never did. I just said that because . . ."

"Because what, Steven?" Charles asked. His jaw clenched when he thought about the night at the precinct, the upcoming court hearing, and that it might have all been for nothing. It was hard to accept the idea of his son being a criminal.

"I was covering for one of the other guys."

"What!" Toni cried.

"He'd been in trouble before and if he got caught again, he was going away. I was just trying to help him." He glanced quickly from his mother to his father.

Charles wiped his face with his hand. Toni's entire posture deflated.

"Is this the truth this time, Steven?" Charles asked.

Steven nodded.

Charles looked at his wife. "I don't know how much this changes things. He was still caught with drugs in his possession. I'll give the lawyer a call in the morning. See what he says." He stared at his son. "Is there anything else we need to know?"

"I'm . . . sorry."

Toni looked at her husband. "So am I," she said softly. She reached across the table and placed her hand tentatively atop his.

A warmth he didn't know he could still feel spread through him in a gentle wave. His throat tightened. He wanted to hold her, make all the ugliness go away, somehow clean up the mess they'd both made, tell her that he still loved her. But he didn't know if he could.

The phone rang, offering him the perfect excuse to disconnect from the almost hypnotic effect she was having on him. He excused himself and went to pick up the phone on the kitchen wall near the door.

Moments later, he held the phone out to Toni, his expression grim. "It's Phillip. He says Victoria's in the hospital."

"I had a great time," Regina said as she and Parker stood in front of her door. He'd followed her home in his car, insisting that he wanted to be certain she made it home safely. Even though she protested, she was secretly pleased by his gentlemanly behavior.

"So did I. Dinner was enlightening. And sitting next to you during a horror film is a true experience," he teased. "I hope we can do it again sometime."

"Maybe," she said coyly, giving him a hint of a smile.

"Uh, I was thinking, I have some free time in the afternoons. I'd be more than willing to come by the store and help out." He lifted then lowered his shoulders. "That is, until you get some help."

"I really couldn't ask you to —"

"You didn't ask; I offered."

She thought about it for a moment. Parker Heywood in her store, in her face, in her presence, the two of them working, sweating side by side. She swallowed. "If you're sure it's not a problem. I can't pay you," she quickly added.

Parker laughed out loud. "Hanging my work in your store is payment enough. What are you planning to do for the opening, anyway?"

"I'm still trying to work that out. I know I don't have much time. But . . . I really haven't had any help. I've been doing it pretty much by myself."

Parker frowned. He vaguely recalled her saying something about "they" didn't expect the place to open, but he'd never pursued it. *Hmmm.* "Didn't your kids or some of your friends want to help? I would think they'd be excited. This is pretty major stuff."

How could she tell him the battle she'd been fighting with herself and seemingly everyone in her life without sounding like she'd surrounded herself with some of the worst people in the world, including her own family? How intelligent did that make her? Yet a small corner of her heart told her that he would understand. During their evening together he hadn't been afraid of appearing vulnerable, opening up some of his old wounds and putting his innermost feelings on display. And the only reason she could think of that he would be that forthcoming was because he sensed he could trust her.

That realization gently pried open that tight space in her heart where she kept her feelings secretly hidden. And looking at him standing in front of her, full of openness and expectation, she knew it would be all right.

"Are you really tired?" she asked suddenly.

Parker grinned. "Depends on what you have in mind, young lady."

"Nothing that exciting. I, uh, was just wondering if you wanted to . . . come upstairs — for a little while. We could finish talking. I mean, it's better than standing out in the streets. And —"

"Sure," he said, cutting off her rambling. "I'm sold. You think your kids are still up? I'd like to meet them."

"I'm sure they are," she said dryly, fighting to keep her nervousness in check. "They're probably watching the clock to see what time I come in. I'd called and told them I was going out for a while this evening," she was saying as she led the way up the front steps. "I didn't have enough time in my day to answer all of their questions."

She stopped at the top of the stairs, turned, and faced him. "This is the first time I've . . . brought someone home, uh, dated — I mean, gone out with anyone since my divorce." She gulped. "The only man they've ever seen me with is my ex-husband." She wasn't quite sure what she was saying, but she hoped he could figure it out.

"So you're not sure if they're going to give me the evil eye or offer me a seat?"

Her mouth quirked up on one side. "Pretty much."

"Relax. It'll be okay. And if things get hairy, I'll just haul you in front of me to ward off the blows."

"Very funny," she said, giggling. She started back up the stairs and was just about to put her key in the apartment door.

"Wait," Parker whispered.

Regina turned, wide-eyed, figuring he'd changed his mind at the last minute.

He stepped closer, his dark gaze sliding over her face. She held her breath, afraid to move. He lowered his head. His locks slid across his shoulders, fanning either side of her face.

"Just in case I don't get a chance to do this later."

Parker tenderly cupped Regina's chin in his palm and drew her to him, and she was certain he could hear the rapid galloping of her heart. He took his time, letting the tension of the moment build. His lips were a breath away from hers, just as the apartment door was flung open.

They sprang apart as if they'd been electrocuted. Regina's head spun. She barely registered what Michele was saying.

"Mr. Phillip called," she said excitedly. "Ms. Victoria is in the hospital and she's asking for you."

# CHAPTER TWENTY-THREE

Toni spoke briefly with Phillip, then hung up the phone, her expression a mixture of surprise and concern.

"What's going on?" Charles asked.

Toni tucked a wayward lock behind her ear. "He says she fell down the stairs and the doctors aren't sure if she's going to lose the baby or not. They don't know why she fell, but they checked to see if there was some underlying cause. Low blood pressure, anemia, or something like that."

"Baby," the male voices chorused.

"That was my reaction," she said in a distant voice. "I didn't know. She never said anything."

Toni blindly sat down, wondering why Victoria never mentioned anything about her pregnancy. Did Regina know? Had they grown that far apart? Just what did her silence about the baby say about the state of their friendship? There was a time when the three of them shared everything. Back then, nothing was out of bounds for them to talk about. Yes, almost everything, she mentally corrected, thinking of her scandalous secret. What else didn't they know about each other? What kind of friends were they, anyway?

That question had intermittently plagued her for months since that night they were together at the Shark Bar. It was almost as if Regina's declaration — emancipation — had thrown everyone's lives into orbit. Her moment of independence. Nothing had been the same since then. Perhaps all that was needed for the inevitable explosion of events and the startling revelations that followed was for the pin to be pulled from the grenade. Regina, in her own deceptively unobtrusive way, was that pin, the one stabilizing force that kept all hell from breaking loose. When the pin was pulled — *ka-boom!*

Now they were all sitting in the debris of their own making. The resulting explosion forced everyone to look at their own lives, and not one of them really liked what they saw. In the past they had focused all of their attention on Regina's shortcomings as a way of not having to deal with the chaos of their own lives. Somehow Regina had always been the easy diversion, but no more. For once they were forced to take full responsibility for their actions and choices.

When she looked around and took note of the room, Steven was gone, leaving her and Charles alone.

"You . . . all right?" he asked with a hitch of hesitation, almost as if he didn't want her to think he cared.

"I suppose so," she answered vaguely, folding her hands in front of her. "She looked up at him. "How did things get so fucked up, Charles? Look at us. We were so in love once. We talked. We shared. We planned." Her eyes searched his face for answers she wasn't sure he could give, any more than she could.

Charles crossed the kitchen floor and leaned against the wooden counter. He folded his arms, feeling uncomfortable, and slowly shook his head. "It's easy to say it was the other person's fault, it was this, it was that." He heaved a deep sigh. "The truth is, it was nothing."

"What are you saying?" she asked, perplexed.

"What went wrong between us, Toni, was our apathy to what was right in front of us. Seeing things and not dealing with them. Feeling things and not talking about it. Turning our backs and pretending our problems would go away. It was as if we thought things would fix themselves if we left them alone, ignored them."

"Maybe you're right, Charles, but I think we have a chance now to do what we should have done a long time ago. I don't want to turn my back on this, on us. I want to try to work things out. If we can. What we have is worth saving."

He looked at her for a long moment. "I don't know, Toni. I really don't. Too much has happened. And I need some time and some space to work it all out in my head. Like I said, when this thing is over with Steven, I'm moving out." He lowered his head a moment, then looked back up at her with deep sadness in his eyes. "Then we'll see what happens."

Toni sucked in air wearily, and her lips trembled as she struggled not to cry. Her options were limited. At least he was thinking about salvaging their marriage, at least thinking about it. She nodded in weak agreement.

"Do you want me to drive you over to the hospital?"

It would be so easy, so typical of her to run out with the intention of making things better for Victoria and Phillip, to offer her insight, her expertise. Maybe Victoria could use her support, some words of comfort. But it was time she dealt with her own issues first. And she needed Charles to see that their marriage was a priority, too.

She sniffed, then straightened in her seat. "Phillip is there. He said she was stable and resting. I can go in the morning if need be."

Charles's eyes flickered for a moment, registering his surprise.

"I thought . . . maybe we could . . . talk some more, figure some things out." She stared at him with hope in her eyes.

Charles glanced away, almost swayed by the soft note of her voice. Then he turned to his wife. "No promises, Toni."

Her heart surged for a moment, then settled. "No promises," she whispered in response.

Regina and Parker took his car and headed to the hospital. He'd totally ignored her insistence that she could go alone.

"What kind of man would I be to let you go running off alone at night, knowing that you're upset, and not offer to go with you? I don't mind, and you're not imposing on me. Okay?" He looked down into her eyes.

"You don't have to do everything alone, Regina. I realize we haven't known each other long. But . . . well, I can't explain it and I'm not going to try," he said, suddenly flustered. "Let's just go, all right? No strings."

Reluctantly she'd finally agreed, but deep down inside she was touched by his act of kindness. And she drank it in like someone who'd been deprived of needed water.

"How long have you two been friends?" Parker asked after about fifteen minutes of riding in silence.

"I met them in college, during a seminar, actually. We were majoring in different subjects, but we'd attended a presentation from the president of the NAACP. The three of us have been friends since then. Antoinette Devon is the other. She was there, too. We call her Toni."

"Are these the same friends you were talking about who didn't think the store would open?"

"Mm-hmm."

"Interesting friends." He hoisted an eyebrow in curiosity.

"Things have been a bit strained between us lately — to put it mildly."

"It happens sometimes," he said. "I'm

sure everything will eventually work out. This Victoria must think enough of you to ask you to come to the hospital."

"You'd be surprised what she thinks of me," she said with a slight edge of sarcasm in her voice. "Toni, too, for that matter."

Parker's brow wrinkled. "Is there something about you that I should know?" he asked in a teasing tone.

Regina gave a half smile. "It's not a very nice picture."

"This may sound like a stupid question, but why are you friends with them, if that's the case?"

"I've asked myself that question more times than I can count over the years. I guess we each give the other something the others need. I was always the one who listened, and Toni always needed to talk. Victoria needed people who didn't have what she did, so that she could remind them of it. Toni and I fit the bill. We sort of fell into being friends, getting together once a month to hang out, chatting on the phone, swapping stories. It became routine."

"But what did you get out of it?"

"I suppose I was a little fascinated with both of them, to tell you the truth. They're so different from me."

"How?"

She was thoughtful for a moment. "Well, Toni is a tiny little thing, full of energy and bright ideas. She's a social worker, very driven, very opinionated. She has a solution for everything. But underneath all of the hurrah, she has a good heart. It just takes a while to find it. Victoria . . . hmm, what can I say? Victoria Hunter is the definition of 'moving on up.' There is a part of her that feels she has to prove something to the world, be accepted, be recognized. She always reminded me of a hurt little girl who needed someone to put a Band-Aid on her wounds. I guess we're all like that in a way. Wanting to be a part of something, but hoping no one sees our flaws."

"Where did you fit in?"

"Don't know if I ever did. I was always the quiet one. The one who just went along with the program. I never asserted myself with them. Toni and Vicky were always outspoken about their feelings; at least it seemed that way. But until the night I kind of lost it, and told them just what they could do with their opinions and criticisms, did I realize we didn't know each other at all."

She gave him an abbreviated version of what had transpired the evening at the Shark Bar and all that led up to it. She

364

briefly touched on their sudden reappearance in her life, their sudden vulnerability, without telling him all of the gory details.

Then she found herself telling him about her childhood, her insecurities and her mother's expectations of her, her marriage to Russell and how unfulfilled she felt. She talked of her dreams and her fears, of feeling alone, but determined to succeed despite all the views to the contrary.

It was so easy talking to Parker. He didn't censure or try to override her thoughts and opinions with his own. And suddenly she realized that this was truly the first time in her life that someone actually listened to her, paid attention to what she said and didn't think that her feelings, her desires, were silly. The experience was so new, so exhilarating, it brought a lump to her throat.

"You're quite an incredible woman, Regina. It's too bad that no one has recognized it before. It's their loss, you know."

She turned to look at him at the same instant he turned to her. Their eyes met and the contact was made. They both felt it. A slow smile spread across his mouth.

"I'm glad I met you, Regina Everette."

"My friends call me Gina," she said softly, feeling warm and tingly inside.

"I'll remember that . . . Gina."

Parker pulled into the lot of Memorial Hospital, a large, sprawling Greco-Roman structure, and they walked together to the entrance.

"I'll wait down here," Parker said when they entered the lobby. "Take whatever time you need. I'll be here."

"Thanks."

"I hope your friend finally realizes the kind of friend she has."

Regina smiled tightly, turned, and headed for the bank of elevators. He watched her standing there among the others, weighing the possibility of a long relationship of some kind with her. And he wasn't sure if he could do it.

# CHAPTER TWENTY-FOUR

Phillip sat in the standard, hospital-issue hard-backed chair at the side of Victoria's bed, holding her hand. He'd never been so terrified in his life as when he saw her lying there on the floor. Hooked to an IV, she seemed so helpless, so frail.

His heart sank to his stomach as hundreds of unspeakable thoughts raced through his mind. His only coherent thought was that he didn't want to lose her; he couldn't. His own life wouldn't be worth living if he did. He needed her to complete him.

All during the ride in the ambulance to the hospital, he prayed, and swore to her that she would be all right. He made promises to God; most of them he knew he'd be unable to keep. Anything to keep her with him.

When she finally spoke, her first words were, "The baby."

"Don't worry about the baby, sweetheart," he said calmly. "You're my only concern. That's all."

She squeezed his hand then, only once, then pulled him to her with a strength that stunned him. "I . . . I don't want to lose this baby, Phil. I can't." Tears streamed from the corners of her eyes.

At that moment, everything inside him seemed to open and give way, and he became filled with an incredible joy. Gently he brushed his mouth against hers.

As he watched her now, sleeping, breathing in that quiet, cool way that always comforted him, he realized that whatever sacrifices he'd made, whatever he'd given up for Victoria, had been worth it. And whatever demons haunted her, they'd battle them together. When this was over, when she was well and strong again, they would talk, really talk.

"Phillip."

He turned toward the soft whisper. Regina was standing expectantly in the doorway. He stood as she walked in, her eyes trained on Victoria.

"How is she?" Regina whispered, afraid of waking her, afraid of the answer.

"The doctors said she has a slight concussion from the fall. They said if she doesn't go into labor within the next twenty-four hours that the baby's chances are good."

Regina breathed a small sigh of relief. "How are you?" She touched his shoulder and looked into the fear that simmered in his dark blue eyes. Phillip was a handsome man by anyone's standards. He had the good looks and bearing of a model. What was most alluring about Phillip Hunter was his easy manner, his sincerity and genuine warmth. He had a way of making everyone who came into his presence feel important and welcome. Barring all the other obstacles that he and Victoria might have to endure, he was the perfect man for her, the ideal partner.

"I'm better. I think," he added with a weak smile. He ran his hands through his dark hair. "I don't know what I would do if something happened to her, Regina."

"She's going to be fine."

"Gina," Victoria called hoarsely.

Regina moved within Victoria's range of sight and gently took her hand. "Hey, girl. How ya feeling?"

"Sore, drowsy. My head is killing me."

"I came as soon as I could."

"I knew you would. I need to talk to you. I didn't want to wait."

Regina leaned closer. Her pulse raced. "What is it?"

"I wanted to tell you . . . how sorry I was, Gina, about everything. The things I said. And even after all I'd done, you were still there for me. I always just took it for granted that you would be. Took you for granted, and I'm sorry."

"Forget it, okay?"

"I decided to keep the baby," she said softly.

Regina smiled. "I'm glad. I think you made the right decision," she said, even as she thought about what the doctors told Phillip and wondered if Victoria knew of their cautious prognosis.

Victoria glanced toward her husband, who was standing on the opposite side of the glass window. "So do I. There are still a lot of issues that I need to face, but I can't sacrifice a child because of them." She smiled and pressed her hand tenderly to her stomach. "I'm going to have to deal with them if I'm going to be a mom."

Regina laughed and shook her head. "Imagine that!" She stroked Victoria's hand. "What made you change your mind?"

Victoria closed her eyes for a moment and sighed deeply. "Finally realizing how much I was cared about. Especially by my husband . . . and my friends. If I'm cared about that much, then maybe I'm worth it, you know? The only person who didn't believe it was me. I guess it began to hit home when I didn't go to that doctor's appointment. Then the baby shower. But when I woke up in the ambulance and realized just how easily life can be changed in an instant, I thought that if I got a second chance I wasn't going to blow it."

"Sometimes a good knock on the head will help you see daylight," she teased.

"It was a long time coming. And you were a part of it, Gina. That's what I wanted you to know. I swore I hated you that night at the club. I thought, How dare she talk to me like that? Who does she think she is? But you know, as much as I didn't want to admit it, you made me start thinking about things, looking at myself. Something I didn't want to do. Something I'd avoided doing for a long time."

She told her about the baby shower and the conversations of the staff, how she'd felt overwhelmed by it all and had come home early. And when she did, all she could think about was making Phillip happy and understanding fully, for the first time, all that he'd given up because of his love for her.

"How could I not give him that love in return?"

"You had to find a way to love yourself first, Vicky. Just like I did. I had to make up my mind that I wasn't going to be held in place by other people's opinions of me. I still have flashbacks from time to time," she admitted with a smile. "But I'm learning how to deal with it. Some days are easier than others. It's going to take work to undo forty years of believing I was less-than. But I'm hopeful. Listen, I'm going to let you get some rest. I know Phillip must be itching to get back in here with you."

"Thanks for coming. I mean that. And for the advice."

Regina nodded, then leaned down and kissed Victoria's cool cheek. "Rest."

"I will." Victoria's voice came as a tired rasp.

Regina turned and walked out, stopping briefly to talk with Phillip, then went down to meet Parker, feeling strangely at peace.

Parker was dozing in a lounge chair when she returned. For a moment she stood there and watched him, feeling comforted and secure. True, they hadn't known each other long, but on so many levels they connected. There was something about him that fed the hope and optimism in her, two qualities often stifled by her strong sense of inferiority. She was never one to believe in that "first sight" thing, but this was different. She breathed deeply. Parker Heywood seemed like a decent man, a sensitive man, someone she could bring into her life.

The thing that struck her the most was that he actually respected her — her opinions and her decisions. At the very least she would feel good to just have him as a friend.

It had been twenty years since she'd been involved with anyone other than Russell. She didn't even know the rules of the game anymore. There were still wounds inside her that needed healing, empty spaces, still some doubts about herself and the urgent need to discover who she really was. Until she could figure all that out, she wasn't sure if she was ready for anything more than friendship. But looking at him, having been in his company, feeling his sincerity, his energy, coming so close to having his mouth against hers, the surge she'd felt whenever in his presence, led her to believe that maybe it would be a lot easier than she thought to yield to this growing feeling inside her, whatever it was.

It was almost as if he were reading her

mind. Slowly his eyes flickered open, and he smiled when he saw her. He stretched his neck, swept his locks away from his face, and stood.

"Hey, guess I was more tired than I thought. How's your friend?"

Regina crossed the space to stand beside him. "I think she'll be all right, no matter which way things turn out."

He looked at her quizzically for a moment.

"I'll tell you all about it one day. Ready?"

"Sure. Let's get you home." He put his arm around her shoulders, and she allowed herself to feel good about it.

More than an hour later, they reluctantly pulled up in front of Regina's house. It was after one in the morning, but neither of them was tired. All during the ride home, they entertained each other with anecdotes about their lives. Regina had him in stitches with her accounts of the nuns during her elementary school days and the wicked punishments they would inflict in the name of preparing her for heaven. She told him of some of her more harrowing adventures as a crime reporter, the drug busts, the political scandals, the gangland rubouts, and some of the seedy places she entered during investigations. How she never became afraid until after the risky assignments were over. How she often threw caution to the wind to pursue a potential lead. But there were rewards as well. Like when she unmasked a slumlord who'd been ripping off his tenants and not providing services. He'd been brought up on charges, the building was eventually condemned, but all of the tenants were relocated to better housing. Some of them still sent her a card during the holidays, she'd said.

Parker enthralled her with tales of the African jungle, the wilds of Uganda, and the savagery of the mayhem in Rwanda, all juxtaposed against the majesty and splendor of some of its modern cities, like Accra and Dar es Salaam — even post-apartheid Johannesburg. He then talked briefly and painfully, she could tell, of his daughter and how much he missed her, how much he wished he were a part of her life. She could tell he spoke from the heart and was not trying to impress her. It was in his eyes as well as his voice — that tear of emotion that was sometimes heard in the wail of blues singers.

And then there was his art. He confessed, almost shyly, that his sole source of solace had been his painting. "I don't know what I would have done if I didn't have my work," he'd said. "It kept me alive. I date occasionally," he admitted. "But to tell you the truth, I haven't thought of really getting serious with anyone again. I've never felt like I was up to it."

"Why?" she asked cautiously, guessing that his reasons were similar to hers — old wounds.

He sighed. "I just feel like if I failed once at something I put my entire being into, what's to say I won't fail again? Maybe what I have to give isn't good enough. I don't think I could bring that into another relationship — take that kind of chance again."

Regina didn't know what to say to that one. *Who knows, maybe he's right.* And she certainly wasn't the one to try to remake someone. She had enough of a load trying to get her own head together. But a part of her couldn't believe that Parker didn't have anything to offer. She knew the kind of damage another person's insensitivity could cause another, the untold emotional and psychological toll it could inflict. But she also knew that the only one who could overcome all that was the injured person. They must want to change, make themselves better. She was the perfect example of that, and she still had a long way to go. She believed Parker had plenty to offer; he'd showed her as much from the moment they met. It was like he'd told her earlier, *It's their loss.*

"Why did you decide on a bookstore?" Parker asked, switching the direction of the conversation.

She laughed lightly. "Every time I walked into one, since I was a little girl, I was fascinated by them. I still am. I did an article once on the rise and fall of the black independent bookstores. From the late seventies into the late eighties they thrived, but then the superstores emerged, slowly swallowing them up one by one. And as they did, they began to swallow up a part of our culture as well. They don't generally carry some of the lesser-known writers of black literature. Our work is generally relegated to a tiny section in the back of their stores and that's it. Nor do they have the personal, earthy touch of the smaller stores. I walk into some of those black bookstores and feel right at home."

Parker nodded in agreement. "I know what you mean. One week they're there;

the next they're gone."

"And for the most part, they can't compete with the big stores in terms of the amount of books they can order, so more and more the publishers ignore them because they're looking for big numbers."

"Part of their demise is our fault, too," Parker added. "We, as black people, don't support our own the way we should. We'd rather go to the mall and get that little dollar off of a book, and then wonder, "What happened to that black bookstore that used to be on this block?" he said in a mocking tone.

Regina laughed. "That's right. So I decided that if I ever went into business for myself, that's what I'd do. But I would add some of the things that the chains offer, a little café, seating for customers so they can browse. Stuff like that."

He turned to her for a moment, studied her profile. "I think that's part of the reason," he said in a gentle probe. "But not all of it."

Regina stared out the window. "Maybe I'll tell you about that one day, too."

"I think you will." He pulled his Jeep into a parking space and shut off the engine. "Thank you," he said softly.

"For what?"

"For letting me be a part of your day, letting me into your life like this. It means a lot."

"I . . . I'm glad you were a part of it, too."

They sat in a momentarily awkward silence, neither knowing what to do next.

"Well, uh . . ." They both spoke at once.

"You first," Parker said.

"Uh, I had a great time being with you . . . and I uh, look forward to seeing you again." Hey, she'd stepped out there and said it. Now what? She concentrated quietly on her fingers.

"So did I. And as long as you want to, I'd like to see you again. Un-work related."

Regina swallowed to relieve the sudden dryness in her throat. Then she dared to look at him and her heart nearly stopped.

"The last time we were here, we got cut off. How 'bout we pick up where we left off?" He angled his body and slid closer, then reached across the seat and eased her to him until his mouth was inches away from hers.

She could feel her body tremble all over when she felt the warmth of his lips touch hers, slow and sensual, tender and strong all at once.

All too soon he eased back and gazed

into her eyes. "Good night, Gina," he said with an undeniable huskiness in his voice.

"Good night," she said softly, and quickly got out of the car before she made a fool of herself. *Quick, into the house.*

The instant she set foot in the door, before she had a moment to think about what just transpired, Michele and Darren were all over her.

"Ma, who was that you were with earlier?" Michele wanted to know. "Who's the man?"

"Are you seeing that dude?" Darren jumped in, sounding suddenly proprietary.

Regina brushed past the both of them and put her bag down. "Just a friend. His name is Parker, okay?"

"Well, Dad called while you were gone," Michele stated in a tone too grown-up for her age. "He said he was coming by tomorrow. He wants to talk to you. It sounds important."

Regina squeezed her eyes shut. *It's always something.*

# CHAPTER TWENTY-FIVE

Russell spent the better part of his night walking the floor of his three-bedroom town house in Montclair, New Jersey. After calling Regina and discovering that she was out with another man, even if it was on some mercy mission, it awakened emotions in him he was sure were dead — jealousy and ownership. He didn't think he was still capable of feeling those things toward Regina. After all, it had been three years since their divorce. They'd both moved on with their lives. Sure, he'd had other women since then, some relationships lasting longer than others. But none that ever made him want to settle down again.

Still, in his mind, he never envisioned Regina with anyone else. Never. He knew it was irrational. She was human, still pretty, even more so now than before. And as ridiculous as it was, to him, she would always be his wife. No matter what any judge or piece of paper said.

And with those crazy thoughts tumbling

around in his head, he sat in front of her house, trying to figure out how to tell her that he wanted her back, that he still loved her.

He opened his car door, stepped out, and checked the security alarm to his Lexus with his remote, then stopped in midstep. What if that guy she was with last night was still there? Anger boiled in his stomach. Would she bring another man into the house and let him spend the night? With his children there? Had she done it before? Was some other man playing daddy to his kids?

He'd wanted to quiz Michele last night when she'd told him that Regina wasn't home. But it was unfair to put his daughter in that type of situation.

He should have called first to make sure it was all right, he thought as he walked up the front steps. But hell, he was here now. He rang the bell and waited.

Moments later Regina appeared at the door.

"Hello, Russell. You should have called first," she said, sleepily.

"Is this a bad time?" He felt his temper rising.

Regina rubbed her eyes and yawned. "You're here now, Russell. Come on up."

She turned and started up the stairs. "The kids are looking forward to seeing you."

"What about you?"

She almost tripped. "Excuse me?"

"Nothing," he mumbled.

She opened the door to the apartment and walked inside, knowing she couldn't have heard right.

"Michele! Darren! Your father is here. Have a seat in the living room. I'm going to get dressed."

"You look fine the way you are."

She looked at him from beneath her lashes, her brows raised in disbelief. She shook her head and disappeared into her bedroom, having a good mind not to come back out until he'd gone.

Whatever was on Russell's mind, she didn't want to know about it, she thought, stepping into the comforting spray of the shower. She wasn't sure where this change in attitude was coming from, but it was unnerving. Yes, something was up. Whenever he was nice to her, there was usually a big surprise around the corner. That behavior happened too often for her to be so easily fooled. She was accustomed to the barking, domineering Russell Everette. She knew how to deal with that side of him — just stay out of his way and do whatever he asked to keep the peace. But this Russell was too much like the charming man she'd met and married, the one who suddenly changed into someone she could no longer live with if she was to retain any sense of herself.

She wasn't sure what he was up to, and the first thought that came into her head was her mother. Millie was not above convincing Russell to sweet-talk her into giving up and giving in. She had no intention of doing either. She hadn't forgotten Russell's bold threat to take the kids away. He was not a man given to idle threats, so this sudden turnaround was certainly suspect.

Regina let the warm water slide across her body. She closed her eyes and raised her face to the water, and an image of Parker bloomed behind her closed lids. There were some issues there, she was pretty sure of it. But overall, she couldn't deny the wonderful feelings she was having about him, even though his words and actions were in conflict with each other. On the one hand, he said he wanted to see her again. He kissed her like he meant it. Then on the other hand, he said he wasn't particularly keen on getting involved with anyone because he didn't feel as if he was up to the task.

She shut off the water and stepped out of the shower. What did it all really mean? she wondered, wiping off with a peach-colored towel. She supposed the same could be said of her. She wasn't too sure about involvement either. But if she had to be uncertain with anyone, she'd like to test the waters with Parker. They could be uncertain together, and maybe, just maybe, they could help each other move beyond the old hurts that held them in place, preventing them from moving on to a better life.

When she reappeared in the kitchen, she was stunned to find Russell at the stove fixing a late breakfast.

She cocked her head to the side and put her hands on her hips. "What are you doing?"

"I figured by the time everyone was up and about they'd be hungry." He smiled that charming smile of his. "I know I am." He whipped the eggs into a mixing bowl, sprinkled some ground cinnamon, and dipped a piece of white bread in the mixture for some homemade French toast. It smelled truly delicious.

He went to the refrigerator and opened it, rooted around for a minute, and pulled out an unopened package of bacon.

Regina's mouth fell open. She shook her head. Maybe she was still asleep and was dreaming. If she didn't know better, she'd swear the man standing in front of her was the same man who used to love to fix Sunday breakfast — the only meal he could really cook — bring it to her in bed. But that was way back when in the early days of their marriage, when the kids were still toddlers. This was now. Her defenses went into high gear.

She marched across the kitchen and took the pound of bacon out of his hands. "I can do this, thank you."

"I just wanted to help. I figured since you were out so late last night, you'd still be tired," he hedged.

She glanced up at him, seeing the question behind the cool control of his innocuous expression. "Is that what this is all about? You're being sweet and attentive because you really want to know where I was last night — better yet, who I was with? If that's the case, why don't you simply ask me, Russell?"

He smiled coldly. "All right, I will. Who *were* you with last night?"

"None of your business. When was the last time I asked you who you were with? Never."

This wasn't going right. This wasn't the way he had it pictured in his mind. He didn't want to ease into the old patterns of interaction, leading to a big blowup. If only he could get things to return to some level of normalcy so they could talk to each other like human beings, without the bickering and arguing. If only.

"You have a lot of nerve, Russell. I don't see you for nearly two years. When you call, on those rare occasions, you're barely civil to me. You turn up out of the blue on my doorstep, threaten to take the kids away one day, and the next you're offering your assistance with the business. What am I supposed to think?"

"That I've been an idiot, Regina. An idiot for letting you go, and an idiot for taking so long to realize what a mistake I've made."

She was dumbfounded. Words escaped her. She couldn't look at him, because if she did she was afraid she might see sincerity in his eyes, and if that happened, she knew she couldn't handle it. Not now, not after all this time. She'd said all the holy words over her marriage a long time ago, done her absolution, and buried it. She ripped open the package of bacon and started lining the strips up in the frying pan. Her hands were shaking.

Russell came up behind her and placed his hands on her shoulders. Her entire body tensed. "When you left me, Regina, I was so blinded by hurt and anger, I couldn't think," he said softly. "I wouldn't allow myself to see how any of it was my fault. As far as I was concerned, I was the injured party."

"Russell, please . . . don't . . . not now," she pleaded. Her voice trembled.

"Shhh, please hear me out. All I wanted to do was hurt you as much as your leaving hurt me. So I stayed away. I wanted you to see how much you needed me. To feel as alone as I did. I just knew you would come back. But you didn't. So I tried to move on with my life. And the longer I stayed away, the easier it was for me to stay angry, not face the truth." He slowly turned her around to give her the full effect of the pain and yearning present in his eyes. He had rehearsed this speech so long in his mind, and he was determined not to mess it up.

She looked up into his eyes, trying to weigh the integrity of his words. Should there be a false note anywhere, she wanted to match that error with the expression. Calmly she stepped back and let him speak.

"The truth is . . . I've never stopped loving you. I know what a bastard I was to you, but it was because I was so afraid of losing you."

"Losing me? I loved you, Russell. The first and only man I've ever loved. All I wanted was for you to love me back, to protect me, and make me feel safe. To keep someone, Russell, you treat them like a human being," she said, the old wounds peeling open. "That means respecting them, respecting their opinions, respecting their choices. You didn't do that. It seemed that you were determined to make me feel small, make me feel worthless. You knew my issues, my weaknesses, and you took them and used them against me."

He dropped his head like a sinner in need of redemption. "I know, I know. But I'd never do that again if you'd give me another chance. I know what I did wrong and I can change."

"Do you really know what you did wrong? Do you know what you did to me?"

"Yes, yes, yes." Russell said the words as if she were actually striking him. He felt the potency of her every word, and the truth of them was not lost on him.

"Russell, I waited a long time for you to change," she added. "But you didn't. If anything you became worse; you hurt me over and over."

"You know I love those kids, love them with all my heart," he said, switching gears as he felt himself losing ground. "I'd do anything to have them and you back in my life. They're a part of me, too, and it's killing me that we can't all be together. Sometimes it takes every bit of my strength just to get through the day, knowing that I'll finish my evening without you all in it. Do you have any idea what that feels like?"

"Russell, I waited, waited, and waited for you to wake up. I gave you everything I had until there was almost nothing left of me. I had to save myself — from myself and from you. I've changed."

"I know you have. You're the woman I always knew you could be," he said, surprised by his admission. "The woman I was afraid you'd become — strong and independent and not needing me."

For a moment, seeing him there, listening to his words, letting them creep past the barriers, the resistance, she almost weakened under the onslaught. The memories, though distant, were sweet — but rare. She remembered the smiles, the gentle touches, the tiny gifts, the love-making, the weight of carrying his children

— the Sunday-morning breakfasts. But it wasn't enough. Not now. And the tragedy of it all was that it could have been.

"The time for us is past, Russell," she said softly but firmly. "I have changed, and maybe you have as well. I hope so, for Michele and Darren's sake. But I can't go back. I won't. And all the talk, the promises . . . they're too late. This is a conversation we should have had years ago, Russ."

"Regina, please, just listen. . . ."

She couldn't stand there a moment longer, not with her insides in a spin and memories running through her mind, tempting her like candy behind a glass counter. She drew in a breath of resolve. "I have some errands to run. The kids should be out soon." She touched his cheek. "Spend some time with them. *They* need you. And if you have changed like you said you have, that's your first step to proving it to them — and to yourself."

She took her keys from the counter and walked out, quietly shutting the door behind her. When she reached the foot of the stairs, she stopped with her hand on the doorknob, and her body trembled as tears ran from her eyes. She was finally free.

# CHAPTER TWENTY-SIX

Toni, Charles, and Steven returned from Steven's first of many court appearances. They didn't talk much on the ride home, and the high tension and anxiety of the morning's proceedings left them drained and irritated. The impersonal approach to justice forced them to view the plight of Steven in a new way, only adding to the fears and doubts that the judicial system was less concerned with finding the truth of the matter than getting another black boy off the streets and behind bars.

"I have a client to pick up in a couple of hours," Charles stated, pulling off his jacket and tossing it on the chaise longue in their bedroom.

Toni rotated her stiff neck. "The lawyer said he can probably get Steven off with probation."

"Yeah, but we'll have to go back to court a few more times before everything is settled."

And then he would be gone, Toni

thought, a heavy sadness settling in her chest like an iron weight. She sat on the edge of the bed, watching her husband change into his chauffeur's uniform, feeling totally lost and vulnerable. He was a good man, she thought. A decent, easygoing, hardworking man. Many women would love to have a man like Charles. And she'd been such a fool to try to change who he was.

"Will you be back later?" she asked tentatively, afraid now that every time he stepped out of the door would be the last time she'd see him.

He stopped dressing and turned to her, saw the fear haunting her eyes, and the hardness around his heart momentarily softened. "Yeah. I'll be back."

"I'll fix dinner."

Charles nodded and turned away, took his tie and jacket and walked out.

Left alone, Toni wondered where her life would go from here. Victoria was ecstatic about her baby and seemingly happy and secure in her marriage. Regina was a hot minute away from opening her bookstore and embarking on a new relationship, according to her. And where was she? She had to be realistic and accept the fact that her life might very well be without Charles in it. And if that were the case, she needed to seriously consider what she would do when that time came.

"I just want you to rest," Phillip insisted, tucking Victoria into their king-size bed. He'd taken a week off from work to look after her, and he didn't intend for her to move one muscle more than necessary. It was his intention not to let her do anything that might jeopardize her health or the baby's.

"But I'm all right, Phil," she said with a smile of delight. "The doctors said I'm fine and the baby is fine." She really was enjoying the royal treatment.

"I know what they said." He sat on the bed next to her. "But let me do this for you. I want to. I want to pamper you, remind you how much you mean to me so you'll never doubt it again."

"I don't," she whispered, stroking his cheek.

"I know this was a big decision for you . . . deciding to have the baby."

"I'm so sorry for putting you through such hell about it. But . . . I was scared and so unsure of myself. It had nothing to do with you. I just didn't think I could be a good mother."

"But why, baby? Help me to understand."

Victoria took a breath. "It's so hard to explain."

"Try."

"I've never really thought very much of myself. I always felt like an outsider, ugly, too dark. But I tried to make up for it by excelling at everything. Having the best clothes, the best job, the best house . . . and you."

"Because I'm white, right?" he said without rancor.

She lowered her gaze. "Yes." She saw him flinch and she ached inside.

"What did that mean to you, Vicky?" His voice sounded hollow.

"It meant that I'd made it, you know. That I had something that was denied me."

"Do you love me, Victoria? I mean really love me?" It was important for him to hear the words, for him to know he was more than a trophy.

"Yes," she said without hesitation. "I do."

Slowly he nodded. "It's going to take more than love, Victoria. Right now you feel vulnerable, so do I, and it's easy to say all the right things. But this is a turning point in our marriage. This baby isn't the answer to the questions you still have about yourself. It's only a step in that direction."

Her heart tumbled over. "What are you saying?"

"We have a hell of a lot of work cut out for us if we're going to make this work, as a couple and as parents. A baby can't undo all those years of feeling the way you do about yourself, or about me. I think we need counseling, not just you, but both of us."

Victoria stiffened. "Counseling? We can do this on our own. We don't need someone else telling us how we feel." Opening herself, showing that part of her that was so damaged was not something she was sure she could do, or if she wanted to. Wasn't her confession of love enough? Wasn't her commitment to have this baby enough?

"I've never asked you for much, Victoria. But I'm asking you to save our marriage. And if it's as important to you as it is to me, you'll do this one thing." He leaned over and kissed her forehead, then left her alone with her thoughts.

"You're the artist," Regina said to

Parker, as she scanned the walls of the store. "Where do you think the paintings should go?"

"Maybe one or two in the café area, just for some added flavor," he joked. "Then set a few up on the walls between the bookshelves and two over the checkout counter."

"Sounds good to me." She pushed out a breath and smiled. "It's really coming together, Parker. In three days I'll have my grand opening. I still can't believe it."

"You should really be proud. You pulled it off. Pretty much by yourself."

"Yes, I did. Didn't I? But you've been a big help, too. And surprisingly, so have the kids, this past week. They both offered to work after school until I get someone in here full-time. So that's a relief."

"Maybe that will give me a chance to get to know them better. Since I plan to be around, too."

She stopped stacking greeting cards in a spinning rack and looked at him. "Do you really?"

"Yes, I do." He sat on an unopened box of books. "I've been doing a lot of thinking, Regina, from the moment we met. I still don't know how good I am at being in a relationship. I know I should let go of the past and move on with my life. But it's not that easy. At least for me."

"Are you still in love with your wife, Lynn?"

He slowly shook his head no, then continued talking in a hushed voice. "I wish it was that simple to explain. At least then it would make sense."

She rested her hip against the glass counter, watching the weight of his confession cause his body to sag for a moment. "Then what is it?"

He frowned in thought, thinking back on what his life had been. "When you've put as much time and effort as I did into a marriage, then watch it fall apart despite all your efforts to salvage it — from counseling, to taking on an extra job to make more money, to giving her everything she asked for — it does something to you. Then, to have your child taken away. I still haven't recovered from it, Regina. And that's being honest. There's this fear inside me that makes me believe that if I failed that miserably once, what's to say I won't again. Lynn just stopped loving me, if she ever did. How can I come into your life, your children's lives, with that kind of baggage — no matter what my good intentions may be?"

There it was again, she thought, that old, "there's always something" lurking in the background to muddy up the works. *Baggage? We all have baggage, no matter who we are, and that should never stop you from moving ahead with your life.*

She sighed deeply. *Change doesn't come without sacrifice.* And the sacrifice for both of them was letting go of the past, the people they once were, and opening their hearts to all the possibilities of what could be.

"Parker," she said thoughtfully, "If I could, I would go back and do so many of the things in my life over again. I think a lot of people would, but we can't. When I decided to leave my husband, then my job, and cut off my friends and family, I knew I was taking the chance of a lifetime. But I did it anyway. I wanted something to call my own, something of my making, not anyone else's. My creation. Opening this store wasn't some quirky business venture on my part; it was my ticket to freedom — shedding my past, going against everything that I've ever been told or led to believe about myself. At some point you're going to have to do the same thing — make that decision to let go."

He looked at her for a long moment,

taking in her serenity, but mostly the inner strength that radiated from her in warm waves. He could easily see how she could be underestimated by her friends and family. Regina wasn't one to boast, to run to the head of the pack and shout, "Here I am." Her actions and her opinions were displayed with a quiet dignity that could easily be mistaken for ineffectuality.

She was challenging him to take a chance on himself, he suddenly realized. Challenging him without throwing down the gauntlet. It was subtle, just beneath the surface — just like Regina, right there in your face without being obtrusive.

"What if you're right about this?" He stood and moved toward her. "What if you're absolutely right, that if I take that leap, I might just find myself on the other side. What are you going to do then when I land right in front of you?"

"We won't know until you get there."

"No promises," he said.

"No strings," she answered, satisfied that she'd finally decided to take another chance — in whatever form it would take.

# CHAPTER TWENTY-SEVEN

A steady stream of people arrived for the opening of Regina's Place after she unlocked the doors at noon. Regina was exhilarated by the turnout but was somewhat exhausted from last-minute work to guarantee everything would be ready for the guests. There had been so much to do, yet she'd pulled it off. Michele and Darren helped to direct customers, offered suggestions for purchases, and even worked the cash register, which took some of the load off her. All their hard work during the past two weeks, handing out flyers and posting notices about the opening, had truly paid off. Whatever skepticism remained about their mother's decision was soon erased.

"This is really great, Ma," Michele had whispered in a conspiratorial tone to her mother, as she looked around at the men, women, and children who browsed the aisles of books. Several of the new book buyers sat comfortably reading on the overstuffed chairs and ottomans that dotted the floor space.

"Yes, it is." Regina sighed with pleasure. "It really is."

"I'm sorry I gave you such a hard time. Darren is, too."

"I'm just happy everything worked out — for everybody. But I'll still need your help for a while until things get settled."

"No problem. Maybe I can get one of my friends to come with me after school or on Saturdays. We can shelve the new books."

Regina smiled, then hugged her daughter tightly against her chest. "I'd like that a lot, sweetie, I really would."

Since it was the only bookstore in the immediate area, everyone, upon entering, commented not only on its exquisite layout and the variety of the stock, but the fact that it was the one business in the thriving commercial district that was long overdue. The last black bookstore in the community closed more than five years ago.

Regina could hardly contain her excitement with the overwhelming success of her first day. Periodically she snatched glances at Parker, who immediately charmed every customer within earshot. Whenever he'd catch her looking at him, he'd throw her a wink or blow an imaginary kiss and she'd feel herself get that tingly feeling all over again. He'd sold three of his paintings, right on the spot, and had taken orders for several of his prints.

Once the store was on solid footing, she planned to open the café in the evenings for after-work gatherings, author signings, and poetry readings.

Toni showed up late in the day with a shopping bag that she quickly filled with books and CDs. As Regina tallied up her purchases, she noted that many of Toni's selections were books on relationships, re-pairing marriage after infidelity, and advice for parents whose kids have been in trouble. There was no need to comment, but it was clear that Toni had finally re-alized that maybe she didn't have all the answers, especially when the trouble was so close to home. It was a first step, Regina thought, hopeful that things would work out for her friend. Because for all of Toni's faults, she was a good woman at heart, a decent person who'd simply lost her way. All of her intentions for her family, herself, and her friends had been well-meant — though often misguided by her own zeal for what she thought was best for everyone else. Unfortunately, her miscues had cost her greatly.

"I was planning to stop by and see Victoria when I closed up," Regina said, handing Toni her bulging package.

"I'd like to come, too. Charles and Steven are out for the evening . . . so there's no real reason for me to rush back." She tried to sound nonchalant, but Regina could hear the hurt in her voice. "And I'd like to see Victoria anyway," she added.

"How are things between you and Charles?"

Toni sighed. "He said once the court thing is settled with Steven he was leaving."

"Oh, Toni, I'm so sorry."

"So am I. But I've come to accept it. I plan to work real hard on myself while he's gone. He said he's open to talking, but he needs some space to clear his head. Maybe he'll find it in his heart to forgive me, and eventually come back home. If he doesn't, I'll just have to accept that. I've been thinking of going home for a while. For real this time. I need to more than ever."

"You'll work it out. You always do. Just hang in there, girl. And you know I'm always there for you if you want to talk."

"I know. I only wish I'd realized it sooner. Live and learn."

Regina patted her hand and nodded.

"Well, I hope to be out of here by eight. In the meantime, let me introduce you to someone . . . special."

Regina took Toni to meet Parker and they hit it off immediately. Toni, being an art buff, was in her element as they swapped opinions on some of the new contemporary artists hitting the scene, including the exhibit of West African masks and sculptures opening at the Whitney. The pair became locked in a vigorous debate over the European and jazz influences in the work of Jean Michel Basquiat and whether the former Haitian graffiti artist had been exploited by that master hustler, Andy Warhol. The friendly exchange ended in a draw, with both art lovers agreeing to go museum hopping one weekend. With Regina, of course.

Toni returned from her conversation with Parker. She leaned over the counter and put her face close to that of her friend, whispering, "Girl, you got a good guy there. He's a keeper."

"Thanks. We're just taking it one day at a time and seeing where it goes. I'm in no rush." She glanced briefly in Parker's direction, and saw he was once again immersed in another conversation with a would-be art buyer.

"Who are the flowers from?" Toni asked, noting the huge arrangement on the front counter.

"They're from Russell, of all people. On the card he apologized for not being here, but sent his congratulations."

Toni's brows rose speculatively.

"Believe me, there's nothing happening with me and Russell," she said, heading off any questions in that direction. "It's a closed case, and I'm finally all right with it."

"Hopefully he is, too. Uh-oh, don't look now, but your mom just came in."

Millicent walked in, her thick hair uncharacteristically tucked beneath a wide-brimmed hat. As always, she was dressed as if she were going to meet the president, with her navy blue Anne Klein designer suit, matching pumps, and purse.

She gazed imperiously around as if she'd inadvertently wandered into the wrong place, but believed that everyone else was lost.

Regina felt a sinking sensation in her stomach and prayed that there wouldn't be a scene. She hadn't seen or spoken to her mother in weeks, not since she'd turned up on her mother's doorstep and told her just what she could do with her interference.

Michele and Darren simultaneously spotted their grandmother and rushed over to embrace her. She kissed each of them affectionately on the cheek.

"Isn't this great?" Regina could hear Michele say. Her mother's response was lost in the noise of the store, but Regina was certain it couldn't have been favorable.

Regina held her breath and straightened up. They were heading toward her, with Michele and Darren practically dragging their grandmother across the floor.

"Hello, Antoinette," Millie greeted. "I see you came out in support of your friend." She had yet to address Regina.

"That's what friends do, Mrs. Prescott. Regina's done a great job. We're all proud of her."

Regina watched her mother with suspicious eyes, wondering what she was up to. She waited for some kind of catty remark to be directed her way.

Millicent's mouth worked back and forth as if her jaw had suddenly rusted shut. "So am I," she mumbled, then looked at her daughter, the hard set of her face suddenly softening. "It looks wonderful, Regina. Really."

"Thank you, Mom."

"I'm sorry that I got here late. I wasn't

sure if I should come, if I'd be welcome."

"Of course you're welcome." She touched her mother's arm. "I'm glad you're here. It wouldn't have been the same without you."

Millicent looked around, amazed and humbled by her daughter's singular achievement. "Look at what you've done," she said in awe. "I've been so wrong about you. I underestimated you."

Regina was stunned. She never expected such an admission from her mother — not *her* mother. This was the same woman who had sided with her ex-husband against her, had threatened to help him take her children from her, had said she was nothing without him. She'd waited so long for her to say the things she'd just heard. Her heart soared.

"Thank you, Mom," she stammered. "You have no idea how much it means to hear you say that."

Toni eased away, taking Michele and Darren with her, knowing that this was a time for mother and daughter.

Millicent folded her hands in front of her, looking mildly embarrassed. "You and those children are all I have in this world, Regina. It took almost losing you for me to accept the fact that you're a grown woman, capable of making your own decisions, running your own life. Russell told me the same thing — in no uncertain terms."

*Miracles still happen,* Regina thought, wondering again what had compelled Russell to speak to her mother on her behalf.

"I've just been so afraid of being alone, Regina. I thought . . . if I could hold you, stay involved in your life, I wouldn't lose you." Her eyes teared up, but she immediately blinked them back.

"Ma, you never have to worry about losing me. We may have our differences but I'll always be your daughter. I love you, Ma. I know you always believed you were doing what you thought was best for me. But there comes a time in every child's life when you have to cut the apron strings and pray that all the good you instilled in them will carry them through. And it did for me, whether you realize it or not. I got my determination from you. Maybe that's why we stay at odds with each other, because underneath it all we're so much alike."

Millicent smiled. "You're not going to work those poor children to death now, are you?" she stated, easily sliding back into her blustery role, a bit uncomfortable with all the sentiment.

Regina looked at her askance, giving her a rueful smile. "Don't start, Mom. Okay?"

"I was only suggesting that maybe you could use a little more help around here, and it may be too much for the children every day with school and all."

"What are you saying, Ma?"

"Well, I *am* retired. I do have *some* free time. . . ."

Oh, Lord, working with her mother. Who would have thought it? Regina came around the counter and put her arm around her mother's stiff shoulders. "Come on, there's someone I want you to meet. And after we close, we're all going to Victoria's house. I'd love you to come along. She's having a baby, you know," she said, making their way toward Parker.

"Victoria! Having a baby! What next?"

Victoria couldn't believe it. It was just like old times, before the Shark Bar scene. Everybody together again. Even Millie and Regina seemed to have mended their fences.

She propped herself up with pillows and listened to her girlfriends chat about Regina's opening, the great crowd, and unexpected guests who popped up at the last minute. Phillip made a swift entrance and departure with her pills and a glass of water. He waited patiently by her bed while she drained the glass and laid her head back on the pillows.

After Phillip left to join Parker, who was relaxing in the living room, Toni teased her friend about the glow in her complexion.

"Vicky, you never looked better," she joked. "I'd kill to get my skin looking that smooth and clear. Motherhood seems to agree with you. How are you feeling?"

"The doctors say I'm getting stronger by the day, but I still have to be careful. No overexertion, no stress, plenty of rest. And Phillip's been just wonderful. You couldn't ask for a better nurse. It takes something like this for you to really see what you have at home."

Regina moved closer to her bedridden friend and took her hand. "I missed you. It would have been great to have you at the opening, but I'm just glad to see you're better. You had us worried for a while there. How's the baby?"

"The baby's growing on schedule," Victoria said with a note of relief in her voice. "All of the tests show it wasn't hurt by the fall. The doctors think my blood pressure did something weird and I got dizzy and fell. But everything's better now." She lowered her voice for only Regina to hear. "Phil and I are going to counseling. I . . .

still have a lot of issues I need to resolve, not just for me, but for both of us."

"That's great, Vicky. Maybe it would have helped me and Russell."

Vicky patted her hand. "We all thought you were crazy, but I was so envious of you."

Regina frowned. "Me?"

Vicky nodded. "You were the only one of us who wasn't afraid to do what was needed no matter how hard it was."

Regina lowered her gaze. "I was scared out of my wits most of the time. Still am." She smiled shyly.

"I'll tell you a secret . . . so am I."

The two women laughed. Victoria shifted her body to get into a more comfortable position in the bed. "So tell me what's happening with Mr. Tall, Dark, and Handsome downstairs," she quizzed with an arched brow. "How's that going?"

"Slowly," Regina admitted modestly, a bit hesitant about discussing her private life in front of her mother.

"He seems like a nice man," Millicent chimed right in. "I hope his art pays well. It takes a lot to take care of a family."

"Ma!"

"Well, it's true," Millie insisted.

Toni and Victoria shared a secret smile,

knowing exactly which direction this conversation was heading.

"I'm not thinking about anything permanent at the moment, and neither is Parker."

"You're no spring chicken anymore," Millicent cautioned. "You need to think about your future — and the future of those children."

"I love spring weddings," Toni teased, adding fuel to the fire.

Regina cut her a nasty look, which she ignored.

"Personally I prefer summer. You don't have to worry about rain," Victoria said, adding her two cents. "Why not have it on one of the islands? That's what Phillip and I did. Remember?"

Suddenly the three women were immersed in planning Regina's glorious wedding, from what type of dress she should wear to who would cater the food. They already had a growing guest list under consideration.

Regina just shook her head in amusement, slipped from the room unnoticed, and went downstairs.

Parker and Phillip were in a hot conversation about Renaissance art when she entered the room. Parker beamed the moment he saw her.

"How are they doing up there?" Phillip asked.

"Oh, they're just planning my and Parker's wedding is all. I figured they didn't need my input so I left them to their own devices," she said with a wicked look in her eyes.

Phillip saw the surprised expression on Parker's face. "Don't worry, man, if they don't have something to get charged up about they're not happy. And I bet Victoria is one of the ringleaders."

"She had plenty of advice to offer," Regina said with a smile.

Phillip shook his head. "Well, if the two of you want to sneak out, I'll cover for you."

Regina looked at Parker. "I'd say a little sneaking was in order right about now, wouldn't you, Parker?"

"You have my vote." He stood and shook Phillip's hand. "Good to meet you, man."

"Hey, stop by anytime."

"Thanks. I'll keep that in mind."

Phillip walked them to the door.

Regina leaned forward and hugged him tight. "I'm so happy for you, Phil." She stepped back and looked into his warm blue eyes that so clearly reflected his joy.

"You're going to make a great dad. And Victoria" — she grinned — "will be Victoria. She'll probably have the poor child in more designer clothes than you can pay for!"

Phillip laughed. "And I'm going to love every minute of it."

Regina and Parker turned to leave. "Good night," they chorused.

"Don't forget to let me know when to get my tux out of the mothballs," he called out, waving to the departing couple.

"Very funny, Phil," Regina shouted over her shoulder.

# CHAPTER TWENTY-EIGHT

All during the ride to Parker's apartment in SoHo, Regina kept replaying the events of the day: the success of her business, the reconciliation with her mother and her friends, her real friends. Hopefully everything would work out for each of them.

Once they were inside and settled, Parker surprised her by opening a bottle of chilled imported champagne. He poured two fingers of the amber liquid into each of a pair of fluted glasses and handed one to her.

"To you, Regina, for fighting the odds and beating them." He raised his glass in a toast, then stopped. "And to us. I hope this is the beginning of something enduring."

She gently tapped her glass against his.

Parker took her free hand and led her to the gray leather sectional couch. "There's something I want to tell you." His voice wavered a bit but quickly regained its power.

*Uh-oh.* "What is it?"

After seating her, Parker sat down where he could continue to read her face. "I've been doing a lot of thinking lately about us, about me, and what I want to do with my life. What I discovered, Regina, is that I really want you with me. Watching you these past few months made me see just what can be accomplished when you believe in yourself — something I haven't done in a long time. I've let what happened to me and Lynn color everything I did, how I functioned, the choices that I made. I'd forgotten that happiness was still possible, that I still had something to offer. But the only way I can be the man that you deserve is to finally put my past to rest."

Her heart tumbled over in her chest. "How?" she whispered.

"I'd given up on trying to find my daughter," he replied. "More out of fear as time went along than anything else."

"What are you afraid of?"

"Afraid that I wouldn't measure up. Afraid that when I did find her she wouldn't care about me one way or the other. Afraid that she'd believe I abandoned her, that I didn't love her enough to fight for her. Afraid that she wouldn't believe how much I love and miss her."

Her expression softened. She tenderly

stroked his cheek, brushed his locks away from the side of his face.

"What I want to tell you is . . . I've found her. I contacted an agency that specializes in reuniting families, and she's agreed to see me. They have contacts and sources nationwide. I don't know how it's all going to turn out, but it's a start."

"Oh, Parker. I know how much your daughter means to you. It'll work out. And even if it doesn't turn out exactly the way you want, you made the effort, you tried, and she'll see that."

"I hope so," he said soberly. "So I took a short leave of absence from teaching. I'm going to California for a few months. That's where she lives."

"Wow, a few months." She wasn't expecting that. "Well . . ." Her voice trailed off.

"When I come back, and I will, I want us to see where this can go with us. But I know I can't do that honestly until that other part of my life is settled. What I need to know, Gina, is if that's what you want, too."

Did she? Could she commit herself to someone again? What if there were more demands made on her than she could fulfill? Could she love someone fully and completely? At times she believed she could. And she thought that Parker could be that person. At other times she wanted to be selfish for the first time in her life, and just take care of Regina. But if there was one thing she'd decided when she went on this new adventure in her life, it was that she wasn't doing anything the same ever again. She'd be taking a chance with him; she knew that. But what was life without risks?

Slowly Parker stood and extended his hand to her. "I want to show you something." He led her to his bedroom.

In the light and shadow that played through the window, he guided her inside. Parker gently put his arm around her shoulders and held her close to his side. Her gaze followed his to the portrait that hung above his bed.

Her heart leaped in her chest and her eyes filled with wonder. There she was captured in all her glory — with an expression that challenged everything before it and said, *I can do anything. Yes, I can.*

# Affirmations for Living

*IF I COULD:*

I would surround myself with people who bring out the best in me.

I would rid myself of the negativity in my life, including friends and significant others.

I would save money for a rainy day.

I would have a kind word for someone each day.

I would do something nice for someone, just because.

I would rekindle old friendships.

I would learn to say NO!

I would go to the gym and stop talking about going.

I would treat myself to something special each payday because I deserve it.

I would take time for myself to be with myself, to understand myself.

I would go back to school to take that class I've been putting off.

I would love myself first, so that I may love others.

I would do all these things and more, IF I COULD . . . and I CAN!

# A READING GROUP GUIDE

# IF I COULD
## Donna Hill

### ABOUT THIS GUIDE

The suggested questions are intended to enhance your group's reading of Donna Hill's IF I COULD. We hope this will increase your enjoyment of this provocative book about one's life choices and search for self-worth.

### DISCUSSION QUESTIONS

1. What effect did Regina's childhood, with all its insecurities, have on the choices she would later make as a woman?
2. What lessons about love and emotional responsibility, concerning marriage and parenting, are revealed to Regina during her journey to wholeness?

3.  Could Regina's husband, Russell, have reacted any other way than he did upon faced with his wife's evolution, both as a woman and his wife? If so, how?

4.  In your opinion, are many women "sexually addicted" to their mates even at the expense of their self-worth? Why do you think this happens to women?

5.  What does Toni's affair with Alan indicate about the nature of who Toni is? What is it about her self-image that made having the affair possible?

6.  Did Toni's infidelity awaken her husband, Charles, to his part in sustaining a marriage and family? Did the infidelity strengthen both Toni and Charles? If so, how?

7.  Is Regina's husband, Russell, indicative of the attitudes of some contemporary African-American men and their view of the roles of men and women in a marriage?

8.  In your opinion is Toni's need to "fix" Charles often a common situation among couples in a relationship? Do women frequently try to improve their mates, and if so,

is this in relation to what society has deemed "acceptable" for men, i.e., status, education, material gain, etc?

9. Is the emotional damage, as seen in Victoria's character — regarding skin color prejudice — a strong factor in black women and men and why they choose lovers and spouses? Do you believe that the color issue is still a factor in African American life and in the way we view ourselves?

10. Does the author deal with the issue of skin color effectively in the book?

11. Do you believe that Victoria's marriage to Phillip was a mask for her own self-hatred and lack of self-worth? What are some of the challenges of interracial marriage as depicted in Victoria's story?

12. Why was Regina's awakening the catalyst for change among the three women?

13. How did Regina's decision not to sleep with Parker indicate her growth as a person?

14. What role does compromise and reconciliation play in each of the stories?

15. Does the way in which the author reveals each of the stories, both

individually and collectively, enhance your grasp of the characters and the situations they faced?

16. Do you see any of yourself, or someone you know, in any of the characters, and in the way they confront issues?

17. Do you find the resolutions to each of the stories both realistic and satisfying as a reader?

# ABOUT THE AUTHOR

Donna Hill was first published in 1987 with the short story "The Long Walk." Since that time, she has been included in five novellas and has published 12 novels, with two more scheduled to be released this year. Her novel, *Indiscretions*, was the first black romance ever to make a bestseller list. She has been featured in national publications such as *Essence*, *The Daily News*, *USA Today*, *Today's Black Woman*, and *Black Enterprise*, among many others and has appeared on numerous radio and television stations across the country. She is the recipient of the *Romantic Times* Career achievement Award for 1998, the 1999 Award of Excellence from *Romance in Color* for her novel "Pieces of Dreams," and the 1999 Sister Circle Book Award. Her work has appeared on the *Emerge*, *Ingram Books*, and *Blackboard* bestsellers lists. Three of her novels have been adapted for television. She works full time as a Public Relations Associate for the Queens Borough Public Library system, and organizes author-centered events and workshops through her promotions and management company, Annod Productions. Donna lives with her family in Brooklyn, New York.